T0129249

A Killing by the Sea

The By the Sea Mystery Series by Kathleen Bridge

Death by the Sea

A Killing by the Sea

A Killing by the Sea

A By the Sea Mystery

Kathleen Bridge

LYRICAL UNDERGROUND
Kensington Publishing Corp.
www.kensingtonbooks.com

To the extent that the image or images on the cover of this book depict a person or persons, such person or persons are merely models, and are not intended to portray any character or characters featured in the book.

LYRICAL UNDERGROUND BOOKS are published by

Kensington Publishing Corp.
119 West 40th Street
New York, NY 10018

Copyright © 2018 by Kathleen Bridge

All rights reserved. No part of this book may be reproduced in any form or by any means without the prior written consent of the Publisher, excepting brief quotes used in reviews.

All Kensington titles, imprints, and distributed lines are available at special quantity discounts for bulk purchases for sales promotion, premiums, fund-raising, educational, or institutional use.

Special book excerpts or customized printings can also be created to fit specific needs. For details, write or phone the office of the Kensington Sales Manager: Kensington Publishing Corp., 119 West 40th Street, New York, NY 10018. Attn. Sales Department. Phone: 1-800-221-2647.

Lyrical Underground and Lyrical Underground logo Reg. US Pat. & TM Off.

First Electronic Edition: September 2018
eISBN-13: 978-1-5161-0521-2
eISBN-10: 1-5161-0521-04

First Print Edition: September 2018
ISBN-13: 978-1-5161-0524-3
ISBN-10: 1-5161-0524-9

Printed in the United States of America

I dedicate this book to my dad, John. I couldn't have a better role model.
Your support and love have meant the world to me. XOXO

Acknowledgments

Thank you to my fabulous agent, Down Dowdle at Blue Ridge Literary Agency. You are not only my agent, but a true friend. My editor, Martin Biro, and his assistant James at Kensington/Lyrical Underground make this writer's life easy with their wise and stellar suggestions. Once again, I would like to thank Chef Lon Otremba for supplying recipes for both of my series. As always, to all my friends, family, and readers—I am so thankful for having you in my life. A special nod of thanks to Karen M. Owen for her contribution to my online presence—I hope someday soon we will meet in person and share a cup of tea.

Oh, 'twas in the broad Atlantic,
'Mid the equinoctial gales,
That a young man fell overboard
Among the sharks and whales.

And down he went like a streak of light,
So quickly down went he,
Until he came to a mer-ma-id
At the bottom of the deep blue sea.

—from *The Oxford Song Book*

Chapter 1

Liz pushed against the revolving door and entered the hotel, glancing around the vintage-chic lobby, as her great-aunt called it. The word "shabby" wasn't allowed when describing the once-grand resort that had opened in 1926.

"It's the Bat! He's out to kill us!" a voice screeched from next to the hotel's check-in counter.

"Relax. Decorum! For mercy's sake."

The statements were spoken with different intonations but originated from the same source. Barnacle Bob wasn't schizophrenic, just used to hearing the lines repeated over and over again—as was Liz. The parrot was reciting dialogue from a play Aunt Amelia was in at the Melbourne Beach Theatre Company's production of Mary Roberts Rinehart's *The Bat*.

"You nailed it, BB. Where's Auntie?" Liz asked.

The parrot ignored her.

"What's wrong? Cat got your tongue?"

Barnacle Bob twirled around in his ornate brass cage. A ruby-red tailfeather floated up and landed on his bald head. BB didn't get along with the Indialantic's felines, Carolyn Keene (aka Caro), Bronte, and Venus. Unlike Barnacle Bob, Killer, the only canine at the hotel, was a cat lover and currently in a relationship with Caro. Whenever Killer entered the same room as Barnacle Bob, the parrot would make meowing sounds, saving him from becoming the Great Dane's tasty treat.

"Adios, amigo. Hasta luego," Liz said to BB, before stepping away from his cage.

"'Ay, yi, yi, yi! I am the Frito Bandito,'" he crooned.

Greta Kimball, the hotel's housekeeper, walked into the lobby carrying Barnacle Bob's breakfast. Venus followed closely at her heels. Greta was tall and thin, in her late seventies, with long white hair she wore in a French braid. When Liz had first met her in an assisted living residence in Melbourne, she'd looked fifteen years older than the woman who stood before her now.

Greta put her face near Barnacle Bob's cage and picked up where the parrot left off. "'I like Frito's corn chips, I like them I do. I like Frito's corn chips, I'll take them from you.'" Then she let out a full-bodied laugh when BB added an "'*Olé*!'" and rang the bell hanging from the side of his cage.

The new housekeeper had been welcomed into the Indialantic's eclectic family with open arms. Five months ago, she'd been rescued from a subpar retirement home by Aunt Amelia—the great rescuer—and received free room and board, along with a small salary, in exchange for her housekeeping duties.

"Good morning, Greta. Don't fall for BB's cutesy act," Liz said. "As soon as you give him his food, he'll go back to the dark side and drag you along with him."

"Oh, I'm not frightened of this little angel."

BB stood a little taller, taking a piece of kiwi from Greta's hand in a restrained manner. Liz still had a red mark on her finger from the last time she'd fed him.

"Well, I'll leave you to it," Liz said as she went through the Spanish-arched doorway in search of her great-aunt.

Ahead, voices filtered out from Aunt Amelia's screening room. Two distinct voices. Aunt Amelia's and her "frenemy" Susannah Shay's. Liz continued down the tiled hall toward them. When she came to the screening room's open doorway, she noiselessly stepped inside.

The room had eight rows of seating and a huge stage with an old-school, theater-size projection screen. At the back of the room was a screening booth with a projector and DVD player. The mini-theater was in shadow, but three spotlights were positioned on the stage.

Until the Melbourne Beach Theatre Company's new renovations were completed, Aunt Amelia's screening room was the temporary site of rehearsals for *The Bat*.

Liz continued down the aisle toward the front of the theater, her elbow knocking a framed photo off the wall. It clattered to the floor with a thud. She bent to pick it up, happy the glass hadn't shattered. A mustachioed Buddy Ebsen, aka Jed Clampett from the 1960s television show *The Beverly Hillbillies*, smiled back at her. His arm was draped over the shoulders of a pigtailed Aunt Amelia. Liz replaced the photo on the wall, where it hung next to a black-and-white autographed shot of Gene Barry as Bat Masterson, gambler and Wild West lawman. He was wearing a derby hat and pointing his cane at a young Amelia Eden Holt. Her hands were up in mock surrender, her head thrown back in laughter. The entire north wall of the room had been plastered with '60s memorabilia—a shrine to her great-aunt's television career.

So as not to disturb the rehearsing, Liz slunk into a seat and looked toward the stage at the two elderly but vibrant women.

"I prefer the play's ending in NBC's 1960 *Dow Hour of Great Mysteries* adaptation of *The Bat*. The one starring Helen Hayes, Margaret Hamilton, and Jason Robards," Susannah's verbose but at the same time calm voice said. "The actors weren't given the identity of the Bat until the final rehearsals—even they didn't know whodunit until the last minute. We should do the same." Susannah, who'd won the lead role in the play as Cornelia Van Gorder, was in her late seventies and professed to be the third cousin once removed of Madame Etiquette herself, Amy Vanderbilt. Prim and proper was an understatement when it came to Susannah Shay. She stood tall with erect posture. Her Cornelia Van Gorder costume entailed a white wig with a bun that hit the nape of her neck; a high-necked, white lace–trimmed blouse with a cameo pinned to the collar; a navy ankle-length skirt, and black-laced shoes straight out of a 1940s Sears catalog. Liz always felt slightly diminished in Susannah's presence, afraid to talk, always on her best behavior, like a seen-but-not-heard child from the Victorian era.

"Margaret Hamilton and I couldn't be more opposite in appearance," Aunt Amelia answered in a high-pitched squeak. Liz's great-aunt had won the role of spinster Cornelia Van Gorder's squeamish, elderly maid. Accustomed to top billing, Liz's great-aunt hadn't been too pleased that her thespian friend got the role she coveted. Susannah had been Aunt Amelia's roommate in Burbank when they worked as television character actresses in the 1960s. Susannah was staying at the Indialantic until her "snowbird" home in a nearby gated community was completed.

"And one more thing," Susannah said. "For clarity's sake, Amelia. I think your character's name should be Lizzie Arlen, like in the Broadway version of *The Bat*, not Liddie Allen, like in *The Circular Staircase,* the novel Mary Roberts Rinehart based the play on."

"If I use the name Lizzie, it will confuse my great-niece." Aunt Amelia winked in Liz's direction. "Also, if we decide to follow the plot in the 1959 televised version of *The Bat*, the one with Agnes Moorehead, Vincent Price, and Lenita Lane, I won't need to worry that the audience will confuse Margaret Hamilton's version of the maid with mine."

"Amelia," Susannah said, adding an exaggerated exhalation. "How many people will remember either teleplay version of *The Bat*? More than half of America didn't even own a television back them." She took Aunt Amelia's hand in hers, then continued in a patronizing tone. "And I doubt that anyone will recall that the elderly actress who played my—I mean Cornelia's—'maidservant' in the *Dow Hour of Great Mysteries* teleplay, was the Wicked Witch of the West. They might remember, however, that you played the maidservant on *Dark Shadows*."

Uh-oh. Liz saw Aunt Amelia's cheeks redden under her bubblegum-pink blush. Unlike Susannah, Aunt Amelia wasn't wearing her maid's costume for her role as Cornelia Van Gorder's scaredy-cat, scatterbrained servant. Amelia Eden Holt had been a beauty in her day and was still a handsome figure, with her bright red hair coifed on top of her head in large soup-can curls, baby-blue pearlescent eye shadow, and black liner that winged outward from the corner of her luminous emerald eyes. She usually dressed in one of her flowing caftans in hues of violet, green, or aqua, and today was no exception.

Susannah didn't seem to notice she'd upset her friend. "I was merely stating that we should leave who will play the Bat a secret until the final weeks of rehearsal. That way, the actor can't ham it up and throw us off our game."

"I suppose that's not a bad idea," Aunt Amelia said. "But I insist on having the name Liddie for my role. What's your opinion, Lizzie?"

Liz knew it wasn't about a name; it was more about her great-aunt's friend winning the starring role in the play. She didn't want to get in the middle of the pair's theatrical histrionics, even if she did think Aunt Amelia would make a great Cornelia Van Gorder. However, in the straight-backed, blue-blooded vein, Susannah Shay fit the bill—as in playbill. From experience, it was certain Aunt Amelia would steal the show—no matter if she had the lead or played the part of the maid. No one put Amelia Eden Holt in a corner, not even the queen of etiquette, Susannah Shay.

"Ladies, ladies, let's not argue," a male voice said.

Sitting in the shadows on the other side of the room was Tom Grayson, the director of the play. Recently, Aunt Amelia had rented him a vacated emporium space for his new business, Treasure Tours by the Sea, thinking it might net her the leading role in the play. Unfortunately, that hadn't happened.

"Let's table this discussion for later," he said. "There's plenty of time for me to decide who'll play the Bat."

Susannah and Aunt Amelia turned toward Tom. They'd both opened their mouths the moment he'd said, "for *me* to decide."

"We've just begun rehearsals," Tom said. "And I still haven't cast anyone to play the parts of Brooks the gardener, Richard Fleming, and the Unknown Man. Auditions will resume next week."

Gregory Grayson, who seemingly owned half of all the businesses and real estate in Melbourne Beach, was the owner of the Melbourne Beach Theatre Company. Gregory had picked his half brother Tom to be the director of the play, thereby keeping it all in the family. Something the rest of the actors weren't too happy about.

Tom said, "Let's call it a day. It looks like Erica is going to be a no show, along with Victor—they're probably off somewhere together."

Erica Grayson, Tom's ex-sister-in-law and Gregory's ex-wife, would be playing the part of Cornelia Van Gorder's niece, Dale. Victor Normand had the role of Dr. Wells.

"Tom," Susannah said, "I think you need to make a decision on which version of *The Bat* we'll be following, along with the name you prefer to use for Amelia. Lizzie or Liddie? I can't be expected to stay in character under these circumstances!"

After an eye roll and a glance in Liz's direction, Aunt Amelia said, "Gracious me."

"Gracious me," was her great-aunt's prearranged code phrase for "get me away from Susannah Shay."

"Auntie, can I please have a word with you?" Liz called from the aisle.

"Of course you can, my dear." She swished past Susannah and met Liz at the door leading out of the screening room. The scent of L'Air du Temps arrived before she did.

They moved into the hallway, and Aunt Amelia closed the door before she spoke. "Thanks for saving me, my love. It all comes rushing back. Susannah and I were usually up for the same parts, even on *Dark Shadows*. However, I scored the recurring role of the Collinses' maid, and she a single-day's performance as one of Barnabas's victims, who was staked to death in the very same episode. Now that I think of it, I'll embrace the role of Cornelia Van Gorder's maid with bells on." She tossed one end of her iridescent peacock-colored scarf over her right shoulder.

"That's the spirit," Liz said. "And I'm sure they'll remember you for your role on *Dark Shadows,* instead of confusing you with the actress who played the Wicked Witch of the West."

"That was a little catty of me, wasn't it? Margaret Hamilton may not have been much in the looks department, but she was undoubtedly the most iconic villain of all time."

Liz laughed. "True. The first time I saw *The Wizard of Oz* she scared me half to death. Her and her flying monkeys, in their not-so-adorable blue and red fez hats."

"I have old pictures of employees wearing similar hats. They were part of the Indialantic's bellhop and elevator operator uniforms in the thirties. Speaking of uniforms, I'm going to have Francie whip me up an exquisite maid's uniform when she returns home. That'll show Susannah."

"Auntie, it's not like you to be so snarky."

"You're right. I've got it!" she said, slapping her hand on the doorframe. "I know what I'll do. I'll have Francie copy the French maid's costume from the movie *Clue*. Most likely, Susannah would rather I wear what actress Shirley Booth wore as TV's favorite maid, *Hazel*." Aunt Amelia noticed the blank look on Liz's face and explained, "*Hazel* was a sitcom from the early 1960s about a family named the Baxters and their maid and housekeeper, who had the perfect answer for any situation. The series was based on a comic strip from *The Saturday Evening Post*. Kind of like *Father Knows Best*. Only Hazel knew best. Hazel wore a dowdy uniform with a little white hat above her plain-Jane face. Don't get me wrong; Shirley was a consummate actress, but her Hazel was a stereotypical portrayal at best. I need to add a little spice to my part as Liddie."

"I'm sure when Francie gets back, she'll make you the perfect maid's costume, Auntie." Francie was a renowned seamstress who made her own patterns based on vintage clothing, which she adjusted to fit today's woman, then sold in shops around the United States. She and her partner, Minna, rented the emporium shop Home Arts by the Sea. Liz couldn't wait to see what Francie came up with.

Aunt Amelia's face lit up and Liz saw her great-aunt's wheels turning on how to change the maid's role into something much more. Much, much more.

"I think we're all set for Pirates' Weekend by the Sea," Liz said. "All we have to do is pray the weather holds and the hurricane decides to visit the east coast instead of the west. The emporium shops are ready to go."

The weekend's festivities were Aunt Amelia's brainchild. It had taken Liz everything she had to rein in a few of her great-aunt's wacky ideas for the event, including a contest for the most articulate macaw. Aunt Amelia's feathered friend Barnacle Bob might be great at repeating 1960s television commercial jingles, but when it came to the rest of the parrot's vocabulary, which included enough curse words to make a stand-up comedian blush,

Liz knew she had to steer her great-aunt in a more wholesome direction. Finally, Liz had persuaded Aunt Amelia to focus on the treasure hunt instead of BB's so-called talents.

In 1945, a mysterious fire had destroyed a section of the Indialantic by the Sea Hotel. Recently, Aunt Amelia, with the financial aid of her nephew, had refurbished the northern section of the hotel and turned it into the Indialantic by the Sea Emporium. Saturday would entail a day of bargains and treasures at the emporium. The vendors from the shops were also donating prizes for Sunday's treasure hunt: bottles of wine from Delicasies by the Sea, sterling silver and turquoise jewelry from Sirens by the Sea, antique books and vintage treasure-themed trinkets from Books and Browsery by the Sea, mixed-media art and knitting lessons from Home Arts by the Sea, and a gift certificate from the new shop, Treasure Tours by the Sea. Aunt Amelia was donating a weekend getaway at the hotel in the newly refurbished Oceana Suite.

Sunday there would a pirates' luncheon and scavenger hunt on the Indialantic's grounds. Pierre, the hotel's octogenarian live-in chef, was still unclear about what a pirates' luncheon entailed. And so was Liz.

"Auntie, have you settled on the menu for the pirates' picnic? I'd love to take a look." Between her great-aunt's grandiose plans for the weekend and Pierre's willingness to agree to whatever his employer and friend requested, Liz needed to be the middleman, for everyone's sake.

"I've discussed it with Greta. Judging by the way she reacted, I'm sure I'm on to a fantastic menu. After I handed her a glass of water, she said she wanted to talk to you first before going over the menu with Pierre."

Oh boy. That didn't sound good.

Aunt Amelia squared her shoulders and stuck out her chin. "Well, I've counted to ten and I'm ready to face Susannah. Better get back inside before she talks Tom into deleting the role of Cornelia's maid from the play. I'm so happy Tom has chosen Katie to play the part of Detective Anderson. I need an ally against Susannah."

Kate Fields, Liz's best friend, had been roped into playing the part of Detective Anderson, taking it on in her usual enthusiastic way by reading and rereading the book the play was based on, *The Circular Staircase*. Aunt Amelia had told Liz that Susannah was up in arms because the role of Detective Anderson in *The Bat* was being played by a female, not a male, like in the play and movies. If Susannah had been born at the turn of the twentieth century, Liz doubted she would have partaken in any suffragette marches. Liz was sure Kate could recite the entire novel verbatim. The last time she'd done any acting was when they'd attended Melbourne Beach

High. Kate had starred as Julia in a modern-day version of *Romeo and Juliet* Liz had written.

"Let's talk later," Aunt Amelia said. "I think I can hear Susannah whispering in Tom's ear from here."

"And I should grab my laptop. Thanks for the idea of making the bell tower my writing lair while the library is being inventoried by Dad. I feel like the queen of the sea with my vantage point of the Atlantic and the Indian River Lagoon. You stick to your guns, Auntie. Don't let anyone steamroll you when it comes to the play!"

Aunt Amelia flexed the muscles on her upper arms. Recently, she'd converted one of the hotel's many unused rooms into a small gym and even begun lifting weights under the auspices of a personal trainer. At eighty, Amelia Eden Holt lived by the adage nineteenth-century female author George Eliot had penned: "It's never too late to be what you might have been." She kissed Liz on the cheek, then strode back into the screening room.

Liz hoped Susannah and Tom had fastened their seat belts.

Chapter 2

Leaning against the boardwalk's railing, Liz looked toward the ocean, sniffing at the briny air like a dog on scent. There wasn't one cloud on the horizon. The silica in the sand reflected the sun in blinding whiteness and the Atlantic's surface looked as if it were sprinkled with glitter. Chapter Seventeen had been giving Liz a hell of a time. Some authors called it the midbook slump. Liz thought of it as the proverbial fork in the road. The part of the story that could go this way or that; poignant and a touch melancholy, like her recent past, or upbeat and full of promise, like her present-day life in Melbourne Beach.

It was a glorious day for the middle of October. She'd been home for six months and not a single hurricane had dared to come near the barrier island. She just hoped that wasn't about to change. Florida's heat and humidity had taken a nosedive, and she planned to take advantage of the postcard-perfect day, hoping the newscasters were once again mistaken in their doom-and-gloom weather prognostications for Pirates' Weekend, only four days away.

Things had been going extremely well—her writing, her healing, her family and social life. However, this morning she'd woken with a prickling behind her eyes and a foreboding that something dark and sinister was moving stealthily toward the Indialantic by the Sea Hotel and Emporium, threatening everyone Liz held dear.

It wasn't like her to have such ominous thoughts. She hadn't had a nightmare about the night she'd been scarred in months. But yesterday, she'd read a blurb in *Florida Today* about her ex-boyfriend's new novel, *Blood and Glass*. The book, described as fiction, was due out any day. Travis's publicist had sent Liz an advance copy, hoping to get a quote for the book jacket. Liz hadn't responded to her, or the slew of paparazzi, requesting an exclusive interview. The book was now locked in the bottom drawer of her father's filing cabinet, unread. Fenton Holt, attorney and protective father, had pointed out that they might need the book in case Liz wanted to file a defamation of character lawsuit against Travis, like he'd done a year and a half ago to her. A lawsuit Travis had lost.

Tugging at the brim of her hat to shade her scar, Liz turned toward the path leading to her beach house. She planned to fetch her laptop and kitten Bronte, then head up to the hotel's bell tower room—her new writing stronghold.

As she hopped over a pair of rotted planks on the boardwalk, she heard the screech of gulls, followed by a guttural, raspy, cawing from the direction of the beach. She felt chilled, as if she were back in New York on a dark, witch-on-a-broomstick autumn day, not under a cheery Florida sun. She hesitated before pivoting her head toward the shoreline. The only other time she'd heard the macabre, redheaded turkey vultures was when they swooped down with their six-foot wingspans to feast on carrion at the side of scenic A1A.

What she saw next made her wish she'd kept walking.

Originally, she'd thought it was some poor, beached sea creature. But as she looked closer, she saw a body facedown in the sand.

A dead body.

Chapter 3

Liz stood sentinel next to the corpse, shooing away birds like Tippi Hedren's character in Hitchcock's classic film. The back of the man's head was covered by a nest of tangled seaweed. As a distraction, she focused her gaze on the numerous holes left on the beach by sand fleas, the anemic-looking insects with crablike legs that islanders liked to use as fish bait. Over the sound of the surf and cacophony of bird noises, someone shouted her name.

Thank God.

Ryan Stone's tall, muscled frame charged toward her. He stopped inches from the body, then grabbed her in a quick embrace. "You're shaking. If you want to wait on the boardwalk, I can stay here." Then he reached under her hat and tipped up her sunglasses. "You okay?"

She shrugged her shoulders, her teary blue eyes locking onto his deep brown ones. "As good as anyone can be." She'd found out last April that Ryan's former occupation as an FDNY firefighter and arson investigator made him a calming presence in high-charged situations. It had been his number she'd called before dialing 9-1-1.

"It's Dylan, isn't it." She didn't pose it as a question.

"I've never met him, but I would say there's a good chance. Did you know him?"

"Yes." She turned her head and tried to focus on the steady ebb and flow of the waves.

Dylan was Minna Presley's nephew. Minna and her business partner and friend, Francie, rented the emporium shop Home Arts by the Sea, a women's lifestyle collective. Five days ago, Dylan, who worked on a fishing trawler, fell overboard and was lost at sea. When the Coast Guard arrived shortly after the distress call went out, near the coordinates the ship had given them, there'd been no sign of him. After days of frantic search, they'd given up hope of finding him alive.

"Why don't you go home? I'll wait with the body," Ryan said.

Before Liz could answer, she heard Agent Charlotte Pearson's authoritative voice, smooth as silk with just a touch of barbed wire. "Step away and let the paramedics do their job."

Agent Pearson, lead homicide detective on the Brevard County PD, came toward them on the sand, not once stumbling on her three-inch pumps. She was dressed exquisitely in a black sleeveless blouse, a white jacket and a skirt, gold at her ears and neck. The detective's shoulder-length blond hair remained sleek and straight, unlike Liz's long strawberry waves which, on a humid day, expanded horizontally into a bedspringlike profusion.

Liz and Ryan stepped back as a troop of officers and paramedics bounded toward them. Liz knew there was no reason for them to hurry. They watched as one of the paramedics gently turned the body faceup. Liz turned away.

It was Dylan.

She'd seen his perpetually smiling face only last week when he'd delivered the day's catch to the kitchen door of the hotel, a fish Friday ritual his Aunt Minna had initiated to the delight of Chef Pierre. Many of Pierre's signature fish dishes were the same ones his Catholic mother had made every Friday when he was a child in the French seaside town of Le Grau-du-Roi on the sandy coast of the Mediterranean. Pierre and Dylan had become fast friends, and Liz dreaded telling the man she thought of as a grandfather about Dylan's senseless death.

They waited until the body was taken away. The white sandy beach that had been frequented by the Indialantic's hotel guests for ninety years seemed tainted by the vision of Dylan's battered remains. One of Aunt Amelia's favorite television guest appearances on *The Alfred Hitchcock Hour* came to mind. The episode, entitled "Day of Reckoning," had her great-aunt playing a partygoer who sees a couple arguing; soon after, the wife falls overboard. Accident or murder? Liz was letting her imagination run away with her, but what were the chances Dylan would wash up on this stretch of the beach? That was the first of more than one question she would have in the following days. And now that she thought of it, why was Agent Pearson, a homicide detective, there?

Liz shivered in the afternoon sun.

Agent Pearson turned to Liz. "I'll tell your father about this. We're scheduled to meet at Island Eats for dinner."

"Sure," Liz answered robotically. She thought the word "scheduled" sounded too formal for a dinner date with the man you were romantically involved with, but she gave the detective a break; as long as her father was happy…"Poor Minna," Liz said with a sob, and Ryan took her hand in his.

"I'll notify Mr. Presley's next of kin. Would that be Minna?" Detective Pearson asked as she shielded her eyes from the sun with her hand.

"No. Minna is, or was, his aunt," Liz answered. "Dylan's mother, Alyse, is widowed and lives in Clearwater, but Dylan had been staying with Minna until he found his own place." Liz covered her mouth to stifle a sob. "If you don't mind, I'd like to be the one to tell Minna."

"Fine. But please wait until I notify the mother. Agent Williams will take your statement."

"There's nothing much to say. I was standing on the boardwalk, heard the turkey vultures, and looked at the beach. Then I came down to keep them away. I didn't touch anything. I know the drill."

"Just be available if we need an official statement."

"You know where I live," Liz said a little too harshly. She wanted to break Agent Pearson's icy reserve.

"Yes, I do." Then the detective turned and headed toward the steps leading up to the boardwalk.

Ryan stood quietly by Liz's side. "I think I'll have a chat with Charlotte. Did you notice the gash on the back of Dylan's head when they turned him over? The shape of the wound was unusual."

"It must be the reason he ended up in the ocean. Probably hit his head on something on the ship, then flew overboard."

"Possibly," Ryan said. His brown, almost black eyes held something she'd seen before. He suspected something and he was keeping it from her. He'd recently been hired as her father's on-call private investigator and spent the rest of his time assisting his grandfather, Pops, in the emporium café and gourmet market, Deli-casies by the Sea.

For the moment, Liz was happy Ryan was by her side. Sadly, it wasn't the first time they'd come face-to-face with a dead body.

"You coming?" he asked.

"No, I need to tell Aunt Amelia. Go ahead."

He hesitated. "Call if you want me to go with you to see Minna."

"I will. And thanks."

"For what?"

"For getting here so quickly."

He bowed at the waist. "Any time, fair maiden."

As she watched him walk away, his dark, tousled hair shining in the early afternoon sun, a familiar flutter rose in her chest. She thought back to last May, when Ryan made the decision to move from Brooklyn to Melbourne Beach. He'd rented the caretaker's cottage from Aunt Amelia. The same cottage Liz had grown up in with her father, following her mother's death. Liz feared Ryan's decision to live on the island might have more to do with their budding relationship than helping her father and his grandfather. There was a definite attraction between them. But she was still wary of knights in shining armor after her disastrous relationship with Travis Osterman, the Pulitzer Prize–winning author of *The McAvoy Brothers*. Travis was the cause of the scar on her right cheek, and had been the reason she'd fled Manhattan and the tabloids for the sanctity of the barrier island. She was determined to concentrate on writing her second novel, help her great-aunt with the running of the hotel and emporium, and assist her father with his legal work, leaving no time for self-pity. *Or romance?* She didn't need rescuing, just time to heal and focus on her blessings.

Had poor Dylan had anyone special in his life? He was close to Liz's age, in his mid-to-late twenties. Or—he had been. A tear escaped; she swiped it away. She must be strong for Minna. *Oh Dylan.* How had this happened?

She stepped closer to where Dylan's body had lain. Something glinted in the sun. She bent and picked it up. She brushed away the surface of what looked like a small gray pebble with the hem of her T-shirt and held it up to the sky. Gold. Her first gold doubloon.

All the Treasure Coast locals knew the story of the Spanish fleet laden with hundreds of millions of dollars in silver, gold, and precious jewelry that had been shipwrecked near the island's Sebastian Inlet. Salvagers, including the most successful American treasure hunter of all time, Mel Fisher, had scored big-time from the bounty of the shipwrecked ships, not only from what was found at the bottom of the ocean, but also on a nearby beach that had once been a survivors' camp for the 1715 fleet.

When Liz was young, usually after a hurricane, she, her father, and her great-aunt would head to that beach, lugging metal detectors, pails, and sifters. Once, Aunt Amelia had found a silver piece of eight, but no one in the family had found a gold doubloon. She should have been thrilled about her find, but it was bittersweet. Dylan was dead, the coin, just a piece of metal.

Was it a coincidence that the gold coin had shown up under Dylan's body? Or was it something more?

Chapter 4

When Liz walked into the lobby, Aunt Amelia was behind the check-in counter, sorting mail into numbered cubbies. "Most of this is trash," she said, her back facing Liz. When she raised her arms, her iridescent violet caftan with its flowing trumpet sleeves reminded Liz of Merlin's robe. All she needed was a wand.

"We did get a postcard from Betty," Aunt Amelia said, turning and waving a glossy card showing 221B Baker Street, Sherlock Holmes's fictional London residence. "This one's as cryptic as the last. It reads, 'Picture yourself the pilot fish with the shark, the jackal with the lion—anything that is insignificant in companionship with what is formidable...'"

Betty Lawson, the hotel's longtime eighty-three-year-old resident, author of a series of 1960s teen mystery books, and esteemed member of the Sherlock Holmes Society of London, was on the other side of the pond, participating in "A Weekend in Sherlockian Norfolk."

"The quote's from *The Valley of Fear*," Liz answered, forgetting for a moment the news she was about to break to Aunt Amelia about Dylan.

Aunt Amelia passed her the postcard. "Basil Rathbone was hands-down the best Sherlock, although that quirky Benedict Cumberbatch you had me watch on PBS puts a different spin on my preconceived vision of Doyle's grand detective of page and screen."

Aunt Amelia came from behind the counter. "Hey, where's your laptop? Thought you'd be blissfully writing away?" Then she looked at Liz's face. "What's wrong? Oh no. It's Dylan, isn't it?" She sat down on a cushioned bamboo love seat.

Liz sat next to her. "I'm afraid so, Auntie. He washed up onto the beach."

"What beach? Whose beach? Not the Indialantic's?"

"Yes."

"Poor Minna." She put her arm around Liz, comforting her as she'd done on the first day Liz moved into the Indialantic at the age of five, mourning the loss of her mother.

The latest issue of *Florida Today* lay folded on the side table. Dylan Presley's face stared back at them. Below his photo was the caption LOCAL FISHERMAN STILL MISSING AT SEA. He wasn't missing anymore, Liz thought sadly. She turned over the newspaper, haunted by Dylan's smiling eyes. Then she thought about Minna.

Dylan had been staying with Minna since July in her and Francie's cottage, a mile south of the hotel. Minna's house- and shopmate, Francie was on a three-country buying trip that included Scotland, Ireland, and England, to procure specialty yarn and fabric for Home Arts by the Sea. Francie was due back in two weeks; her last stop would be Cornwall, where she promised to do some research for Liz's novel, then she was going on to London to rendezvous with Betty before they both headed back to the States. It was unfortunate Francie wasn't home to comfort her friend.

"Pierre is going to be devastated," Aunt Amelia said.

So far, they'd kept Pierre, the hotel's octogenarian chef, in the dark about the fact that his young friend was missing. Pierre had a memory loss. He'd shown improvement since he'd been on a regimen that included both Eastern and Western medicine. However, they were ever watchful for any regression. Now, with this heartbreaking news, Liz worried it might send Pierre into a tailspin.

"I'll tell Pierre bright and early in the morning, before the paper's delivered. Does Minna know?" Aunt Amelia asked.

"No. Agent Pearson said to wait until she notifies Dylan's mother."

"Oh my. Minna's big opening at the new gallery is this evening. Did you know, a percentage of each piece she sells will be going to a local works program, helping vets get above-minimum-wage jobs?"

"That sounds like Minna. I told Agent Pearson I'd tell Minna about Dylan."

"Maybe you should wait until after everyone leaves the gallery? I have rehearsals tonight, but if you want me to go with you to the gallery to break the news, I'm there."

"Thanks, but Kate's picking me up. That's if it's okay she won't be here for rehearsals?"

"Of course it's okay. Plus, we're still working on the scene you saw earlier, and it doesn't involve Detective Anderson. This is such a sad state of affairs. To have poor Dylan wash up on the Indialantic's beach."

Aunt Amelia went on to find Greta and tell her the news. Liz went home to check on Bronte. She hadn't told her great-aunt about the gaping wound on the back of Dylan's head. Or the strange way Ryan had reacted. She'd also kept quiet about finding the gold doubloon. First, she would find out if it was authentic.

Chapter 5

"So, what's the plan?" Kate asked, as she pulled her aqua junkin' van onto A1A and headed north. Kate wasn't her usual bubbly self after Liz told her about Dylan.

"I think I need to play it by ear. Charlotte called a few minutes ago. She contacted Dylan's mother and is going to do a press release first thing in the morning, after the coroner confirms cause of death." Liz envisioned the back of Dylan's head and her stomach lurched at the same time Kate made a sharp, blinkerless turn into the parking lot behind the Beachside Gallery. The contents in the back of the van shifted; vintage books, assorted estate sale finds, and a surfboard crashed to the left side of the cargo area. Liz gripped the door handle, fearing the van might tip.

"Minna was so looking forward to the gallery opening," Kate said. "She even confided in me that she'd talked the manager of the gallery into displaying some of Dylan's amazing photographs alongside her mixed-media art." A tear slid down Kate's tanned cheek.

Liz wasn't used to seeing Kate anything but puppy-dog happy.

"I know; Minna told me," Liz said. "I think she had this vision of Dylan turning up unharmed, walking into the gallery to see his photographs on display. Maybe I should've told her before the opening?"

"I don't think there's any right time to tell someone something like this."

Liz looked over at Kate's perfect profile. Her hair was pulled up in a long, sleek ponytail, and her vintage floral sundress accented her strong, athletic body. She wore little makeup, just lip gloss and mascara on thick eyelashes above hazel eyes that usually sparkled with flecks of amber. But not tonight.

Liz had been excited by the gallery opening and, earlier in the week, had splurged on a simple turquoise sheath dress from Sirens by the Sea.

Kate put the van in Park and turned off the ignition. "The lot is packed."

Liz glanced out the van's window and felt a tightening in her chest. Since moving from Manhattan to Melbourne Beach, she hadn't attended many public functions. The Indialantic by the Sea Hotel and Emporium had become a refuge and safe harbor, and there was little reason to leave her cozy nest. Everything she could possibly need—food, clothing, friendship, family and the therapeutic ocean—were in comforting arm's reach. She pulled down the van's visor and looked in the small mirror.

Kate said, "Love your hair that way. Soft and ethereal. From another decade."

Liz had corralled her unruly slave-to-humidity tresses into a loose bun and had let tendrils frame her face. Not that she was trying to hide the scar on her right cheek—well, perhaps a little. Recently, she'd gotten the go-ahead from her plastic surgeon to apply makeup with sunscreen to the four-inch scar.

They got out of the van and stood in line outside the gallery with a crowd of Melbourne and Vero Beach beautiful people. Most were dressed in light cottons and linens, and the air was scented with expensive perfume. The former home of a photography studio, the gallery still had brown Kraft paper taped to its showcase windows, hiding the interior of the newly designed space. There were a few torn spots where passersby had tried to peek inside. Last week, on her way to Beachside Books, Liz had been tempted to do the same.

An overly perfumed woman elbowed her way in front of them. She held an invitation in her French-manicured hand. Pictured on the front was a photo of one of Minna's works.

"Darn!" Liz said. "I left our invitations at home."

"I'm sure that won't be a problem," Kate replied as she grabbed Liz's wrist, pulling her toward the door.

A skeletally thin man dressed in a short-sleeved shirt and bow tie, round tortoiseshell glasses, and plaid shorts, came out of the gallery door. He shooed away the crowd in front of the plateglass window and ceremonially ripped off the brown paper. The crowd "oohed," as he exposed the interior of the new gallery. Thirty-foot walls peaked to a multipaned glass ceiling that let in peachy sunset light. The walls were set up similarly to those in Home Arts by the Sea. Canvases were stacked on top of each other on the wall. A rail near the ceiling gave access to the art by way of a white thirty-foot ladder on rollers, making it possible to traverse all three sides of the main showroom.

When they finally made it to the entrance, the bow-tied man asked for their invitation.

Kate said, "We're friends of Ms. Presley. I'm sure she'll vouch for us."

"I'm sorry. I can't let you in without an invitation." He shrugged his narrow shoulders, then glanced in the direction of the interior, packed with invitees. Minna was lost somewhere in the center. All they could see was her short, spiky hair tipped in shades of blue and green. Minna's hair color changed from week to week.

Kate stepped closer. "I insist you tell Ms. Presley that Kate and Liz are here and have forgotten their invitations."

The man ignored her, then ushered in an impeccably dressed man in a white linen suit and chunky gold wristwatch. Evidently, he didn't need to show anything but his ostentatiousness.

"Snob," Kate said. "Come on, Liz." She grabbed Liz's forearm and pulled her away from the doorway. "I have a plan," she said as they walked around the corner toward the parking lot.

Fearless Kate and her well-intentioned plans had been their undoing in the past.

When they reached the back of the gallery, they followed a small gravel alley. One of the waitstaff, dressed all in white, sat on a folding chair inhaling a cigarette. Liz counted to twenty before he exhaled, then he got up, threw his cigarette stub in a potted palm, and went inside. Kate sprinted to the door just before the latch caught. In high school, she'd been the recipient of a few trophies as state champion short-distance runner. Now she motioned for Liz to hurry. When Liz reached her, she whispered, "It's not like we're doing anything illegal. We were invited."

They stepped into an empty back room with a sink, microwave, refrigerator, and marble counter. On top of the counter were silver trays holding bubbling champagne, a raspberry at the bottom of each flute. Kate grabbed two glasses and handed one to Liz. She lifted her glass and clinked it against Liz's. "Here's to Dylan. May a flight of angels guide him safely home."

Just as Liz said, "Amen," Gregory Grayson charged through the doorway from the main showroom.

"What are you two doing back here?" He was only about five-foot-seven, but his deep voice made him seem seven-foot tall. Liz almost didn't recognize him until she saw his frosty blue eyes. Not that she had personally met the man who owned most of the barrier island, but she'd seen his face plastered in the society pages and business section. It seemed not only did Gregory Grayson own Aunt Amelia's Melbourne Beach Theatre Company but also the new Beachside Gallery. On top of that, Liz knew he'd recently bought the luxury glass-bottom treasure diving yacht docked behind the Indialantic by the Sea Hotel. Apparently, there were a slew of tourists and islanders who didn't mind spending three hundred dollars an hour to dive for treasure, then be catered to by a five-star chef and a white-gloved crew.

As part of his shop, Treasure Tours by the Sea, Gregory's brother Tom was in charge of booking daytime excursions on the yacht. Tom also sold tickets for local Treasure Coast and Space Coast events and attractions. Aunt Amelia told Liz that since the shop's opening a month ago, Treasure Tours was booking well into the winter holidays.

Kate stuck out her hand. "Mr. Grayson. So nice to meet you again. I'm sorry for our impertinence, but we were looking for the powder room and came upon a room full of champagne. You can't blame us, can you?" She added a giggle, then petted the sleeve of his white muslin Thai tunic. The expression on his face didn't fit his relaxed Zen clothing, but then he smiled, and his face changed from cold and impenetrable to warm and welcoming.

Kate gushed, clearly in awe of the man. "Are you the owner of the gallery? Your brother Tom runs the next shop over from mine at the Indialantic by the Sea Emporium."

"I'm one of the owners of the Beachside Gallery. You must be Minna's partner? She's sold five of her works in the first twenty minutes. You should be proud of her."

"I'm not Minna's partner; that's Francie Jenkins," Kate answered. "She's in Europe on a buying trip. I run Books and Browsery by the Sea—used books and whatnot."

Gregory arched his brow when she said "whatnot" but didn't ask her to explain.

"I'm also playing the part of Detective Anderson in *The Bat*."

He looked at her with a blank stare.

"The next production at the Melbourne Beach Theatre. *Your* theater," she reminded him.

"Well. Break a leg," he said.

He must not be a hands-on owner if he didn't know what his theater company was up to, Liz thought. No doubt he trusted Tom with the play choices.

Liz stood back and observed their tête-á-tête. Not a big drinker, she realized she'd already finished her champagne, even the succulent raspberry at the bottom. At least her hand had stopped shaking. She didn't want to be rude but needed to find Minna before someone blurted out the news about her nephew.

Gregory wordlessly handed Liz another flute of bubbly.

"Thank you."

"I don't think we've met?" He extended his hand, then thought better of it and gave her a double-cheeked air-kiss, Manhattan-style.

Liz returned the requisite bobbing motion, then stepped back. "Liz Holt. Nice to meet you. Congrats on the gallery." There was something mesmerizing about him. His eyes were so Paul Newman blue that it was hard to tear her gaze away. He could have been in his midthirties, but she knew he was closer to fifty.

"I'd better get back outside and find one of Craig's minions to pass out the champagne before it goes flat. Craig's shirking his duties, although we do seem to have a bigger turnout than expected." He bowed slightly, then left the room.

Liz assumed Craig was the manager of the gallery.

Kate said, "See, no problem about an invitation. He's something special, isn't he?"

"I guess. Let's go out to see Minna and get it over with." Liz tipped up the champagne glass. As soon as the liquid hit her lips, she remembered something her therapist from New York had said: It was okay to have an occasional drink when feeling happy and grounded. Drinking when depressed or sad: not a good idea. She put the flute on the counter, the crystal clattering against the marble.

Chapter 6

It was too late.

When they stepped into the showroom, Jake, Dylan's new friend and crewmate on the fishing trawler, was talking to Minna.

The room was packed. Liz tapped Kate's left shoulder and pointed. They both watched as if in slow motion as Minna received the heartbreaking news. She jerked back as if slapped, then started to crumple to the floor. Jake put his arms around her and kept her upright.

Liz grabbed Kate's wrist and pulled her forward, parting the crowd, not caring what designer shoes she stepped on or what bruises might be caused as she elbowed her way toward Minna. When they reached her, Minna looked at their faces, wanting them to tell her it wasn't true. Liz pushed Jake away and supported Minna, Kate got on the other side, and they escorted her into the room with the champagne, only now it was filled with a half-dozen servers getting instructions by the same guy with the bow tie who wouldn't let them in without their invitations. After the bow-tie guy finished, she overheard him tell one of them, "Mr. Grayson almost fainted when he walked in and saw how I arranged the art for the opening. I could tell he thought it was genius that we included Minna Presley's nephew's photographs."

Suddenly, the bow-tie guy noticed Minna. He was by her side in an instant. He grabbed a glass of champagne off a tray and put it in her hand. "Congrats! Amazing show."

Minna stared blankly ahead. Kate took the glass and placed it back on the tray. "Ms. Presley needs a moment. Can everyone please vacate the room?"

"Of course," bow-tie guy said. "You heard Ms. Presley. Everyone grab a tray and vamoose!" Each took a tray and exited. "Please let us know if you need anything, Ms. Presley."

"Thank you, Mr. Ruskin," Minna said on autopilot.

Once the room had cleared out, Liz pulled a chair to where Kate held on to Minna, then gently pushed her down.

In between sobbing and gulping for air, Minna said, "Not Dylan. Oh, my poor sister-in-law. Poor Alyse."

"Agent Pearson has contacted Alyse," Kate said. "Liz and I planned to tell you first. Somewhere private." Then Kate joined Minna in the sobbing.

Liz took Minna's hand in hers. With tear-filled eyes, she said, "I'm so sorry, Minna."

Minna looked from one to the other, started to speak, but couldn't get the words out.

"Do you want me to tell Mr. Grayson that he should send everyone home?" Kate asked.

"Yes." Then, as if zapped by lightning, she shot up from her seat. "I've changed my mind. Please come with me. I need your support."

They moved into the main showroom. Apparently, the word had gotten out about Dylan's death. The crowd quieted, and everyone took a step back as Minna, followed by Kate and Liz, went to the center of the room, where Gregory Grayson stood.

Minna grabbed a flute of champagne from one of the waitstaff and said, "Can I have everyone's attention?" She made her way toward the wall on the western side of the gallery. Gregory, Liz, and Kate followed.

Daylight had faded into night, but a gibbous moon shone through the glass ceiling. Spotlights hung from thin metal beams, highlighting a wall of similarly framed photographs. One spotlight centered on Minna's pale face. "I've just learned that my talented, warm, loving nephew has passed away. Dylan insisted that one hundred percent of the proceeds from his work should go to the VWC, the Veterans' Works Charity, even though he could have used the money." She pointed to a framed photo of the exterior of a ship's wheelhouse; in the reflection of the glass was a man holding a camera. Dylan. Even while capturing the shot, a huge smile covered his handsome face. Minna lifted her glass and barely got out the words. "To Dylan...a life well...and too short...lived." Unable to retain her composure, the champagne flute slipped through her fingers and crashed to the floor. Kate caught Minna before she landed on shards of broken glass. Gregory took one of Minna's arms and Kate the other, then they escorted her into a room a few feet away.

Liz stood frozen, looking at the broken glass. For a moment, she was back to the night she was scarred.

"Such a tragedy," someone said from behind her.

She pivoted her head and saw Jake, Dylan's friend from the fishing trawler. Dylan had signed on to the boat three months ago, his first foray into commercial fishing, and even though Jake was younger—only in his early twenties—he'd taken Dylan under his wing. On the few Fridays Dylan wasn't available to deliver freshly caught seafood to the hotel, Jake had filled in. Liz would be lying if she said she wasn't angry with him for breaking the news to Minna in such a public place. And how had he known about Dylan's death? Agent Pearson had said she was waiting until tomorrow to announce it. Then Liz remembered what a small island they lived on. News traveled fast. She still wanted to give Jake a piece of her mind for the indelicate way he'd handled things, but when she turned, he'd disappeared. Just as well; this was no time for recriminations. She hurried toward the room into which Minna, Kate, and Gregory had escaped, opened the door, and stepped inside.

The room wasn't what she expected. It was only twenty feet wide and four feet deep. In front of her was a cushioned Lucite bench. Hanging above it was a framed modern-art print of intertwining octopuslike tentacles in shades of aqua, coral, and eggplant. Wide aluminum filing cabinets covered the rest of the wall space. She guessed they held portfolios of lithographs or silk-screened works of art. She could have sworn this was the door the threesome had opened. Where were they?

Suddenly, the wall behind the bench moved inward and she saw Gregory, Kate, and Minna.

"Ms. Holt," Gregory said. "I'm sorry if we frightened you. This is my specially built safe room. It's totally hurricane proof. I put one in all my buildings on the island."

Liz closed her open mouth and glanced into the room behind them. It was set up much like her loft in SoHo, everything you needed in one space, only without a tall ceiling or windows.

She made a mental note to look in to building a hurricane-proof safe room in the Indialantic. Although she had a hunch it would be too costly; the hotel was barely getting by as it was. She thanked God for the emporium shops. Aunt Amelia had wanted to open more of the Indialantic's hotel suites to the public, but Liz and her father thought it would be too much work for an eighty-year-old, even if she was the most active senior they knew. Plus, Liz wanted the hotel part of the Indialantic to stay the same—more of a boardinghouse filled with people she thought of as family.

Aunt Amelia had told Liz that in the '40s and '50s the cellar of the hotel was used as a shelter for elderly or handicapped Melbourne Beach residents who weren't able to vacate the island during fast-approaching hurricanes. Cellars were a rarity here, and she suspected that after all these years the Indialantic's subterranean level would be more like the catacombs of Paris from Hugo's *Les Misérables*. She remembered seeing a set of blueprints of the original layout of the hotel before the fire. Perhaps instead of building a hurricane-proof shelter, they could use a portion of the hotel's cellar as a safe room.

Kate was the last one out of Gregory's safe room. The thick panel made a suction noise as it automatically closed behind her. She came to stand next to Liz and said, "I told Minna I'd drive her home; you can take the van and meet us there."

"No need," Gregory said, his voice full of authority. "I'll have my driver give her a ride home."

"She might not want to be alone," Liz said.

"I'm fine, Liz," Minna said. "I've been grieving for Dylan every day since he was lost at sea. I need to go home to call my sister-in-law."

"Well, then," Liz said, "I'll drive your car to the Indialantic and park it in the emporium's lot. I can drop it off in the morning to check on you then."

Minna handed Liz her car keys, took Liz's hand in hers, and squeezed it. "Thanks, friend." Then she turned to Gregory and Kate. "Thank you, all."

A few minutes later, Liz, Kate, and Gregory watched Minna pull away in a chauffeured silver Mercedes Maybach. Gregory went back inside the gallery, and after Liz kissed her on the cheek, Kate headed to the rear parking lot.

As Liz walked toward Minna's BMW, parked on the street in front of the gallery, she heard a familiar voice with perfect diction. "Miss Elizabeth. Please tell me I didn't miss the gallery showing of Miss Minna Presley's works?"

She turned and saw Susannah Shay. "No, I think it's still going on."

"Good. Rehearsals were a dismal failure. Something is bothering Amelia; as her great-niece, you might want to look in to it."

"Will do, Susannah." Liz knew what her great-aunt was upset about. Dylan.

Liz saw Susannah bristle at her use of her first name. Liz had heard through the grapevine—Aunt Amelia being one of the grapes—that Susannah had requested that Liz address her as "Miss Shay."

"Thank goodness," Susannah said. "Now that I am moving to Vero Beach, the cultural capital of central east coast Florida, I need to make my appearances. I thought I might buy a piece or two for my new pied-à-terre. Minna Presley is a juried artist. Her bio and reputation are stellar. I had my people look in to her background. I always say, 'A person's past is a good indication of their character.' And there's no such thing as reinventing yourself unless you are atoning for past transgressions."

It must feel good to be so perfect. Liz thought about her notorious past in Manhattan. She had a feeling Susannah was wielding one of her double entendre's like the expert markswoman she was.

"Well, I had better go inside and make my purchase," Susannah said. "I need something in tones of peach and cream to match my living room's color scheme." She walked away in her Chanel tweed suit and pumps, using perfectly measured steps, as if she had a stack of imaginary books balanced on her head.

Liz went to the BMW, got inside, and headed for home. As she drove, she looked to her left at the shimmering sea, the waves highlighted by the light of the moon. The same sea Dylan had loved to photograph, the same sea in which he'd died.

Chapter 7

Wednesday morning, Liz kissed Bronte on her pink nose. The kitten turned away and hopped onto a stack of books in the bookcase flanking the window seat. Kate had named her Bronte because she used to hide in the classic book section in Kate's shop, which housed books by the Bronte sisters. Liz felt guilty she and Bronte wouldn't be able to perform their early morning ritual of sitting on the deck watching seabirds scavenge the Atlantic's shoreline. Having the Pelican Island National Wildlife Sanctuary only a few miles away, Bronte reaped the benefits of any errant avians escaping eastward for a flyby.

The gray-and-white tiger kitten was almost eight months old and small for her age. Liz hoped she stayed that way. Bronte was a lover, not a fighter. She made lots of hissing noises and chattered her teeth if any birds came near but never ventured off the deck in pursuit. Not that Liz would leave her alone outdoors. Too many threats from bobcats, alligators, giant crabs, and poisonous snakes.

Making sure Bronte's water and food bowls were full, she grabbed her handbag and set the alarm on the panel next to the French doors. After what had happened last spring, Fenton Holt was more concerned about human threats to his daughter than animal. She'd promised her father to always set the alarm, something she'd gotten used to doing while living in Manhattan but would never get used to in Melbourne Beach, the small, sleepy island where she'd grown up. Her father had also installed alarms and security cameras at every entrance and exit of the hotel and emporium. Aunt Amelia, trusting soul that she was, insisted on only setting the alarm in the evenings before bed, saying, "You can't teach an old horse new tricks," then waited for everyone to tell her she wasn't old. Which they always did.

Liz stepped onto the deck. It was the first time she could remember not making a beeline for the wood railing to soak up the ocean vista. Even though her beach was farther south than the Indialantic's, yesterday's horrific scene kept replaying in her head. She hurriedly went down the wooden steps to the driveway, then took the path leading to the Indialantic. She wanted to a snag a few of Pierre's croissants, filled with sweet citrus cream cheese, to bring to Minna when she dropped off her car. Ryan was scheduled to meet Liz at Minna's at ten, then give her a ride back to the Indialantic. Afterward, she hoped to be able to squeeze in a couple of hours of writing.

Working on her second novel was something she'd avoided for a long time. Now, it was all she could think about. An idea would pop into her head and she'd write it down on a napkin, paper plate, whatever she could find, including her inner arm. Liz was witnessing the opposite of what had happened when she'd tried to sit at her laptop in the months following her traumatic night with Travis. Now, it seemed she couldn't get the words out fast enough. Instead of writer's block, she had writer's can't stop. But when she woke this morning, instead of thinking of what plot point would come next in her gothic suspense-historical mystery, *An American in Cornwall*, all she could think about was that homicide detective Charlotte Pearson had shown up for what everyone assumed was an accidental drowning. She couldn't wrap her mind around the fact that Dylan had a huge gash on the back of his head and there'd been a gold coin beneath his body. She planned to stop by her father's to see if his girlfriend had gotten the coroner's report for Dylan's cause of death. Recently, Charlotte had been a little more accommodating than she'd been last spring, but she still was reserved when it came to sharing PD info with her boyfriend's daughter. And it was true Liz wasn't the warmest toward Charlotte, for reasons her therapist back in New York would have a Freudian field day.

A few minutes later, Liz pushed through the revolving door at the entrance of the hotel and saw Greta with a feather duster in her hand.

"Oh Liz, I'm so glad I caught you. We need to go over your auntie's pirates' picnic menu before anyone else sees it." Greta took out a folded piece of paper from her skirt pocket and put it on the counter next to the Indialantic's hotel register, which dated from 1926. When Liz was younger, she and Aunt Amelia had stretched out on the floor on the lobby's massive Persian rug, while her great-aunt would call out names from years past, when the Indialantic by the Sea Hotel was the premier resort for the rich and famous. She explained who was who and even told Liz how they'd been dressed based on volumes of albums filled with pictures taken by the house photographers. Some of the names in the register included nefarious mobsters and rumrunners; however, for obvious reasons, you wouldn't find their photos in any of the albums.

Liz picked up the menu and whistled. It was worse than she'd anticipated. Aunt Amelia had listed different dish ideas for the picnic using pirate terms: "cannonballs" for meatballs was the best of the bunch, although "peg legs" for pickles was a contender. Then there was "golden seashells" (mac and cheese), "bounty of the sea" (fish sticks), "Polly's crackers" (just plain crackers), and "shark bait" (cubed cheese). "Thanks, Greta. This obviously needs a little tweaking. I might have an idea that will make everyone happy. With only three days to go, we're cutting it close. I'll take this and see if I can't change the ordinary to the sublime with a little help from Pops and Chef Pierre."

"You're the best, Liz. You always know how to pacify your great-aunt's grandiose ideas and at the same time see the forest for the trees. Let me know if you need any help. Just give me the shopping list. What I can't pick up at Deli-casies by the Sea, I can get in town. How many are you expecting?"

Liz was a gourmet cook, taught by the best, Pierre. Due to his recent memory loss, she'd taken on the responsibility of prepping the hotel's meals. Lucky for Liz, Greta was not only a great housekeeper but also a good cook and took over when Liz couldn't. Greta and Pierre had become fast friends, and Liz was grateful for her help.

"Auntie said there are forty-eight people who've bought tickets for the picnic and treasure hunt."

"Let's hope the weather holds. I used to be able to tell ahead of time if foul weather was approaching by the pain in my hip. But since I got my new one, thanks to your father's help with my subpar insurance company, I'll be ready to dance the pirate jig on Sunday no matter what."

Fenton was known in the area as a defender of the underdog and always took on small cases for little pay. One of the reason's Aunt Amelia came up with Pirates' Weekend was to garner some extra cash to keep the Indialantic solvent. After they'd installed central air-conditioning in the hotel and emporium, the electric bills were four figures a month, not to mention the new metal storm shutters they'd purchased for a staggering amount.

After saying good-bye to Greta, confident she'd set her mind at ease, Liz walked through the large dining room and into the kitchen, where she was assailed by the voices of Aunt Amelia and Chef Pierre, whom Liz called Grand-Pierre, a play on the French word for grandfather, *grand-père*.

Pierre had been at the hotel before Liz and her father had moved in with Aunt Amelia, and he'd become her surrogate grandfather.

As soon as Liz opened her mouth to say, "Good morning," Pierre stuffed a petit beignet in her mouth. Pierre and her great-aunt were "food pushers," with one key difference: Liz didn't mind anything Pierre shoved her way. Aunt Amelia's meals, on the other hand, were something that made hot school lunches seem like they'd been prepared by Michelin thirty-two-star Chef of the Century, Joël Robuchon.

"Lizzie, what happened?" Pierre asked, his toque slightly askew. He had flour on his waxed and curled mustache, making him look like he'd just stepped in from a Florida snowstorm.

For a minute, she thought he was talking about Dylan.

"You left the copy of *The Murder at the Vicarage* on the back veranda."

Pierre was the one who'd gotten Liz hooked on Agatha Christie as a teen. Recently, with the blessing of her therapist, she'd been on a mission to read every book and short story Dame Agatha had written, and Pierre was her main supplier. However, between writing *An American in Cornwall* and a recent love affair with Sherlock Holmes, Miss Marple, Poirot, Tommy and Tuppence, and the rest of the crew had fallen by the wayside.

"I'd wondered where that book went to," Liz said. She looked over Pierre's head and gave her great-aunt a questioning look. Aunt Amelia shook her head in the negative. She hadn't told Pierre about Dylan.

A sonic boom sounded from the butler's pantry. Nine thirty. Aunt Amelia handed Liz a pair of earplugs, then put another pair in her ears. Pierre had always been immune to the daily ear-piercing sounds coming from the pantry. After almost thirty years of living with it, her great-aunt still had to protect herself from the noise. Every morning at the same time, Barnacle Bob screamed and carried on for thirty minutes in parrot. Something common to most macaws, and the reason a lot of the birds found themselves abandoned on the doorsteps of veterinary clinics and bird rescues worldwide. Another reason for their abandonment was that they refused to talk—not a problem in Barnacle Bob's case.

Instead of doing his squawking at sundown, as most macaws did, Barnacle Bob chose the morning for his reverie. Aunt Amelia called Barnacle Bob her "little rooster."

Liz gulped down a quick cup of coffee and told Pierre and Aunt Amelia that she had to run. She wanted to leave the two alone, so Aunt Amelia could talk to Pierre before he heard the tragic news elsewhere, as Minna had from Jake. She prayed Pierre would be able to handle the loss. Was it only last Friday, when she'd seen him and Dylan in the hotel's gourmet kitchen? Pierre had been showing Dylan how to make his signature Cajun-seasoned grouper filets, dredged in the perfect amount of flour and cornmeal, then fried in the huge cast-iron frying pan Pierre brought with him from France thirty years ago.

Once, when Liz was Pierre's sorcerer's apprentice, she'd made the mistake of scrubbing the cast-iron pan with dish detergent and a scouring pad. Later, she found out dish detergent was a big no-no. Pierre had instructed her that the key to cooking on a cast-iron pan was to let the seasoning build up from meal to meal and only to clean it by rinsing with hot water, then wiping with a paper towel. He'd told her that, if needed, she could use a paste of coarse kosher salt and water to remove stuck-on food. For her tenth birthday, Pierre had given Liz her own pan, which she'd been using faithfully for eighteen years with nary a soapsud touching it.

Before leaving the kitchen for Minna's, Liz placed six of Pierre's stuffed croissants on a small cake plate with a glass dome. Then she gave him a smooch on the cheek, blew an air-kiss to Aunt Amelia, and opened the door leading outside. As she stepped through the doorway, she heard Pierre say, "I think I'll make some savory croissants for a change. What's your opinion, *ma chérie*? Fill them with camembert and a sprinkling of cayenne for Dylan to try when he comes tomorrow for his cooking lesson?"

Liz turned and forced a smile on her face, then gave Pierre a thumbs-up before she closed the door, happy he didn't see the tears welling in her eyes.

Taking the path that snaked past Pierre's fragrant kitchen garden, she headed toward the back of the hotel. The grounds were green and profuse with flowering vines and flowers, their scent mixing with the salty air. She came to her father's office/apartment and knocked on the door. The shingle hanging outside his door read, FENTON HOLT, ESQUIRE.

He opened the door and, after giving her a hug, ushered her in. "Coffee?"

Her father was as bad a cook as Aunt Amelia, and that included his coffee-making abilities. "I'm good. Just had some of Grand-Pierre's."

He laughed. "I didn't make it myself. I snuck into the hotel's kitchen this morning and siphoned some from the carafe. I drank it all, but I can make you instant. I can't ruin that."

"No, I'm good. And I'm spoiled," she said, grinning.

Her father walked behind his desk and sat his tall, lanky form in the leather desk chair she'd bought him for Christmas. Liz took a seat across from him. As she opened her mouth to speak, he spoke for her. "Dylan. I know; it's such a devastating loss." Her and her father usually finished each other's sentences. After he lost his wife, and Liz her mother at age five, their father/daughter relationship was closer than most.

"Any word on cause of death?" she asked.

Fenton looked down for a moment, his reading glasses slipping to the tip of his nose and focused on a stack of legal papers. Her father had been Brevard County's lead defense attorney before he retired for health reasons and now took on small cases for islanders. He glanced up at her with watery eyes. "No word, yet. You sound like Ryan."

"What? Ryan has already spoken to you about Dylan's death?"

"You just missed him. He seemed concerned about the wound on the back of Dylan's head."

Liz thought back to yesterday's scene, then sank back into her seat. "What did Charlotte say about it?"

He stared out the window at the view of the Indian River Lagoon and the Indialantic's dock. "I haven't had a chance to talk to her. She's scheduled to do a press conference at ten."

Liz looked at the wall clock. "It's a minute to ten. Let's watch."

They entered her father's apartment, which had access to the interior of the hotel, and sat together on the sofa surrounded by towering bookcases, mostly filled with law books, police procedurals, and fiction and nonfiction crime-and-thriller books. Liz grabbed the remote control from the side table and switched on the television. Sally Beaman, the local cable news reporter, came onto the screen. Liz had gone to Melbourne Beach High with Sally. A former homecoming queen, her beauty paled when the screen switched to a close-up of five-foot-ten Charlotte standing behind the podium. Liz looked over at her father. His eyes didn't leave Charlotte's face. He really was smitten.

When the news conference was over, her father clicked off the TV. "Not anything groundbreaking. They still haven't ruled on cause of death. I'll fill Charlotte in on Ryan's thoughts about foul play later."

"There's one more thing," Liz said. She told her father about the gold doubloon.

He raised his eyebrows over green eyes that were the same color as Aunt Amelia's. "Now, that's a strange turn of events. Do you have it with you?"

Liz dug in her handbag and retrieved the coin, encrusted with centuries of petrified marine life, and handed it to him.

"It sure looks authentic. If you want, I have a former client I can show it to."

Before Liz could answer, the phone in the office rang. Fenton got up to answer. From his "uh-huhs" and "you sures?" she could tell it was Charlotte. It took everything Liz had not to charge into the office and force him to share the phone receiver with her. A few minutes later, he hung up and came back into the room.

"Well?" Liz asked.

"They still have some tests coming back. I'm meeting Charlotte for dinner; maybe by then she'll know more. She has a lot on her plate after a drug dealer was charged with homicide when a teen died from fentanyl-laced heroin. This is one case where I'm happy I'm not lead public defender. I don't think I could have taken the dealer's case."

"Tragic, and I'm glad they're prosecuting. However, I'm sure if you were still in office, you would have taken the case. Presumption of innocence was spoon-fed to me since I was wee small, Father dear."

He smiled. "You're probably right."

She glanced at the clock. "I'm going to drop off Minna's car. She went home in Gregory Grayson's Mercedes last night and I drove hers here."

"That was nice of both of you," he said.

"What do you know about Mr. Grayson? He has his finger in a lot of pots. He must've come into the picture during the time I was in Manhattan. Reputable or dis?"

"I don't know anything 'dis' reputable," he said, putting quotation marks in the air. "If anything, he seems pretty transparent. He's the new owner of Auntie's theater company and the luxury treasure diving yacht, along with some other projects I saw posted at town hall. Why do you ask?"

"He's also the owner of Beachside Gallery and has a hidden safe room in the gallery, supposedly in case of hurricanes. We should have one at the hotel. Has anyone been in the Indialantic's cellar in decades?"

Fenton scratched his clean-shaven chin. "Yes, we have the hotel inspected yearly, but the inspectors don't spend a lot of time down there for obvious reasons. It's amazing that after all the hurricanes and gales the Indialantic's withstood, only once was there any water damage."

The cellar under the hotel had been boarded up in the 1940s. It was rumored that at one time it was used to hide the bootlegged liquor of local rumrunners without the okay from Liz's great-grandfather. "You never let me down there as a kid. I think we should consider building our own hurricane-safe room."

"Not a wise idea; there's a reason Floridians don't have basements or cellars."

"Flooding?"

"But it's a good idea to build something. I'll look in to it," he said. "Speaking of storms, there's one churning its way toward us from the

Caribbean, just in time for your Pirates' Weekend. It might make landfall on Sunday or Monday."

"Not *my* Pirates' Weekend. Auntie's. How many times have the weather forecasters been wrong? This old hotel has withstood almost a hundred years of tropical weather; I'm sure she has a few more years left in her. That reminds me: How's getting historical status going?"

Seeing that many famous celebrities had stayed at the Indialantic by the Sea over the years, her father was trying to get the hotel deemed a national landmark to garner extra cash for repairs. Back in the day, some infamous guests like mobster Al Capone, and some celebrities like Ginger Rogers could be seen behind dark glasses in their private cabanas on the beach. Currently, Susannah Shay, a celebrity in her own mind, was the only guest until her condo was ready. The last time they'd opened the hotel to the public hadn't turned out too well, as in a murder.

"It's looking good," he said, searching the room for something. Liz knew what: his reading glasses. She pointed to the table by the couch. where he'd taken them off to watch the newscast. It was an old pattern of hers, looking out for him, like he always did for her. "Well, my offer still stands if you need me to help you inventory the library. You know it's my favorite room."

"You worry about your novel. Ryan and I have it covered. Ryan's a hard worker in the library's inventory process—unlike you, he doesn't pause to read passages from each book."

Chapter 8

After saying good-bye to her father and leaving the gold coin with him to show to his connection, Liz stepped onto the lane that followed the rear of the hotel, passing the open courtyard that separated the hotel from the emporium.

"Per Mr. Grayson, I have full authority!" Liz heard someone shout from the direction of the hotel's dock.

"Over my dead body!" someone else answered.

She turned her head toward the Indian River Lagoon and saw two men standing on Gregory Grayson's glass-bottomed treasure diving yacht, *Visions of Gold*. One of the irate men glanced toward shore. It was Tom, proprietor of Treasure Tours by the Sea, director of *The Bat,* and Gregory Grayson's half brother. The other man was Victor, who'd been given the role of Dr. Wells in the play. Liz waved, but they didn't notice. She watched Tom shove Victor, who landed on a cushioned deck chair, then kicked out his right leg, his foot connecting with the area between Tom's legs. Tom let out a howl so loud, even Rosie, the Roseate Spoonbill they'd named for obvious reasons, took off from the piling next to the boat like a bat out of one of Aunt Amelia's *Dark Shadows* crypts.

Liz ran across the highway, wondering whether to board *Visions of Gold* or stay safely on the dock. The decision was taken out of her hands when Erica Grayson emerged from the cabin. "What are you fighting about? You're making a scene."

Liz had only seen Erica once, during rehearsals for *The Bat*. On stage, she had appeared to be a sweet young ingénue, wearing little makeup, her dark hair pushed off her face, dressed in a muted floral dress that hit beneath the knee, something that might be worn to a fête on the grounds of a vicarage in Miss Marple's St. Mary Mead. It was hard to believe this was the same woman.

Erica stepped to the rear of the deck and put her hand on Victor's shoulder. She wore a flesh-toned lace bikini that left little to the imagination. Liz could tell her firm breasts were definitely fake. When Erica turned to point her finger at Tom, Liz had to turn away before she broke out in laughter. Erica's thong-covered, or barely covered, caboose—Aunt Amelia's word— appeared to have been inflated with a bicycle pump. Liz wondered how she could stand upright on her skinny, storklike legs and spike sandals. During rehearsal, she'd only seen Erica from the back row. Up close, her face looked waxy, like the hard plastic 1960s Miss Revlon doll Kate had on display in her shop.

Erica noticed Liz and grabbed an off-white sarong from a chair. She tied it around her waist, then came to the brass railing to ask, "Can I help you?"

"Is everything okay? I'm Amelia Holt's great-niece, Liz."

Erica tipped up her sunglasses, exposing bloodshot eyes. She focused her stare on Liz's right cheek, then she turned to the men. Liz couldn't picture Erica and Gregory as a couple. Him in his Thai tunic and sandals and her like someone from a *Real Housewives* episode. Perhaps east didn't meet west, and that had something to do with their getting a divorce. Of course, Gregory's zillion-dollar Mercedes wasn't exactly a Zenmobile. A better question would be why Erica was on her ex's yacht. And would Gregory be happy that Erica's boyfriend Victor was lounging around with her? She didn't have time to contemplate things because Tom came down the gangway and onto the dock.

"Liz. What can we do for you?" He moved with the agility of someone who weighed about a hundred pounds less. He had a teddy bear physique and reminded Liz and Aunt Amelia of Ernest Borgnine from the '60s sitcom *McHale's Navy.* Her great-aunt had had a one-episode part as a Navy nurse catering to a boatload of sailors who'd come down with the chicken pox. Liz and her great-aunt played an ongoing game in which they assigned '60s TV monikers to hotel guests and emporium shopkeepers. They'd both agreed on Tom's alias.

"I heard the shouting," Liz answered.

"Oh, that. Just a little roughhousing." Tom was a close talker. He took a step toward her, and she could see it was time for a nose hair trimming. "We're getting in character for *The Bat.*"

Liz glanced toward the deck. Both Erica and Victor were looking at her. As far as she knew, there weren't any scenes in which someone got kicked in their private parts. "If you're sure everything's okay…"

"Sure I'm sure. Gregory is coming by later to do an inspection for *Visions of Gold*'s maiden launch on Friday. Hope it goes better than last night's gallery opening."

"Were you there?"

"Yes. Such a tragedy. I can tell you're a close-knit group, and that poor young man who drowned had a promising career in photography. Did you know him well?"

"Well enough to know he was a wonderful person." Liz looked at her watch. "I'd better get going. Good luck on the inspection. Auntie is so excited about Pirates' Weekend, especially your donation of free passage on *Visions of Gold*."

"Of course. Colorful character, Amelia is. So happy to have her in my production. She will lend a little spice to the cast—not that Susannah isn't a consummate performer; a tad bland but memorized her lines in three days. Can't ask more than that."

"No. You can't. You must be excited about the launch."

"I'll be happy when it goes as planned. There's a lot of pressure for me to prove myself to Gregory, seeing Treasure Tours by the Sea was my idea."

"Have you and your brother shared in other ventures over the years?"

"Oh no," Tom said, moving in even closer. "Gregory and I just met for the first time. Of course, living in Florida, I couldn't help but be aware of his successes. When I read about him refurbishing the Melbourne Beach Theatre and his purchase of *Visions of Gold,* I couldn't help but think it might be the right time to connect, knowing I have expertise in both areas. You see, my mother passed away recently. She wouldn't allow me to even mention my and Gregory's father's name. She never asked for a penny from him. I was ready for a change of scenery and a chance to finally meet my brother." He extended his arm to encompass the beauty around them.

"It is quite breathtaking, isn't it?"

He smiled. But he wasn't looking at his surroundings; he was looking straight at Liz.

"It certainly is." She took a step back. "Well, have a nice day, Tom."

"You too, Liz." Then he went up the gangway.

As she walked away, she heard, "Liz, wait." She turned. Tom was on the upper deck, leaning over the gold railing "Can you please pass on something to Amelia? We had a couple of cancellations because of the possible weather pattern making its way toward the island. I'd like to invite two of my leading ladies, Amelia and Susannah, to partake in the maiden voyage of *Visions of Gold.* If you could please tell them, I'd appreciate it."

"Oh, they'll both be so excited," Liz called up.

He gave her a gap-toothed grin and went into the cabin. Erica and Victor had disappeared from the deck, and Liz wondered about their relationship. None of her affair, just something to gossip with Aunt Amelia about over high tea in the Indialantic's inner courtyard.

She left the dock, crossed the road, and strolled to the emporium's parking lot, where she'd left Minna's car. Coming in her direction was Brittany Poole, proprietress of Sirens by the Sea. Liz had no choice but to continue.

"Brittany," Liz said as she passed.

"Liz," Brittany said in return, then continued toward the road, in the direction of the dock. Not even an inkling of a smile. Brittany's platinum blond hair was weighed down with hair product, helmetlike. She'd be so much more attractive without all the makeup. Liz's father would say Brittany was insecure and hiding from the world through her face paint. He always saw the good in people. Liz wished she could, and she usually did, but not where Brittany was concerned. She'd been burned too many times by her when they were preteens and teenagers.

Kate had told her that Brittany had been trying to strike up a friendship with Tom. But he didn't seem interested. Brittany was a gold digger, and Liz had no problem believing she was going after him to get closer to his brother Gregory—the richest man on the island. Tom would be a stepping stone to Gregory, now that he had become one of the most eligible and wealthy bachelors in Florida. She was glad Brittany had set her sights on someone besides Ryan. Every time Liz entered the emporium, Ryan was either doing some grunt work in her shop or Brittany was hanging out on one of the stools in Deli-casies, being catered to by Ryan from behind the barista counter. Liz never saw Brittany in the gourmet deli and café when Pops, Ryan's grandfather, was the one working.

As she walked to the parking lot, Liz saw clouds hovering above the Indian River Lagoon to her left. To her right there were clear blue skies, but the surf was rough, and she could hear the loud pounding of the waves against the shore. The lagoon was gray, the Atlantic teal blue. Typical island weather. When Liz reached the lot, she took out Minna's keys, pressed the Unlock button, and got in. She reached her hand down to adjust the seat back and felt something metal. A key ring with two small keys. She put them in the console drink holder and took off for Minna and Francie's cottage.

It was getting late, and Ryan was waiting for her. He wasn't the most patient person, but a lot better now than when she'd first met him in April, when she'd thought he was the biggest jerk on the planet. He continued to be a mystery. There was something he seemed to be holding back. Something from his past, perhaps? Liz wasn't sure she wanted to know. It might be better to leave the past in the past—for both of them.

Chapter 9

As Liz drove south on A1A, blasting one of Minna's preset jazz stations, she distracted herself from thoughts of Dylan by admiring the island's untamed beauty. Minna's Beemer was a lot smoother to drive than Betty's ancient Cadillac, which Liz keep at her beach house now that the eighty-three-year-old's driver's license had expired. All her facilities were intact, Betty just didn't drive much, saying, "Since the emporium shops opened, living at the Indialantic is like living in your own ecosystem. Everything at your fingertips."

A few minutes later, Liz pulled in front of Minna and Francie's yellow cottage, which had worn aqua shutters with cut-outs of seahorses. Ryan's black Jeep was parked in front, along with a motorcycle. She got out of the car and went to the passenger door, just as Jake, Dylan's friend and co-worker, bounced out of the cottage like he'd just chugged a couple of Pops' triple espressos from Deli-casies. She grabbed the plate of croissants off the seat, shut the door, and hurried to meet him.

"Hey, Jake."

"Aren't you one of Minna's friends from last night?" He flip-flopped toward her, then stopped in front of his bike. His aviator glasses were mirrored, and she saw herself frowning in their reflection. Something was off about the kid, even though he was impishly cute, with his freckles and sun-bleached blond hair. He was *too* up, *too* smiley. Maybe it was the sight of the huge, menacing squid tattoo on the underside of his forearm that bothered her. It didn't look like the squid she used to make her calamari. This was an inky sea monster with tentacles waving in all directions, lurking to catch its prey. "That's quite the squid tattoo," she said.

"It's not a squid, it's a kraken. She's my protector and good luck charm for when I'm deep sea diving.

"She?"

"Served me well so far."

"If I remember well, aren't kraken supposed to grab onto ships and pull them down to Davy Jones's locker? I would think that would be bad luck for someone who spends most of his time on a boat."

"Nah, the opposite. Or at least that's what the guy who gave me that tattoo said." He added a laugh.

She stuck out her hand and he pumped it. "Liz Holt," she said. "We met before, when you were delivering seafood to our chef, Pierre, at the Indialantic by the Sea." Jake reminded Liz of a grown-up Dennis the Menace. She was sure her aunt would agree, and then she'd tell Liz again about the time she played a nosy neighbor on the '60s sitcom.

Jake grinned. "The French guy, right? Wears that funny hat?"

"A toque. Yep, that's Pierre. How's Minna doing?"

He shrugged his shoulders. "Seems okay. I better go. Have an all-night job later, have to take advantage of the pre-storm surf." He turned toward his bike.

Liz had been avoiding The Weather Channel, hoping when she looked that Tropical Storm Roberta would have made an about-face. "Jake, can I ask if you were with Dylan when he went overboard?"

He didn't turn around to answer her, just climbed on his motorcycle. "I was below, in the cabin. Dylan was on deck."

She stepped closer and put her hand on his shoulder. "It must be tough. He was your friend. I'm just trying to figure out what happened."

"He was my best bud."

She wished he'd take off his sunglasses so she could see his eyes—a window to the soul, Aunt Amelia always said. She chided herself for being so distrustful of his sunny nature. Must be from living in Manhattan for so long. Not to mention avoiding all the piranha paparazzi who'd circled prior to the ruling that vindicated her in the defamation of character lawsuit her ex had waged against her. Liz had been deemed not guilty, though every headline said the ruling was a travesty of justice, Travis's readers siding with the Pulitzer Prize–winner and author of the best war novel of the century.

Jake put on his helmet. A surfboard was strapped to the back of the motorcycle with a bungee cord. "He didn't have a chance," he mumbled. "Wish I could have saved him. Would've jumped in if I was there…that's how close we were." He grabbed the gold cross hanging from around his neck and kissed it. "Catch you later. Tell your French guy, I'll bring him his seafood on Friday. I'm sure Dylan would have wanted me to." He started the bike's engine and took off.

She watched him head south on A1A, toward the Sebastian Inlet, home of international surfing competitions, then walked to the cottage, up the stairs to the porch, and rang the doorbell. Ryan answered.

As soon as he saw Liz, a huge smile appeared on his handsome face. "Pretty timely, Ms. Holt. Not like you at all," he said, adding a wink.

She exhaled when she saw him, not realizing she'd been holding her breath. She wasn't a swooning female who got the vapors, ready to melt into the next available male's arms in emotional situations, but Ryan was one of those take-charge, never-let-them-see-you-sweat kind of guys. No doubt a throwback to his years on the FDNY. He'd given up a lot to live on the island, and they were taking it slow. Maybe too slow on her part, but she was gun-shy after her disastrous relationship with her narcissistic ex.

"Big jerk," she said, grinning. "How's Minna?" Now that they'd moved onto being friends, she almost missed the verbal sparring matches they'd had at the beginning of their relationship, when Ryan had believed every disparaging thing the tabloids had said about her.

He pushed open the screen door and stuck out his head. His breath smelled minty. "She's sleeping right now. A neighbor's sitting with her. Hold on, I'll tell the neighbor I'm leaving."

"Wait. I don't want to disturb Minna, but I brought her some of Pierre's stuffed croissants. Can you give them to the neighbor or put them in the kitchen?" She held them toward him, along with Minna's car keys.

He took them in his large hands. "Okay, I'll be right back."

Liz sat on a white-painted rocking chair on the porch. The aqua cushion was covered with Francie's elderly tortoiseshell feline's hair. Now that Liz was a newbie cat owner, it didn't bother her in the least. She couldn't see the Atlantic, but she could smell it. Liz didn't want to go inside and bother Minna; she would call her later, in the early evening, and see if she could bring over one of Pierre's gourmet meals.

What started out as a beautiful morning was now clouding up. The billowy white-marshmallow clouds were being overrun with gunmetal-gray storm clouds. Three days until Pirates' Weekend. Would the forecasters be right for a change? Would Tropical Storm Roberta morph into Hurricane Roberta? And what about a funeral for Dylan? Would it be here or in Clearwater? She knew Aunt Amelia and Pierre would want to make the trip.

Lightning zigzagged in the sky. She heard thunder at the same time Ryan tapped her on the shoulder. She jumped, the back of the rocking chair banging against the plateglass window. Another clap of thunder sounded.

"Sorry I startled you," he said. "We'd better get to the Jeep before the deluge."

They ran to the car, the humidity wicking its way through her long hair, expanding it into a mass of strawberry-blond ringlets. All she needed was a folk guitar and a gig at a coffee house in Greenwich Village. Too bad she couldn't remember the lyrics to Joni Mitchell's "Big Yellow Taxi." Or, unlike her great-aunt, carry a tune.

The rain started halfway to the Jeep. Gallant Ryan followed her to the passenger door and opened it. "Buckle up." His wet navy T-shirt clung to his rock-hard upper arms and chest.

He shut her door, went around the Jeep, and got inside.

"Hey, check out that Mercedes. A Maybach," he said.

Liz glanced out the window and saw Gregory Grayson stepping out of his car, holding an umbrella. No chauffeur this morning. It was nice of him to check on Minna. "It's Gregory Grayson, the owner of the Beachside Gallery. I don't know where he came from, but when I was eighteen, before I left for Columbia, no one had heard of him. Now, ten years later, he seems to own all of Melbourne Beach."

"Is that a bad thing?" Ryan asked. "Is he one of those megadevelopers who demolishes quaint old buildings, then builds condos or strip malls?"

"Bite your tongue!"

"You can bite my tongue anytime," he said with a big grin.

She slapped his arm. "Susannah Shay would have your hide for that innuendo. She actually came to dinner last night wearing white gloves— said she's trying to stay in character."

Ryan grinned, "And she's been trying to rid me of my New York accent, even though I don't have one. I only lived in Brooklyn for a couple of years. So, back to Gregory Grayson. Is he a big jerk like me?"

"No, Gregory actually seems to be a good guy."

Ryan's smile turned to a frown.

"You're a good guy too, Ryan Stone. But Gregory took the failing Melbourne Beach Theatre Company out of debt and is remodeling it. And now, with the new gallery and his treasure diving yacht, I think he's making a positive impact on the island."

Ryan gave her a wary glance. "You're on a first-name basis with him? You sure sound like a fan."

"I only met him once. Don't know him at all. And I'm not the type to get suckered into trusting someone by their outside appearance or accomplishments; learned that lesson long ago."

For some reason, Liz hadn't told Ryan about her ex's soon-to-be released book based on their turbulent relationship. The wounds were still too raw. Plus, she hadn't read it and didn't plan to in the near future. She changed the subject. "How's Minna?"

"I only saw her for a few minutes before her neighbor came over and put her to bed. She watched the news conference about Dylan. Might have done more damage than good. But she didn't seem to have any questions about cause of death, like I do."

"I saw my dad before I came here. He told me about your concerns about Dylan's wound and promised to tell Charlotte when he sees her." Then Liz filled him in on the gold doubloon.

"That was a lucky find," he said as he turned into her driveway.

"What do you think of Jake?"

"Who?"

"Dylan's friend from the fishing boat. I just talked to him as he was leaving Minna and Francie's."

"So that's his name."

"He's the one who told Minna about Dylan last night, before Kate and I had a chance. I wonder how he found out."

"I was in the kitchen when he came in," Ryan said. "I heard him tell Minna he wanted to return something to Dylan's room, then about five minutes later, I heard him say good-bye. Five minutes is a long time to drop something off."

"Are you always so suspicious?" she asked.

"Goes with the job. Or should I say my old job."

"Actually, your new job as Dad's private eye. Should I call you Magnum, P.I.? This isn't Hawaii, but close enough to it."

"That would be a stretch."

"Jake seems young and immature. Wonder what he was returning."

"I guess you could ask Minna."

Liz looked over at his attractive profile. His dark, almost black hair needed to be cut. There was stubble on his chin and his dark, intense eyes made him look like a pirate—all he needed was a gold-hoop earring.

She pressed her finger to his cheek. A dark eyelash stuck to her finger and she held it in the air. "Make a wish and blow."

Their eyes locked, and he gently blew on her finger. The lash hung in the air for a moment, then disappeared.

"Don't ask what I wished for or it won't come true," he said.

Liz didn't have to ask; he reached over and kissed her on the lips. Kiss number forty-five. But who was counting? She said, "I just came up with the best idea for Sunday's treasure hunt. Why don't you dress up as the Treasure Coast's favorite pirate, Henry Jennings?"

"Oh no, you don't. Aunt Amelia asked me to do the same thing. And what kind of pirate name is Henry Jennings?"

It was endearing that he called her great-aunt "Aunt Amelia." He'd done it without hesitation the first time her great-aunt had asked him to.

Ryan started the engine, put the Jeep in gear, and pulled away from the curb.

"Jennings was actually a savvy Englishman from Jamaica who plundered the survivors' camp of the 1715 Spanish fleet that sank here," Liz said. "You know the story."

He performed a U-turn on A1A, heading north toward the Indialantic. "I know the story of the Spanish treasure ad nauseum, hence the name given to this area, the Treasure Coast. But I don't know anything about Pirate Jennings."

"Jennings started out as a businessman, then he was captain of a ship in the West Indies. His job was to hunt pirates. Soon, he realized it was more profitable and exciting to be a privateer/pirate himself compared to a seaman. He recovered three hundred thousand pieces of eight a hop, skip, and a jump from where we are right now. And you'll never believe what became of him at the end of his career."

"Hanged by a noose?" Ryan asked. "Walked the plank?"

"No. He accumulated prestige and wealth, then surrendered to the governor of the Bahama Islands and lived out the rest of his life in luxury as a respected citizen."

"Classy pirate."

"Indeed. You must play him. He was quite the colorful character. There's a book about him in Kate's shop. Ask her about it. He wasn't your typical pirate. A scoundrel, like you. You can help me leave the clues to the scavenger hunt and make sure no one cheats. Wait until you see the grand prize. Auntie won't tell me what it is, but I can tell it will be spectacular—she never does anything on a small scale."

"I'll get back to you on that one," he said.

When they reached her beach house, Liz reached down to retrieve her handbag from the floor. A four-by-six glossy card with four shots of a sexy woman dressed in revealing clothing stared up at her. She quickly put the card in her handbag. "Thanks for the lift," she said, then bounced out of the Jeep like her rear end was on fire.

Ryan wasn't the most wholesome of men, not a bookish academic like Travis, with perfect manners Susannah Shay would admire, but she'd never guessed he was into escorts or porn stars. Probably a misunderstanding, like in romance movies on the Hallmark Channel—the girl in the photo was probably his cousin. Sometimes when Ryan was helping Fenton on a case, he had to go to some seedy locations; maybe the card had been put on his windshield.

During the past few weeks, she'd noticed Ryan disappearing at odd hours, mostly at night. She'd asked her father if he had him working on something for a client and he'd told her no. The only thing he had Ryan working on was helping him inventory the Indialantic's massive library. Once, she even asked Pops if he knew where his grandson kept disappearing to. All Pops had said was, "He's working on a case."

When she reached the steps to her deck, Ryan opened the passenger window and called out, "That's it? No glass of wine on the dock at sunset?"

Liz glanced up at the stormy sky and pointed.

"You know this schizophrenic island weather," he said. "It'll clear up. Might be the last good sunset in a while, with bad girl Roberta making her way up from the Caribbean."

"Let me see how much writing I get done. If you'll play a pirate, I'll meet you on the dock. And I'll tell you what: I'll even bait your hook next week."

He frowned and gave her a puppy-dog whimper. "Do I really have to dress up?"

"Take it or leave it."

"Okay, bossy pants. I guess I'll take it."

Liz remembered the first time she'd suggested they watch the sunset over the Indian River Lagoon, he'd scoffed and said, "The guys on the FDNY would have a field day if they knew I watched sunsets and sipped pink wine." So they'd compromised. Once a week they shared a sunset and a glass of rosé, and once a week they went fishing at Honest John's Fish Camp and shared a beer. Liz's alcohol limit was four drinks a month. Alcohol had been one of the reasons for the scar on her right cheek.

Chapter 10

Liz climbed the steps to the bell tower, holding a basket with Bronte snuggled inside. It was the same basket she had been left in six months ago, when she was found on the steps outside the emporium's doors. In her other hand was her laptop and a boxed lunch packed by Grand-Pierre, like the ones he used to make for her after she'd complained that the hot lunches in her middle school's cafeteria were subpar.

Almost every lunch hour at school, a group of kids would pass by Kate and Liz's table and ask, "What's it today? Calves' brains?" Some were simply curious, some being obnoxious teens, but Liz and Kate hadn't minded. All they cared about was what gastronomic delight awaited them. Sometimes there was homemade pâtè de campagne with sliced cornichons and coarse French mustard on sourdough bread. Other times, something as simple as a workman's lunch: a crusty baguette, slabs of sharp cheddar, and a small container of Pierre's mango and curry chutney.

Some of their best school lunches were simply hotel leftovers from one of Pierre's meals prepared the night before. Brazen Kate had made an arrangement with one of the lunch ladies that they would share Pierre's gourmet leftovers as long as they could use the school's microwave to heat them up. Pierre always included enough food for at least three.

It had been a while since Pierre had made Liz lunch, and the act made her hopeful that his memory might be improving. It was usually her fixing Pierre one of his childhood favorites from when he lived with his mother in a tiny seaside town in France. Pierre's memory might be spotty, but only this morning, he'd told her a new story about his early days at a Cordon Bleu cooking school. When, as a young man, he worked below a tall American woman with a singsong voice: Julia Child.

Liz paused near the top step, out of breath, hearing footsteps behind her. No, erase that: dog steps. She turned and saw Killer, followed by Caro.

"No dog and cats allowed in my writing lair," she scolded.

The Great Dane turned his head and looked at her Scooby-Doo style: "You talkin' to me? What about that kitten in a basket?" Unlike most Great Danes, his ears were unclipped. He and his feline cohort in crime, Caro, both had black fur with white tuxedo-shirtfronts; the only difference in their markings was that Caro had a white milk mustache on her upper lip.

Liz peered down at them, although Killer was almost at eye level, and said, "I'm sure, now that Betty and the Captain are away, you two will want to cause trouble." Caro meowed, and Bronte opened her eyes and mewed back. "Oh, come on up. But no distractions; I'm way behind on my daily word count."

A few minutes later, she was at the small wooden camp table she'd designated to be her workstation. She couldn't get a Wi-Fi signal in the bell tower, so she had to save her work, then run down the stairs every couple of hours to connect to Wi-Fi and email the document to herself or send it to the cloud for safekeeping. There were easier places to write, but nothing with a view so glorious and an environment so quiet. Although today she was having a hard time concentrating. Her thoughts kept going back to Dylan's death. An entire scene she'd written, set on the Cornwall moors, that had her protagonist walking among the heather and looking out over the cliffs to the rough sea, just wasn't working. It was too stereotypical of Gothic romances. She scrapped it by cutting and pasting the passage onto another document she'd titled "Cut Stuff." Not wanting to "throw the babies out with the bathwater," as one of her writing instructors had told her class must be done on occasion. Saying if you kept going over and over it, get rid of it. Adios. Trust your instincts and move on.

She glanced up at the belfry, which still held the original bell from when the Indialantic had been built. A long, thick corded rope hung from the bell's clapper, like the one Hugo had described in his novel *Notre-Dame de Paris*, better known as *The Hunchback of Notre Dame*. When Liz was small, she and Pierre would come up to the bell tower and he would read the novel to her. Sometimes in French, sometimes in English. The story had taught her to be tolerant of other people's differences.

She lightly traced the scar on her cheek with her finger, then stood. All three pets were snoozing. She tiptoed over to the arched opening that faced east, surveying the ocean panorama she'd grown up viewing every day. It still took her breath away twenty-three years later. The waters were calm under a partly sunny sky, but the waves at sea looked higher, reminding her of Jake and the surfboard she'd seen strapped to the back of his bike. Was he telling the truth that he wasn't anywhere near Dylan when he went overboard? And why was Jake below deck during the squall and Dylan above?

She brushed away her melancholy thoughts and went back to the other side of the small room, to the arched opening that faced the Indian River Lagoon. She had a fantastic idea. She would invite Ryan up to the bell tower for their next sunset-over-the-lagoon date. She could bring up a large floor pillow and some wine and cheese from Deli-casies. Turn it into their make-out lair. Her face heated at the thought, and she glanced toward the dock, where her father's vintage Chris-Craft *Serendipity* bobbed in its slip. Next to Serendipity was *Queen of the Seas*, the Indialantic's tour boat.

Visions of Gold took up the south side of the dock. It was a magnificent vessel, state of the art, nothing like the treasure salvagers Liz had seen docked in the harbor. Liz leaned out the open archway, breathing in the salt on the breeze. From this vantage point, the view went on for miles. Glancing to the north, in the direction of the emporium, she saw Charlotte talking animatedly with Victor Normand, the actor from her great-aunt's theater troupe. The homicide detective didn't look happy, and neither did Victor. Charlotte, dressed in a navy linen shirtdress that showed off her long, tanned legs, passed him something, probably her card, then regally walked away.

Unbeknownst to her father, when she'd first heard he was dating Charlotte, Liz had Googled her. She came from a megawealthy family on Orchid Island, a tony little enclave of Vero Beach. The family owned beachfront property and had a stable of world-renowned polo ponies—one of which was ridden by Britain's Prince Charles years ago. Charlotte's affluent background explained the exquisite way she dressed and her cool persona. What didn't make sense was why she would become a homicide detective instead of resting on her family's laurels. *Oops.* Now that she thought about it, that raised Charlotte a notch on the likability scale, reminding Liz never to judge a book by its cover, as people had done to her on more than one occasion. Putting that aside, what would a homicide detective and Victor have to talk about?

Something rubbed against her leg. Bronte. She looked down. "Are you reminding me we have to go to our tea party?" At the word "go," both Killer and Caro stretched and yawned. Caro had been curled in Killer's arms, Maxi-Me and Mini-Me. Liz went to the desk and put her laptop in its case, then grabbed Bronte's basket and her lunch box, where not a crumb remained. It was a quarter to three and she'd promised Aunt Amelia that she would meet her in the hotel's inner courtyard in fifteen minutes. She opened the arched wooden door and started down the stone steps to the hotel's second floor, feeling like the Pied Piper as the Three Musketeers followed closely behind. Bronte took up the rear, pausing at the top of each step before leaping down. It was the first time she'd gone down the tower stairs on her own. Liz was proud. Her baby was growing up.

* * * *

"Pass the cream before Susannah finds us," Aunt Amelia whispered.

They sat under the thirty-foot palm tree in the hotel's interior courtyard. Ryan had been right; the storm clouds had vanished and the sun shone down on them in all its splendor. High tea was something Liz and her great-aunt had shared sporadically in the past. Since Susannah's arrival, it had become a weekday ritual—one Liz tried to avoid like the plague. Today, Susannah was in Vero Beach picking out carpeting for her new master bedroom. Liz was hopeful that meant she would be moving into her condo toot sweet. Susannah wasn't a terrible person; it was just impossible for Liz to relax and let her hair down around the woman.

Liz passed the cream as requested and took a sip of her orange-infused green tea. Pops supplied the imported loose tea from his shop and Pierre added dried orange peel from the Indialantic's tree to make it Aunt Amelia's special blend. She was a substandard cook, but Aunt Amelia made a mean pot of tea. The entire tea service was the same as the one the hotel had when it opened in 1926. However, this wasn't the original set. After the fire in 1945 destroyed the hotel's china closet, only a cake plate remained, a chipped cake plate at that. Recently, Kate had gone on a mission to replace the Crown Ducal Bird of Paradise chintzware tea set after she saw an old photo of guests enjoying high tea in the courtyard, a ritual Liz's English great-grandmother, Maeve from Cornwall, had initiated almost a hundred years ago.

Liz took a nibble of her second French macaron. Pierre always made his macarons in three lightly tinted colors; pink, mint, and French blue—Marie Antoinette's favorite shades. Liz always chose the mint, Aunt Amelia the pink, and when Betty returned, she would snare the French blue. Also on the bistro table was a plate of mini almond crêpe cakes with mascarpone. Susannah would be really irked if she learned she'd missed out on one of her favorites.

"Okay, Auntie, let's get the lowdown on the cast members in *The Bat*. Earlier, I saw Tom push Victor on *Visions of Gold*'s deck; then, in retaliation, Victor kneed Tom in the groin. Also, Erica Grayson appeared out of nowhere. On top of that, I just saw Victor talking to Charlotte."

"Our Charlotte?" she asked. She didn't need a peaked brow; today, hers was shaded in thick dark auburn, reminiscent of film star Joan Crawford's. Aunt Amelia had told Liz that Bette Davis once called Crawford's brows African caterpillars. "Bette was probably just jealous because hers had to be drawn on," her great-aunt had said. "That's showbiz." Susannah Shay and Aunt Amelia seemed to have a similar relationship to Davis and Crawford, but Liz doubted either one of them recognized it.

"Yes, Auntie. *Our* Charlotte," Liz said, slathering lemon butter on her scone. Pierre had taught her how to make the perfect butter for his scones—butter, lemon juice, and confectioner's sugar. As simple as that.

"Kneed in the groin. Kneed in the groin," Barnacle Bob spouted from his perch on the back of Aunt Amelia's chair.

"BB, simmer down," her great-aunt said with a click of the tongue. "Shame on you." She was the only one able to take him out of his cage and have him return without protest. Liz kept her distance 24/7.

"Pretty Boy. Pretty Boy."

Aunt Amelia covered her mouth with her hand to stifle a giggle. Yes, at eighty she still giggled. Then she handed Barnacle Bob a slice of kiwi.

"That's why he's so incorrigible; you're rewarding him for his bad behavior," Liz said.

"Hmmm, I remember some pretty naughty things you did as a child, and my leniency didn't seem to bother you then."

"Touché," Liz said, then gently clinked her teacup against her great-aunt's. "Okay, spill. But before you fill me in, we first need to assign character names to the Melbourne Beach players. We already have Tom as gap-toothed Lieutenant Commander Quinton McHale."

"I forgot Ernest Borgnine's character's name was Quinton, just like Quentin Collins, half man/half werewolf, played by the gorgeous David Selby on my show. Boy, did I have the hots for that guy, me and the rest of the cast."

It had only been recently, after Susannah Shay had arrived, that Aunt Amelia had begun calling *Dark Shadows* "my show."

"Oh, by the way, I have news for you," Liz said. "Tom invited you and Susannah on the maiden voyage of *Visions of Gold*. Apparently, there were a few cancellations."

"Ooh la la! How fabulous. Maybe I can bend his ear on upping the lines in my part. He specifically invited Susannah, right?"

"I'm afraid so, Auntie."

Aunt Amelia frowned, then brushed away her disappointment and said, "I wonder what you wear on a luxury treasure diving yacht. I'm certainly not diving for treasure, but it will be fun to watch the others through the glass bottom. Susannah told me that *Visions of Gold* cost over a million dollars."

"How would Susannah know that?"

"Oh, Susannah's the biggest snoop on the planet. One day it's going to get her in trouble."

"I'm curious about Erica Grayson. What vintage television actress does she remind you of?" Liz asked, steering the conversation away from Susannah Shay.

Aunt Amelia looked up at the sky, palm fronds leaving shadows on her face. "Julie Newmar!"

"Nailed it! The Catwoman from TV's *Batman*. You're good," Liz said, and they fist-bumped.

"I was actually on set when Miss Newmar appeared in an episode of *The Twilight Zone* called 'Of Late I Think of Cliffordville.' It was right before her stint on *Batman*. She inspired my cat-eyeliner technique."

Liz looked at her brightly made-up face, with her pearlescent baby-blue eye shadow and thick black liner. She wondered how her great-aunt's role as Cornelia Van Gorder's dowdy maid was going to pan out.

"Okay," Liz said. "My turn. Let me think about Victor. Let's see; he's in his early forties, a meticulous dresser, and tall, dark, and handsome. I think he has what they called in your day, Auntie, a 'chiseled jaw.' How about Carl Betz from …"

Aunt Amelia jumped up, disturbing Barnacle Bob, who flew to the center of the iron bistro table and landed on the plate of macarons. "Dr. Alex Stone! From *The Donna Reed Show*. Agreed, one hundred percent!" she said, sitting down. Then she extended her arm for Barnacle Bob to hop on. "Plus, Victor's playing a doctor in *The Bat*. How apropos."

"Stone, the same last name as Ryan," Liz mused. "Shouldn't it have been called, *The Donna 'Stone' Show*, instead of *The Donna Reed Show*?"

"Never thought about it. Maybe, because the series started in the midfifties they were afraid no one would watch unless they used a movie star's name in the title."

"Like *Seinfeld*," Liz said.

"What-feld?"

"Never mind." Amelia Eden Holt rarely watched anything that wasn't from the late '50s to the early '70s—her peak years as an actress. Each viewing came with a charming anecdote. Her great-aunt had almost fifty television credits on IMDB. And those fifty hadn't included all the television shows she hadn't gotten credit for, proving how big a character actress she really was.

Aunt Amelia poured more tea into Liz's cup. "Donna Reed was a big star in the forties. *It's a Wonderful Life* was the movie that gave her a name."

Like half of the world, *It's a Wonderful Life* was the Holts' favorite holiday movie. So much so that every time Barnacle Bob rang the bell inside his cage, Aunt Amelia would say, "An angel just got its wings." Then, as soon as Aunt Amelia left the room, Barnacle Bob would say, "The Devil made me do it," a line from the TV show *Laugh-In*, from when Amelia Eden Holt played one of Goldie Hawn's background go-go dancers. Liz had watched the episode with her father, great-aunt, and Barnacle Bob in the screening room. Most of the humor and lingo was lost on Liz, but Aunt Amelia sure knew how to shimmy and shake her shoulders in her fringed minidress and thigh-high gold sequin boots.

"So why do you think Tom and Victor were fighting? Do they both like Erica?" Liz asked.

"I have no idea. But you could always ask Miss Etiquette. Susannah makes it her goal to get the lowdown on our small troop. I wouldn't be surprised if she hired a private detective to make sure none of the actors had a spotty past, *Playboy* centerfold, or partook in a sex scene. She's such a prude but didn't mind stuffing her brassiere for her part as a wanton bar-patron-turned-vampire on *my* show."

That was a little more information than Liz needed to know about Susannah. "How about Erica? How long was she married to Gregory? Any children?"

"No children. I think they were married for only a couple of years, got divorced recently. Erica has been a thespian in the Melbourne Beach Theatre Company for three years. I think that's how she and Mr. Grayson met. And why he bought the theater, no doubt. Thank God for that. Wait until you see the plans for the refurbished theater."

"Does Erica do anything else but act?"

"She doesn't have a job that I know of, but I think she is part owner of *Visions of Gold* and the Beachside Gallery. Judging by her abundance of jewelry and exotic cars, she must've done well in the divorce settlement. Although Susannah says her taste is garish and nouveau riche, unlike Susannah's once-, twice-, or thrice-removed cousin and New York social-register icon Amy Vanderbilt. It's an understatement that Susannah and Erica don't get along. But I have to admit, they're fun to watch."

"Meow," Liz said, and Barnacle Bob, scaredy-cat of cats, gave her a dirty look.

"You're right, Lizzie dear. Susannah is my friend, not my rival."

Liz had a feeling her great-aunt's fingers were crossed behind her back. "Tom?"

"Tom recently moved here from Jacksonville. He ran a small theater up there, and a travel agency. He told me he came up with the idea of Treasure Tours by the Sea when he read in a Florida paper that his brother Gregory had just bought a luxury treasure-diving yacht. Apparently, Tom and Gregory never met until he moved to Melbourne Beach, even though they both knew of the other's existence. There's a ten-year age difference between them. Gregory's mother was his father, Philip Grayson's first wife; Tom's mother was his second."

"It seems hard to believe Tom never met his brother before. Jacksonville is only two hundred miles away. Is Tom ..."

Greta ran into the courtyard, her French braid untwisted, her breathing labored "Amelia! She's coming."

Liz assumed she meant Susannah.

"Greta, you grab the tray off the cart and clear the table. Hide it on the other side of the tree. Barnacle Bob, come with me. Pronto!" The parrot hopped onto her shoulder and they scurried through the open French doors and into the hotel's dining room. Aunt Amelia called back to Liz, "Save yourself!"

Liz darted out the other doorway that led to the lobby, then crouched down behind the check-in counter. She heard the swoosh of the revolving door and what she assumed were Susannah's footsteps sounding off the terra-cotta floors. She was safe.

Or at least she'd thought she was, until her phone rang. She took it out and looked at the screen. It was Minna. Liz tapped it to answer, just as an overwhelming odor of mothballs descended upon her. She looked up. Susannah looked down. There was a disapproving twist to Susannah's mouth. "Miss Elizabeth, what are you doing? I thought your auntie agreed with my suggestion that cell phones should be switched to the Vibrate position at all times, so as not to disturb the hotel guests."

Liz stood and put her finger to her mouth to hush her.

Apparently, no one hushed Susannah Shay. She huffed off, mumbling about having a word with Amelia about her insolent great-niece.

"Minna. Hi. Sorry about that," Liz said into the phone.

"I wanted to thank you for the scones and dropping off my car. I just woke up. Can you believe it?"

"I hope the rest did you good."

"It did."

Liz heard a scuffling on the other end of the phone, and "What in the world!" Then silence.

"Minna. Minna? Are you there? Everything okay?"

No response.

Chapter 11

Liz hurried through the lobby doors. Minna and Francie's cottage was only a mile away. She had a choice of running to her beach house and getting Betty's blue-bomber Cadillac DeVille or using one of the hotel's golf carts, parked a few feet away. She chose the golf cart.

It was a bumpy ride following the road on A1A, especially because she drove one-handed, the other hand grasping the phone to her ear. Every few minutes, she called out, "Minna, are you there?"

She saw the smoke when she was about eight hundred feet away from the cottage. She stopped the golf cart and dialed 911, reporting a fire at Minna's address. "Yellow house…aqua shutters. Hurry!" They told her help was already on the way. She hung up and pasted her foot to the floor.

When she got to the cottage, she parked the golf cart on the grass near the front steps, got out, and charged inside, calling, "Minna! Minna!"

Smoke filled the cottage. She heard someone coughing and went to the front bedroom. Minna was on the floor, looking under the bed. When Liz walked in she glanced up. "I can't find Turtle." Turtle was Minna's roommate's eighteen-year-old tortoiseshell cat.

"Where else does he hide?" Liz knew all about cats and their secret hiding spots.

"He might be in Dylan's…the guest room, off the kitchen."

Liz ran down the hallway. The smoke was less dense at the back of the cottage and she had no problem finding the room. "Here kitty, kitty," she called as she ran inside. She searched under the bed, but no Turtle. Next, she went to the closet. Turtle was curled in a tight ball on a nest of clothing, his amber eyes wide open in fright.

"Come on, Turtle, let's get some fresh air." Liz reached for him, and he retreated farther from her reach. Finally, she picked up the whole pile of clothing with Turtle on top. She cradled the cat inside the clothing like a baby in a receiving blanket. Liz yelled, "Minna! I found him." Then she hurried to the front of the house, where she saw Minna in the living room searching under the sofa, coughing from the smoke coming from the south side of the cottage.

"Thank God," she said, before getting up from the floor and rushing over to Liz and Turtle.

"Is there anything else you need? I hear sirens."

"No. I've got my file box of important papers and my handbag."

Every resident who lived on a barrier island, especially during hurricane season, had a file box at the ready that held insurance, bank, and other important papers. "Good. Let's get the hell out of here."

They rushed out the front door and down the sidewalk, just as the first fire truck showed up.

Minna placed her handbag and file box on the sidewalk, then stretched out her hands to take Turtle. When safely in her arms, she nuzzled her nose in the cat's fur. "Turtle, Francie would never forgive me if something happened to you." She looked over at Liz. "Thanks for finding him."

"No problem," Liz said, still holding the pile of clothing Turtle had been laying on. "I better move the golf cart so the fire department has access to the front of the cottage."

Minna nodded her head, tears making tiny rivulets through the soot on her cheeks. Liz left Minna's side, walked over to the golf cart, and threw the clothing into the small cargo area in back.

After Liz parked the cart on the neighbor's sidewalk, she returned to Minna, who was talking to a first responder. "Anyone inside?" Liz heard him ask.

"No," Minna answered.

"Before we go in, do you know where the fire originated?"

Minna looked at him with a glassy stare. "The front left bedroom. My bedroom."

"Are you okay? Do you need a paramedic?"

"No. I'm fine."

"Take a couple of deep breaths."

She did.

"Good. No coughing," he said, and took off to join the rest of firefighters who'd just bounded by, carrying a humungous black hose.

Flames leaped up from a window on the left side of the cottage. Minna closed her mouth and let out a small whimper, Liz grabbed her and the cat in an embrace. When they pulled apart, Minna said, "I was talking to you on the phone in the kitchen and smelled smoke. How did this happen? I don't smoke cigarettes. Don't even have matches or candles in my bedroom."

An officer from the Indian River Police Department approached them. "Are you the owners?" he asked. He was in his fifties and had a kind face, with laugh lines around his eyes.

"I'm the owner," Minna replied. "Minna Presley."

"The artist. Right? My wife bought one of your pieces recently. She's a big fan." He put his hand on her shoulder and asked gently, "Do you know how the fire started?"

They all glanced toward the cottage. Four firefighters aimed the black hose, shooting gallons of water at the flames licking up the front left side of the cottage. Within seconds, most of the fire had been extinguished.

"No. I have no idea how the fire started," Minna answered.

"Okay. No worries. The wind is mild, and this is the best team of firefighters for miles."

"Thank you," Minna said.

They gazed at the activity on the south side of the house. "Look!" Minna said. "A rainbow."

There was the positive Minna Liz knew and loved. She looked to where Minna had pointed. In the stream of water arching from the hose, Liz saw a bright rainbow of colors. "That's a good sign that everything will be fine, Minna."

Once, when Liz was with her ex at a celebrity book signing party in the Hamptons, everyone had rushed onto the lawn to view an amazing rainbow. Travis had said, "Rainbows are just a refraction of sunlight in droplets of water when your back's facing the sun." Liz hadn't cared about the scientific elucidation. It was like telling a small child that the fat man in the red suit and white beard didn't exist. Some things were meant to go unexplained.

"Minna! Are you all right?" a male voice said from behind them.

They turned to see Gregory Grayson, his Mercedes idling behind a fire truck.

"Yes," Minna replied.

He looked at the cat in her arms. "I was on my way back to check on you. I stopped by earlier. Did your neighbor let you know?"

"She did. Thank you for being so concerned."

They all looked at the cottage.

"The fire seems to be contained," Gregory said. "Is there anything important inside?"

"No. Oh yes; I should have grabbed Francie's jewelry box. But as you said, the fire is contained, and it was on the opposite side of the house from her bedroom."

"Where's her bedroom and where's the box?" he asked.

"Francie's jewelry box is...Oh my! I can't even think! I believe it's under her nightstand. The first room to the right, when you walk into the cottage." Before she could say more, Gregory charged up the walkway and into the house.

A few minutes later, two firefighters, each holding on to Gregory's arms, escorted him out of the cottage. He tried to shake them off to no avail as they half-dragged him toward Liz and Minna. Another firefighter followed behind, holding a pink jewelry box. Gregory's tanned face was flushed. "Let me go! I wasn't trying to steal anything!" Gregory shouted. "Do you know how much money my company, Gray Isle, donates to the Barrier Island Fire and Rescue?"

"No, but we do know how much Minna Presley contributes through her charity auctions. And we know you don't live here," the taller of the two firefighters said.

"Please release him," Minna said. "He was only going into the house on my request."

The third firefighter, a woman, went to hand Minna the jewelry box. Minna still held Turtle, so Liz said, "I'll take it."

The firefighter looked at Minna, and she nodded her head. "I'm so sorry, Gregory," Minna said. "Thanks for going inside."

He caressed her arm. "No problem, Minna. As long as you're safe. I think they'll be able to save most of the cottage."

They all looked up. Only a light wisp of smoke escaped from a window on the left side of the cottage.

"Minna, I insist you come stay at the hotel," Liz said. "At least until it's clear for you to go back."

"And I'll send a construction crew over to assess the damage," Gregory said.

The female firefighter turned to Gregory. "No one is stepping inside until we determine the origin of the fire." She took out a business card and handed it to Minna. "We'll secure the side windows and doors. You can call tomorrow to see when you're allowed back."

Minna took the card.

"Come on, Minna, let's go. You need Aunt Amelia to take you under her wing," Liz said.

Minna looked down at a docile Turtle.

"Of course Turtle can come," Liz said. "Auntie will welcome him... welcome both of you with open arms. We have three cats at the hotel already. Barnacle Bob is going to have a conniption, but Killer the canine will be over the moon," she said, trying to lighten the mood.

"You two go," Gregory said. "I'll stay behind to see if I can get any intel on the fire."

Liz grabbed the file box and Minna put her handbag over her shoulder.

"Thanks again, Gregory," Minna said, glancing at the cottage before they turned and went in the direction of the golf cart and Minna's BMW.

As they walked, Liz saw Gregory's chauffeur get out of the Mercedes and run to his boss. He wore a baseball cap and dark Ray-Ban sunglasses, and she was floored when she saw the driver was Victor Normand. Liz watched Victor approach Gregory. He towered over him. "Do you really think it's wise," Victor said, "running into a burning house? I'm glad you're okay, Mr. Grayson."

"Thanks for your concern, Victor."

Victor gave Gregory a threatening look that only Liz seemed to notice. Then he went to the rear passenger door and held it open. Liz had a feeling Gregory didn't have a clue Victor was involved with Erica. Or maybe if he did know, he didn't care.

Minna hadn't witnessed the exchange, and Liz scurried to open the passenger door of the BMW. Minna placed Turtle on the seat and Liz put the file box and Francie's jewelry box on the floor in the backseat. Liz said, "I'll meet you back at the Indialantic."

Minna got in her car and Liz watched her pull away. She hurried to the golf cart, got in, and headed north to home. Halfway there, she realized something.

Why hadn't she called Ryan—one of FDNY's finest?

Chapter 12

Thursday morning, Minna, Kate, and Liz were at Deli-casies by the Sea lapping at the homemade whipped cream atop their caramel macchiatos. Filling in as temporary barista was Ryan, while Pops prepared conch salad in the kitchen for his TGIF seafood menu.

Liz had explained to Kate what had gone down the day before at Minna's cottage. She had also called Ryan last night, and they'd gotten into their first disagreement.

"Why didn't you call me as soon as you arrived at Minna's?" he'd asked.

She hadn't liked his tone of voice. He wasn't her father. She'd said, "I called 911, and so had Minna. I wasn't in any danger; the smoke was contained on the south side of the cottage, coming from Minna's bedroom."

"You know that now. You have no idea how fast a fire can spread. And you had no idea of the origin or reason for it."

"Tell me you wouldn't have done the same."

There had been silence on the other end of the line. Why *hadn't* she called Ryan? They'd ended the conversation on a pleasant note. But, even now, she could hear the coldness and anger in his voice. Was it concern or a macho guy thing?

Liz watched Ryan at the controls of the espresso machine and thought back to when they'd first met, when her impression of him was of a dark, brooding, and insolent adversary. Liz looked at him as he passed a foamy cup of espresso to Minna. Now, all she saw was his concern for Minna. It seemed Liz was the one being a big jerk.

"Oh Minna, how terrible," Kate said. "How much can a person take? You're welcome to come stay with me at my beach shack until the damage is assessed."

"Kate, you're too kind. Turtle and I already found shelter at the Indialantic. But I really appreciate the invitation."

Last evening, Turtle had been safely deposited in Aunt Amelia's sitting room and given her own cat bed next to Barnacle Bob's cage, much to his displeasure, while Greta had been dispatched to freshen up the Oceana Suite.

Ryan's dark eyes transferred to Minna. By the firm set of his jaw, Liz could tell he wouldn't rest until he got down to who or what had started the fire. "Minna, did you hear any loud sounds of glass breaking before you smelled the smoke?"

"Not that I can think of. The last couple of days have been such a nightmare. I'm just glad Francie is in Europe and Turtle is safe. My sister-in-law decided to remain in Clearwater, even though I'd invited her to stay in the guest room. Dylan's room." She smacked herself on the forehead. "I'm such an idiot. No wonder she didn't want to come, I should have offered her my room—but then...the fire."

"Oh, I'm sure that's not the reason she didn't come," Kate said.

"You're right. I talked to Alyse this morning. The police haven't finished with the autopsy, so she doesn't know when the funeral will be, or where. Until then, she's staying in Clearwater."

Liz looked over Minna's head at Ryan. He'd caught it too. Something must be up if they still hadn't released the body. "Minna, if you want, I can talk to Auntie, and maybe we can postpone Pirates' Weekend until after the funeral."

"That's sweet of you, but with everything so up in the air, you all should keep to your plan. And until I can get back inside my home, I can help you."

"That's not necessary," Liz said.

"I insist," Minna said. "It'll be a good distraction."

"What about the artwork you had in the house? Was anything damaged?" Ryan asked.

"Most of my work is at Beachside Gallery, or Sun Gallery in Vero Beach. I can't imagine what started the fire. The air-conditioning system is on the other side of the cottage. I don't use a blow dryer or curling iron, as you can see." She grinned, and they glanced at her short, gel-spiked brown hair with its green and blue tips.

It was a relief to see a smile on Minna's face. "Well, if the fire department doesn't find the origin of the fire, I know a good arson investigator." Liz looked at Ryan and winked.

"I'll head over there tomorrow to check it out," he said.

"Thank you, Ryan." She dug in her handbag and passed him a set of house keys. "Now I'm going to relieve Ashley at Home Arts."

"How's she working out?" Liz asked. Ashley was a local high school student who usually worked as a barista for Pops and Ryan in Deli-casies. Because Francie was away, Pops and Ryan had loaned her out to Home Arts by the Sea.

"She's amazing," Minna said. "She even knows how to use a sewing machine and knits quirky items the youngsters are in to." She slid off the barstool and grabbed her macchiato. "I'm going shopping at Sirens by the Sea to pick up some basics I'll need until I can get back into the cottage."

Pops shuffled up to them, holding a big bowl. Liz could tell he was still hurting from his second knee operation. "Who wants to be a taste-tester?"

Kate raised her hand, "I do!" The other three seconded the motion.

He spooned something onto small plates and handed them out.

"A bonus," Pops said, "if you can tell me what the secret ingredient is." Pops was renowned for his amazing cold salads.

It was Ryan's turn to raise his hand.

"Not fair, Ryan Stone," Liz said. "You had a preview of all your grandfather's ingredients." She took another bite. She thought she knew the main ingredients and called out, "Dried cranberries, green onions, roasted squares of butternut squash, spinach, toasted pecans and orzo pasta, mint, with an orange honey vinegar dressing. Am I right, Pops?"

A smile traveled from ear to ear through the roadmap of wrinkles on Pops' face. He had tufts of white hair on top of his head and large ears. Liz and Aunt Amelia hadn't come up with a '60s actor he reminded them of; his ears screamed Johnny Carson, but that was as far as the resemblance went. "You're close, Liz," Pops said. "Very close. Only one mistake."

Liz looked down at her plate and the elliptical shape of the orzo. "I know! Pierre used it once. It's very hard to find. Pearl couscous. Nailed it!"

"Indeed you did, Liz, butternut squash salad with pearl couscous," Pop answered. "Anything missing?"

"Not at all," Minna said. "A beautiful fall salad. Pops, I'll take a half a pound for lunch."

Pops went back to the kitchen, then returned with a container filled with more than a half-pound of salad. He put the container in a Deli-casies bag, along with a miniloaf of sourdough bread, and handed it to Minna.

"What do I owe you, Pops?"

"On the house. I heard about the fire. I'm so sorry for all your troubles."

"Everyone is so kind. You're going to make me cry."

Kate stuffed a mini tropical fruit tart in her mouth. Pops was a great salad maker and a cheese and wine connoisseur, but the hotel's chef, Pierre, provided

Deli-casies's baked goods and most of the desserts. "Yeah. Everyone's nice with one exception: Brittany."

Ryan, Kate, and Liz turned their heads to their right at the four-foot partition that divided the emporium shops from each other. The shop adjoining Deli-casies was Liz's archnemesis Brittany Poole's clothing and jewelry shop.

"Keep your eye on her, Minna," Liz said, lowering her voice. "Brittany has a penchant for ripping off the price tags, then making up her own dollar amounts. Fantastical dollar amounts."

"Don't worry," Minna said. "She still hasn't paid me the balance from the piece she bought at Sun Gallery, so I have an open tab in Sirens."

Last April, Brittany had bought one of Minna's works, then given the gallery owner a bounced check.

"And get a copy of your owed balance. I've found Brittany's math skills sorely lacking," Kate added.

Ryan rolled his eyes, making it clear he didn't want to get involved in female gossip. Only in Brittany's case, every word they'd spoken was true; no gossip required.

After Minna returned to Home Arts to relieve Ashley, Kate said, "Liz, I want to show you my new purchase. Come next door."

When Liz didn't respond, Kate kicked her ankle.

"Okay. Let's see it," Liz answered.

They said good-bye to Ryan and Pops and went next door to Books & Browsery by the Sea. The shop was crammed with vintage items and towering barrister bookcases.

"Follow me," Kate said, her long brown ponytail swinging back and forth as she walked. "We need to talk about what's going on."

"I'll follow, if I'm able," Liz said, sidewinding crates of used books and a sundry of unidentifiable objects Kate had rescued from the garbage, thrift shops, and garage sales.

They both plunked down on the overstuffed magnolia-print sofa at the back of the shop.

"Okay, how do you think Minna looked?" Kate asked.

"Not good. Between Dylan and now a fire. I don't know…"

"Don't know what?" Kate asked.

Liz filled her in on the wound at the back of Dylan's head. She left out the gold coin; she didn't want to talk about it until she knew if it was authentic. Liz didn't want Kate to start postulating until she found out from Charlotte why the body hadn't been released to the next of kin. Then she told Kate the details about the fire and how Jake and Gregory Grayson had showed up at Minna's cottage. "Actually," Liz said, "Gregory was at Minna's twice. Once when I dropped off her car, and then at the fire."

"He must be enamored with Minna. Lucky lady," Kate said.

"Not so lucky," Liz reminded her.

"You're right."

"Oh, I almost forgot. Guess who Gregory Grayson's chauffeur was this morning? Victor."

"Victor as in Dr. Wells in *The Bat*?"

"The same. How are you getting along with everyone in the cast?"

"I haven't rehearsed any scenes yet. The day I auditioned for my part, I caught Erica and Victor coming out of the room adjacent to the screening room. This production is becoming like your great-aunt's *Peyton Place*," Kate said with a laugh.

Peyton Place was a 1960s nighttime TV soap opera. Aunt Amelia had had seven or eight small parts in the drama, all uncredited. Liz had watched only one episode, with her great-aunt playing a bystander in a courtroom scene in which Lee Grant, playing Stella Chernak, admitted to committing perjury when she accused one of Peyton Place's elite, Rodney Harrington, of murdering her brother Joe.

"Aunt Amelia has renamed that room the Enlightenment Parlor," Liz said. "It currently looks like a sultan's tent from *Aladdin,* with cushions scattered all over the floor and beaded curtains."

"Aww. One of our favorite cartoons from Disney. Any magic carpets in the Enlightenment Parlor?" Kate asked.

They both laughed. Having been friends since first grade, Liz thought of Kate as not only her best friend but also a sister.

"That's what I love about your great-aunt," Kate said. "She's always growing and open to new experiences. How did she get stuck with such a stick-in-the-mud for a great-niece?"

Liz stuck out her tongue. "Someone has to rein in some of your and Auntie's harebrained schemes. I take after my father, pragmatic and steady."

Kate stood and reached for an old cloth-covered book with gold print that was sitting on the checkout counter next to an antique brass cash register. "Look what I found at a Cocoa Beach sale last weekend." Before handing it to Liz, she opened it to the center of the book and spoke into its pages, "I appreciate you showing yourself to me, dear friend." Kate was normal in every way. Perhaps a little high-spirited. But her one idiosyncrasy was that she talked to books. It had all started when they were in elementary school and Fenton had allowed them into the Indialantic's library for the first time. Kate later told Liz that when she stepped inside, she had to cover her ears because of all the noise coming from the thousands of books in the floor-to-ceiling bookcases; they'd all started conversing with her at once. Of course, that was after they'd watched the Disney cartoon *Beauty and the Beast,* which had talking candelabras and teapots. As the years passed, Kate had continued to talk to, praise, and chastise characters from literature, reveling in the author's voices in obscure books no one had ever heard of.

Liz examined the tan leather volume. Printed in gold on the cover was *Capt. Jeremiah Jennings.* A musty odor assailed her, and she sneezed.

"Bless you," Kate said. "Isn't it amazing? It's from a captain's journal a family member transcribed into book form. The best part is that the captain lived around here. Close to the original site of the Cape Canaveral lighthouse. It's all about our barrier island, treasure, and pirates. There are even maps, like this one." She splayed open the book and pulled out a loose page with a sepia-colored map and handed it to Liz. It was a crude rendering of a piece of land with the Atlantic Ocean to the east and the Indian River Lagoon to the west. There was an "X" marking the spot in an unusual place. If this was a treasure map, the loot was buried on the shore of the Lagoon, not on the shore of the Atlantic, where the 1715 Spanish fleet bearing a queen's treasure sank. Liz recognized the geography of the shoreline: Snag Harbor Cove, just a stone's throw from Indialantic by the Sea. "Very cool. It'll make a wonderful prop for the treasure hunt."

"Great idea," Kate said. "I'll make a copy. It will add a dose of authenticity to the festivities. The map's probably fantasy on the mapmaker's part, but still so much fun. That's what I love about garage sales; you never know what you'll find. After Uncle Fenton is finished with the library's inventory, I'll add this to the collection." Liz's father wasn't Kate's blood relative, but the ties were strong nonetheless.

The hotel's library was very special to Liz and Kate. It was where their love of literature was fostered under the tutelage of Liz's father. After her mother died and Liz and her father moved into the caretaker's cottage behind the hotel, the library became a refuge from the heartache. Most of the library's collection of books came from her great-grandmother's family castle in Cornwall, Isle Tor. In 1926, when Liz's great-grandmother's family estate was turned over to the National Trust because of back taxes, Liz's great-grandfather, the owner of the newly built Indialantic by the Sea Hotel, commissioned a ship to bring the library to America as a wedding gift to his beautiful auburn-haired bride, Maeve.

Recently, Fenton had had the hotel's huge library, complete with a large fireplace, climate-controlled to preserve the integrity of the rare volumes dating back to the sixteen hundreds. He'd also enlisted the help of his part-time investigator, Ryan, to assist with the library's inventory in anticipation of the Indialantic being awarded Historic Landmark status. Her father felt the rarity of the volumes in the library, which had been in the hotel since its inception, would push the scales in their direction and provide the necessary funding to cover the library and the hotel's improvements. Liz had volunteered to help, but her father had refused, happy she was back to writing after a long period of writer's block.

"I wonder if the author is related to our island's pirate, Henry Jennings," Liz said.

"Wow, never thought about that. I can't wait to read it. I'll be sure to let you know."

"Dad will be thrilled. He loves local history."

"Guess what I scored at a going-out-of-business sale?" Kate asked.

"I couldn't possibly guess."

"A pillory for Pirates' Weekend. It will be great for picture taking."

"A pillory?"

"You know, the thing you stick your head and hands through for public humiliation."

"Oh, like stocks? That's an unusual score, even for you."

"How's the menu coming along for Sunday's picnic?" Kate asked, sitting back down.

Liz grabbed a Chinese wooden puzzle box from the shelf next to her. "I think you'll be surprised. Pleasantly, I hope." She took apart the puzzle. "Can I buy this from you? I remember, as a child, doing these puzzle boxes with Pierre. I'm curious whether, with his recent state of mind, he'll remember how. He still plays chess with Pops a couple of times a week to keep his mind sharp. I think Pops lets him win."

"That's sweet. How'd Pierre take the news about Dylan?" Kate took one of the loose wooden pieces and stuck it into the puzzle.

"Auntie said he cried, then dried his eyes and pretended nothing was wrong. She was sure he was doing it for her sake. Trying to be strong. I want to be there on Friday when Jake shows up to bring seafood to the kitchen."

"Jake?"

"Dylan's friend on the fishing boat. The one who told Minna about Dylan at the gallery."

"That blond cutie?"

"Too young for you. Or maybe not. There's something off about him, though. Ryan thinks so too."

Kate looked over at her, just as Liz put the last puzzle piece in place. "Wish Dylan's death could be as neatly tied up as this puzzle," Liz said, placing the puzzle box back on the shelf.

"Thought you wanted to take the puzzle box for Pierre."

"My brain's in a fog." Liz snatched the box off the shelf, just as piano keys chimed from her cell phone. Her father's assigned ringtone. She pulled out her phone and answered. She talked to her father for a few minutes and, after she hung up, said, "Dad. He has news but wants to tell me in person."

"That doesn't sound good," Kate said, frowning.

Liz got up from the sofa at the same time Victor Normand strode by Kate's shop, heading in the direction of Treasure Tours by the Sea.

"Boy, he looks mad about something," Kate said.

Liz told her about the scene on *Visions of Gold*.

Kate stood. "Let's go investigate; we need to keep our minds off Dylan. Let's see what Victor's so irate about. Maybe it has something to do with *The Bat.*"

Liz was about to protest but thought better of it. Once Kate set her mind to something, she wouldn't let it go. Kate really did take after Aunt Amelia more than Liz did.

She followed Kate toward the west side of Books & Browsery. When they turned the corner at the last row of six-foot barrister bookcases, they crouched down to be hidden by the four-foot partition that separated Kate's shop from Treasure Tours by the Sea.

"Your brother just told me you said he should fire me," Victor shouted. "If you know what's good for you, you'll keep your nose out of my business. Mr. Grayson can decide for himself who to hire and who not to."

Liz could almost feel the dampness in the air from the spit attached to Victor's words.

"What kind of hold does Erica have on him?" Tom asked. "I'd heard their divorce was far from amicable. How did you get the job of his chauffeur?"

"Oh, you don't know? Erica is part owner of the yacht. Thought your brother would have filled you in on that little fact."

They lowered their voices, and Kate shot up like the creepy clown jack-in-the-box on the shelf next to them.

Liz pulled her back down. "Shhh...don't let them see you."

A few minutes later, they heard Victor stomping toward the emporium's front vestibule.

Kate stood. "Wow. There's drama in the drama club," she said with a laugh.

Liz got up from the floor and wiped the dust off her jeans.

"Don't look at me that way. I purposely only clean once every two weeks. People think they're getting a bargain and discovering treasure when it's dusty. Speaking of treasure," Kate said, walking to the other side of the shop, "come see the other item I chose for Sunday's hunt."

After Liz admired a brass spyglass Kate had found at a flea market, she left the emporium and stopped at her father's office. Once they'd filled each other in on their day, he said, "Charlotte had the coroner do a tox screening on Dylan. I'm heartbroken to say he had an unusual drug in his blood. Rohypnol. It's now being ruled a suspicious death and possible homicide." Her father got up from his desk and walked around, putting a comforting hand on her shoulder.

"A Roofie? As in the amnesiac date-rape drug?"

"Yes. Charlotte says there's no reason for a person to take Rohypnol unless they're an insomniac. It's not even made in the United States. After I hung up with her, I looked it up. It's a small pill, dissolves quickly, and has no smell or taste. And no one can remember anything after being drugged." He went to the watercooler, filled a paper cup, and handed it to her.

"Where does it come from?"

"Mexico is the biggest supplier."

She took a sip of water, trying to wrap her brain around the fact that Dylan had been drugged before he fell, or was thrown, off the fishing trawler. "I need to see Ryan." This time she wouldn't keep him out of the loop, as she'd done by not calling him about the fire at Minna's.

Fenton met her gaze. "Charlotte and the Brevard County Sheriff's Department are on it."

"Well, maybe for this murder, we can do a little more sharing of information with your girlfriend."

"I can tell you this: Charlotte asked me about Dylan and his relationship with Jake, that young man I met in the kitchen a few Fridays ago."

"I knew it. Something's weird about that kid." Charlotte was interested in Jake and Victor. At this point, Liz just didn't see a connection between Victor and Dylan's death—or should she say murder?

"Don't go getting involved in the Brevard County Sheriff's Department's business. If drugs are involved, you have to keep your distance. Charlotte was very emphatic that we keep out of her investigation. Promise, daughter dear."

Liz stood and said, "Love you." Then she walked out the door. She figured if she didn't say the word "Promise," she wouldn't have to be held to it. For Minna and Dylan's mother's sake, Liz needed more information on Jake, and she knew someone who could help her: her father's own part-time private investigator.

Chapter 13

Ryan and Liz walked into Beachside Gallery. The skinny bow-tied man who wouldn't let Liz and Kate inside on the night of the opening without their invitations was talking to a couple admiring Minna's art. There were huge spaces where her mixed-media pieces once hung. If Liz had to guess, she'd sold more than half of them.

Liz made a beeline to the wall displaying Dylan's photos. Ryan followed close behind. She stopped in front of one of the black-framed photographs. "That's the name of Dylan's fishing boat, *Poseidon*," she said, pointing. She noticed that a number of Dylan's pieces had also sold. "It must be such a bittersweet feeling for Minna, knowing her and her nephew's pieces sold but he wasn't around to celebrate their success. Wait until she hears he was murdered."

"You told me Charlotte said it was a suspicious death, a *possible* homicide. It's better if we investigate this way, instead of grilling Minna about her nephew." He examined the photo that showed the ship's stern trailing a foamy wake through rough seas the color of midnight.

"My father said Charlotte will keep the findings about the Rohypnol in Dylan's system quiet."

"Are you interested in that photograph?" the bow-tied man asked. He'd crept up behind them. How much had he heard? "The photographer recently passed away," he said, shaking his head. "A local man, held in high esteem in our community."

"How much is this photo?" Liz asked.

"Two-fifty," the man replied.

"Are all the proceeds still going to charity?"

"Yes," the gallery assistant answered.

"Sold," Ryan said.

"You got a good deal, sir. After an artist or photographer dies, prices usually go up. It's the way the art world works."

"And how much is that one?" Liz pointed to an underwater shot taken from the bottom of the ocean looking up at a school of jewel-toned fish. It was daylight at the ocean's surface, and a blurry outline of the side of the fishing trawler could be seen through the watery lens.

"Same price," he said.

"I'll take it."

The man handed each of them his card. *CRAIG RUSKIN, Gallery Manager,* was printed in gold on white cardstock. Then he took the two pieces off the wall. "Come to the front desk and I'll wrap these for you."

They followed Craig to the desk at the entrance of the gallery. He took their credit cards and processed the sales, glancing up as the bell on the door announced that a customer had entered. He called out, "Ms. Franklin, I'll be right with you." He frenetically wrapped Ryan and Liz's purchases, practically shoving them at them, then hurried away to an elderly woman standing in front of the largest of Minna's works. Craig Ruskin obviously worked on commission.

The bell rang again as another customer entered the gallery. When Liz turned away from the desk, she saw Erica Grayson, Gregory's ex-wife and the actress playing Dale in *The Bat.* She was dressed more sedately than on the deck of *Visions of Gold* but would still stand out in a crowd. Liz noticed Ryan giving her a second look as they passed by. Erica glanced at him and smiled. She ignored Liz. Seeing Ryan's reaction to Erica reminded Liz of the photo of the sexy woman she'd found on the floor of his Jeep. It was still in her handbag. When Liz had modeled during college, she'd had a similar card, only hers was legit, called a comp card. It was meant to show different looks for booking jobs. Printed on it were the model's name, age, clothing size, height, and weight. The cards were passed out during casting calls or agency go-sees. The poses and clothing, or lack of clothing, on the card she'd found in Ryan's possession were a lot different from Liz's.

Ryan held open the door, but before stepping over the threshold, she turned her head at the sound of Erica's clattering high-heeled sandals on the gallery's polished wood floors. At the far side of the gallery, Erica looked around before opening the door leading into the small room with access to the hurricane safe room. Through the doorway, she saw Gregory usher her in, then he kissed her before closing the door.

Once outside the gallery, Ryan said to Liz, "There's something wonderful about Dylan's work. What drew you to the piece you chose?"

"I love that it was shot underwater," Liz answered as they walked hand in hand. "Minna told me Dylan's favorite photos were the ones he took of the ocean. I'm going to hang it in my beach house. I have the perfect spot."

They followed the sidewalk, passing a Russian bakery, two women's clothing stores, a bank, a highly rated restaurant, and a coffee bar. Liz smiled to herself, because the emporium had all the same choices, including a gallery on the thirty-foot wall inside Home Arts that featured art made by members of the collective and an ATM.

Liz looked across the street at Surf and Sun, just one of six surf shops in the area. Two, tanned shirtless guys who looked like lifeguards were boarding up the large plateglass window in the front of the shop. The rap, rap, tap of their hammers echoed down the street. Melbourne Beach's Fifth Avenue was a little different from the one in Manhattan, but it had everything needed in a beachside town.

Ryan followed her gaze. "Hey, eyes off. Be careful of the drool," he commanded in a joking manner, referring to the shirtless males.

"Yes, sir!" Liz looked up and down the street; some of the quaint shops had already added their hurricane shutters. Where had she been? In a weather vacuum? "Things aren't looking too swell for Pirates' Weekend. Good thing we have a rain, or should I say hurricane date."

They got inside Ryan's Jeep, and as they pulled away, Liz filled him in on the amazing hurricane safe room Gregory had built inside the gallery, and that Erica Grayson had just gone through the door to the room leading to it. "It was like she owned the place, or at least half of it, if Auntie's gossip is true. Don't you think it's unusual for a divorced couple to still be so close? It's not like they have children."

Ryan knew all about the production of *The Bat* because both Aunt Amelia and Kate had tried to get him to try out for one of the parts.

"I don't know, it depends on the relationship," he said. "Maybe they're still friends?"

Liz took a deep breath. Ryan had never shared anything about his past relationships in New York, but he knew everything about hers. Every nuance about her relationship with Travis had been plastered all over the tabloids.

"What's next, Mr. Investigator?" Liz asked.

"After I go check on the damage from the fire at Minna's cottage, I think I'll research the *Poseidon* and try to get on board. Dylan's shipmate never saw me at Minna's cottage, I just heard him, so there won't be a problem of being recognized."

"Maybe *Poseidon* is being used for more than fishing. There's been smuggling going on around here for a long time. Dylan might have found out about a drug operation, so someone spiked his drink with a Roofie, then bashed him on the head and threw him into the ocean."

At the traffic light, Ryan moved over the gearshift and kissed Liz on the nose, "That's what I love about you; you're always thinking, and one step ahead of the bad guys."

"Don't patronize me. I've been by my dad's side when he cracked open many a case. Before I left for college, I was his right-hand woman."

"I wasn't being patronizing, bossy pants," he said, adding a smile that showed off a dimple. "Do you know where Captain Netherton is staying in DC for his Coast Guard convention? He might have some connections who can tell us what went down on the day Dylan disappeared off the *Poseidon*."

The hotel's sightseeing cruiser, *Queen of the Seas* was skippered by Captain Netherton every Monday, Wednesday, and Friday. The captain also lived at the Indialantic and was given free room and board in exchange for piloting the cruiser while narrating an exciting spiel about the Treasure Coast's history and folklore. There was something charismatic about the seventysomething distinguished captain that even Liz was attracted to. Captain Clyde B. Netherton was a suave and gallant ladies' man, lookalike of the actor Edward Mulhare, who played Captain Daniel Gregg in the 1960s TV show *The Ghost & Mrs. Muir*. He was currently in Washington, D.C. at a reunion with his old U.S. Coast Guard buddies. Both Betty and Aunt Amelia were enamored with the debonair captain.

"Great idea!" Liz said. "Aunt Amelia is in touch with him via email even though I showed her how to text on her new phone. He's due home soon. I miss him, and I know Killer really misses him. Aunt Amelia's been left in charge of Caro, Killer, and now Turtle. Bronte stays with me and Venus has officially adopted Greta."

"Boy, you said a mouthful. Add that wacky parrot and you've got the start of Aunt Amelia's Ark, instead of Noah's."

"Come on, you love Barnacle Bob. Admit it."

"I wouldn't go that far. But I would've loved to have met the person who taught him all that foul language."

When they arrived at the Indialantic, Liz said, "Are you going to be okay on a boat?"

"Don't worry about me," he said, grinning. "I've gotten a lot better since going out on the *Queen of the Seas* with Captain Netherton. He even let me steer last time we went out."

She got out of the car and said, "Next time we go out on Dad's Chris-Craft, I'll let you take a turn at the wheel. And I'll leave the puke bucket at home."

"Touché, and I'll let you put those creepy-crawly sand fleas on your own hook next time we go fishing."

Liz stuck out her tongue, closed the car door, and headed for the revolving door leading into the hotel's lobby. Last night she'd been right. The sky had been too cloudy for a sunset rendezvous with Ryan, and tonight didn't look much better.

Praying she wouldn't run into Susannah, she held her breath as she pushed against the door and walked into the lobby.

Instead of Susannah, Gregory Grayson stood at the check-in counter, his hand poised over the large brass bell. He turned at the sound of the swishing revolving door.

"Mr. Grayson?" Liz said.

"Please, call me Gregory."

"Gregory. Can I help you with something?"

"I was calling for a bellhop. I wanted to check on Minna. See if she got any information about the fire and if I can offer the help of Grayson Construction."

"We haven't had a bellhop in years, but it's kind of you to check on Minna." She wondered how he'd gotten to the hotel; his chauffeured Maybach wasn't out front. "Did you check the emporium?" she asked.

"Yes. Kate told me she was here, at the hotel." He looked around the well-worn lobby, with its art nouveau and deco furnishings.

Liz thought it was the perfect backdrop for old Hollywood screen star Carmen Miranda to come sashaying into the room, a basket of fruit teetering on top of her head, singing "The Chiquita Banana Song." Obviously, by the frown on his face, Gregory didn't see the old charm of the Indialantic.

"I could send my foreman over here if you're interested in a little rehab work." He looked up at the thirty-foot ceiling. "This old lady has good bones but could use a few nips and tucks. Is that Otis in running order?"

He was referring to the polished brass accordion-gate elevator next to the check-in counter. Back in the day, it had carried many notable personalities up to their suites. Now, the elevator was just eye candy until Aunt Amelia could afford to fix it. "No. It's on our wish list. My great-aunt loves everything the way it is. We all do," she said, sticking out her chin.

"Has your aunt thought of selling?"

"My great-aunt would never sell."

"The emporium seems to be doing well. I like the open-space concept."

"My father hired one of his clients to draw up the plans, and another one laid the floors and partitions. Kate from Books and Browsery and Minna and Francie had a lot of input on the small touches. Most of the lighting, including the Baccarat chandelier, came from what was salvaged after the Indialantic's fire in 1945."

"A community effort, it sounds like. Well, my offer still stands; anything you need, just call."

"Thank you. Let me see if Minna's here. Please have a seat." She pointed to the settee. "I'll be right back."

He sat, gingerly, as if he was afraid the bamboo frame might collapse under his weight. Then he reached over to the side table and grabbed one of the Indialantic's brochures.

On the front of the brochure was an old photo of the hotel in its heyday, with its white stucco Spanish façade, orange-tiled roof, and the bell tower with flags flying and palm trees swaying. In the foreground were the ocean, striped beach cabanas, the boardwalk, and the old beach pavilion—now Liz's beach house. She'd found the original hand-colored photo in an album and had taken it upon herself to reproduce it for the front of the brochure. She'd also set the copy on the backside with the hotel's rates and the names of the emporium shops, along with their web addresses and hours.

"I also own a printing company," he said after scanning the front and back.

Of course. What didn't he own? "Thanks; I'll tell Aunt Amelia about your offer. I'll be right back." She exited the lobby through an arched doorway that opened to a short corridor. Gregory Grayson sure liked to fix things. She just didn't know if he was being magnanimous or a tad snooty. At the end of the hallway, Liz pushed open the door to the dining room and stepped inside.

Speaking of snooty, Susannah sat stiffly upright at a table for one, looking like a hologram from a different century in her Cornelia Van Gorder costume. In front of her was her daily luncheon choice: a wedge of Boston lettuce with a slathering of green goddess dressing and a cup of tepid, not-too-hot Lipton tea. Two tea bags, not one.

"Miss Elizabeth," she said. "I've been waiting for Mrs. Kimball to bring me my dessert. Can you be a peach and see where's she's gone to?"

"My pleasure," Liz answered, wondering if she should bow. "And please"—*please, please*—"call me Liz. Did you manage to find one of Minna's mixed-media pieces for your new condo at the gallery opening? And speaking of your condo, Aunt Amelia says it sounds wonderful. Will it be completed soon? I know Auntie will be sooo sad to see you go." There was a reason Liz wasn't an actress, but Susannah didn't seem to notice.

"Oh, no worries there, my dear. I won't be leaving in the near future. I've been very unhappy with the contractor's work. There were no marble saddles put on the thresholds from the bathrooms to the bedrooms, and the kitchen cupboards were hung in a slipshod manner. And, yes. I found two pieces of Minna's for over my sofa. I was surprised no one else had grabbed them. It was a good thing I brought swatches of the upholstery fabric with me." Susannah dabbed the corner of her mouth. "I also managed to snare one of the photograph's done by Miss Presley's nephew. Actually, the whole thing was kind of a scene," she said, an evil twist to her thin lips: Susannah Shay's version of a smile. "I had to wrestle it away from a young man who said he was a friend of the poor deceased photographer."

"Good for you," Liz said. "Just curious; what did the man look like?"

"Blond, freckles, in his twenties. He had an odor about him that was quite unsavory. If you want to look at the photograph, I've hung it in my suite."

Jake. What had Jake wanted with one of Dylan's photographs?

"Don't tell Amelia, but I had to replace that crude watercolor of a seascape she had in the sitting room. It's small touches, like tasteful art, that elevates the ordinary into the extraordinary."

"I'll have to remember that," Liz mumbled under her breath.

As she walked away, Susannah called after her, "And ask Mrs. Kimball to remember to put the crème fraîche on the side of the dish, not on top of the pie. You must be very explicit with servants, my dear Elizabeth. Make sure it was prepared by Chef Pierre, not store-bought. I can spot Reddi-wip or Cool Whip within an instant of tasting."

"I'll tell Greta straightaway," Liz said, biting the inside of her left cheek.

"As I've told Amelia, on more than one occasion, you really should call the woman Mrs. Kimball. There's no need to blur the lines between employer and employee."

Liz wanted to say that Greta Kimball was part of the Indialantic by the Sea's family. But instead she bit her other cheek and went in search of Minna.

Chapter 14

When Liz charged into the kitchen, Greta was standing at the sink. She noticed Liz's eye roll and laughed. "Let me guess: an etiquette lesson from our favorite doyenne, Cornelia Van Gorder, aka Miss Perfect, Susannah Shay?"

"You got it. She wants me to tell you to only use crème fraîche whipped by Chef Pierre himself."

"That woman's a piece of work, to be sure," Greta said. "You and I know Pierre would never serve anything store-bought. Right, Chef?"

"*Mon Dieu, comme si!*" Pierre said, and they all laughed.

Pierre sat at the farm table without his toque, wisps of gray hair sticking up from his head like bull's horns, a match to his curled and waxed mustache. Minna stood next to him, holding a glass of water.

Liz went to the table, pulled out a chair, and sat next to Pierre. Turning her head toward Minna, she said, "I'm glad I found you. You have someone looking for you in the lobby."

"I do?"

"Billionaire Gregory Grayson," Liz answered.

Minna's face flushed a becoming pink and she nervously raked her long artist-fingers through her short, spiked hair. "Chef seemed a little winded, so I was just about to give him a cool glass of water." Minna handed Pierre the glass.

"*Merci,*" he said, taking it in shaky hands.

"It's a good thing Pierre made a fresh dessert this morning for our demanding guest," Greta said. She took a slice of Key lime pie from under the clear-domed, pedestaled cake plate, then placed it on a white dish with "I" and "H" monogrammed in the center. She walked to the commercial-grade refrigerator, removed a bowl, and brought it back to the counter. Liz watched as she scooped a large dollop of crème fraîche from a bowl and held it over the pie.

"On the side, Greta. On the side!" Liz called out.

"Ugh," Greta replied. "Glad you caught me or I would've had to eat the pie myself and make her highness another. As you can see, since my hip operation and moving into the Indialantic, I've developed a little spare tire. And it's all your fault," she said, glancing at Pierre.

Pierre smiled, then turned to Liz. "I have yet to view Amelia's menu for Sunday's pirates picnic."

"Not to worry, Grand-Pierre. I've printed out the menu. I'll bring it over later for your stamp of approval. Then you, Greta, and I will meet Saturday to prepare what we can ahead of time."

"Of course, *ma cherie*. We'll make Amelia proud. Although I still don't think of pirates picnicking. Pillaging, yes. Picnicking, no." He took a sip of water and stood. "Excuse me, ladies. I must retire for my afternoon nap or there will be hell to pay with Amelia." He shuffled toward the back of the kitchen, in the direction of the service elevator that would bring him up to his suite.

After he was out of earshot, Greta said, "When your auntie mentioned to Pierre that Jake would be here on Friday, he acted like he'd never met him before. I'm not sure if he'll have the same bond with the new young man as he did with Dylan. Oh, by the way, the pantry and fridge are stocked with everything we need for *your* version of Amelia's menu, everything except the seafood."

"Thanks Greta," Liz said. "I'll look things over later."

A phone rang, and everyone checked their pockets.

Minna pulled out hers and put it to her ear. "Minna Presley." She listened to the person on the other end, then said, "Thank you, Ryan. I'll be right there." Then Minna handed the phone to Liz. "Ryan wants to talk to you."

Liz took the phone. "Ryan? Is everything okay?"

There was so much background noise, his voice was barely audible. "Can you come with Minna to her cottage? There's something I want you both to see."

"Of course." She looked at Minna. "We'll be right there."

After Liz handed back the phone, Minna said to Greta, "Would you mind telling Mr. Grayson that I've been called away on an emergency?" Then she looked at Liz. "Ready? I'm parked in the back."

"Sure," Liz said, "I'll just grab my handbag from the pantry."

"Shoot," Minna said. "I have my car keys, but my handbag is back at the emporium. Liz, do you mind driving? With my luck, I'll get pulled over for driving without a license."

"No problem. I so enjoy your wheels compared to Betty's ancient blue bomber. But don't tell her I told you that."

Greta left to give Gregory Minna's message and Liz and Minna exited via the side door. On their way to the parking lot, they passed Pierre's kitchen garden, which he'd purposely planted next to one of the Indialantic's numerous lemon trees. As they walked, Liz glanced to the left at the Indialantic's dock and saw that *Visions of Gold* was missing from its slip. Aunt Amelia and Susannah had lucked out with a free ticket for the yacht's maiden voyage. Even though Aunt Amelia had grown up on the island, she'd never sprouted a pair of sea legs or a mermaid's tail. But Amelia Eden Holt would never miss the opportunity for a new adventure. As Liz looked again at the empty slip, she realized that technically, tomorrow wouldn't be *Visions of Gold*'s maiden voyage; today was. She wondered where it had gone.

* * * *

Once inside the BMW, they took A1A a mile south and stopped in front of Minna's cottage. No one had spoken on the short trip. Both worried about the reason Ryan had called.

Liz pulled behind a Brevard County sheriff's patrol car and parked. Ryan was standing in the driveway behind his black Jeep, talking to a uniformed officer. They got out of the car and Ryan waved them over.

"I'm not into premonitions, but this doesn't look good," Minna said.

"Everything will be fine Minna. I promise." *Who was she to promise anything?*

When they reached the driveway, Ryan said, "Minna, this is Officer Collins."

Officer Collins extended his hand and shook Minna's.

"Is this about yesterday's fire?" Minna asked, looking searchingly at Ryan's stoic face. "Ryan, what's going on?"

Ryan took a moment before answering, as if choosing his words carefully. "Before I came by, as we discussed yesterday, I put in a call to Barrier Island Fire and Rescue. They'd determined the fire was started by someone wedging open your bedroom window and throwing an ignited, diesel-soaked rag onto your bedding."

Liz gasped. "Oh my God, it was deliberately set?"

Ryan answered, "Most definitely."

"Who would do that?" Minna croaked. "And why?"

Ryan reached over and took Minna's hand. "There's more. When I approached the front door, holding the set of keys you gave me yesterday, I saw it was open. Before stepping inside, I walked the perimeter of the cottage and made sure everything was secure. I came back around to the front door, stepped inside, and..."

"And what?" Liz said impatiently.

"The place was ransacked."

Minna took a step forward, "Ransacked?"

"Yes," Ryan said. "I called the police before going any farther than the front room."

Officer Collins looked at Minna. "If you don't mind, Ms. Presley, I'd like you to come with me and tell me if anything is missing." The officer was young and shifted nervously from foot to foot until Minna answered.

"Of course. This is all becoming too much. Can Liz come along?"

Officer Collins looked unsure if Liz going inside was considered proper protocol. He searched Ryan's face. Ryan gave him an almost imperceptible nod; then Officer Collins said, "I don't see a problem with that."

Ryan wasn't law enforcement, just a former firefighter and arson investigator and, currently, her father's part-time investigator, but unlike the young cop, Ryan always remained calm and confident under stress. He was like the eye of the hurricane; no matter what was swirling around him, he remained still, analyzing, weighing his options, then speaking. She had seen him vulnerable only once, but that was enough to let her know he was human.

Liz took Minna's hand in hers and they followed Officer Collins onto the covered porch, then stepped through the open front door. Ryan followed behind. The cottage smelled of smoke, but the odor wasn't as strong as Liz expected, which was good news. But what they found in each room was complete chaos. "Ransacked" was too nice a word to describe the carnage before them.

Minna went from room to room, wringing her hands. One minute crying, the next red-faced, filled with anger. Dylan's room was the worst. Liz and Ryan made eye contact as soon as they stepped inside. Dylan's death was no accident. He knew something or had something his killer wanted.

"Minna, what was Jake returning the day after Liz found Dylan on the beach?" Ryan asked.

"His duffel bag, with his camera, from the *Poseidon*. Dylan was always with one of his cameras." She glanced around Dylan's room, then stepped toward an orange zippered bag laying on its side. Next to the bag was a camera with a telephoto lens. The mattress of the bed had deep slash marks in it, and Minna let out a little whimper at the sight of all the stuffing oozing from each gash.

"Please don't touch anything," Officer Collins said from the doorway.

Ryan walked up to Minna and put his hand on her shoulder. "You said Dylan had more than one camera? I don't see any others."

She jerked her head around, searching the room. "His underwater camera was here. I know because after the gallery opening, I came home and cried myself to sleep on his bed."

Minna looked so drained that Liz didn't think she had a single tear left in her. "Come, Minna. Let's go back to the Indialantic. I'm sure Ryan and Officer Collins can lock up."

When they got back to the hotel, Minna went to check on Home Arts and Liz searched out Aunt Amelia, who was in her new exercise room. Liz told her about what had happened at the cottage.

"Deplorable!" Aunt Amelia said. "What a tragic turn of events. I'm so happy we put her in the Oceana Suite. It's the perfect place for her to relax and restore with its ocean view. If you don't mind, Lizzie, can you please bring fresh towels to her suite and Susannah's? Greta promised to clean Barnacle Bob's cage, a task I wouldn't wish on my worst enemy. I'm scheduled to meet Paolo, my trainer. He seems to be running late." Her great-aunt wore a pink leotard, tights, and ballet slippers. A pink chiffon scarf was tied around her forehead.

"Of course," Liz answered. "No problem. And you're right, Greta deserves a medal."

After leaving Aunt Amelia, Liz made her way up to the second floor, where she removed a stack of fluffy white monogrammed towels from the walk-in linen closet. Then she continued down to the Oceana Suite. Liz, Aunt Amelia, Kate, Minna, and Francie had helped to redecorate, while at the same time keeping to the suite's timeless charm. The results were amazing. No one would ever have known that last April, the suite had been a crime scene.

Liz left a stack of towels on the bed, then continued to Susannah's suite, the Windward Shores. When she walked inside she was surprised by the clutter. From Susannah's outward appearance and demeanor, Liz thought she would keep the suite military clean.

On the sitting room desk there was an open laptop next to a printer. Piles of paper were overflowing from a tray on the desk. Curious, Liz couldn't help but look at a printed page that had fallen to the floor. It was an email from the Polson Agency in Jacksonville.

> *Dear Ms. Shay,*
> *I found the information you asked for on a Thomas Grayson.*
> *There isn't much. He grew up in Jacksonville, went to Florida*
> *State College. As per my investigation, he has been working*
> *at an accounting agency for the past twenty years. I can find*
> *no record of him ever owning a travel agency or working in*
> *community theater.*
> *Please submit the remaining balance on my retainer at your*
> *earliest convenience.*
> *Best,*
> *Anthony Polson*
> *P.S. I am still working on the other matter.*

Liz returned the letter to the floor. Above the desk was the photograph of Dylan's that Susannah had fought Jake for on the night of Minna's opening. It was exceptional. The deck of a fishing trawler was pictured at nightfall. An open, recessed section near the stern was awash with hundreds of fish laying on chipped ice shavings, some still in the throes of life—or death. Their scales reflected the camera's flash in a kaleidoscope of sparkling jewel tones. Dylan had had an amazing eye; everywhere she looked there was a fusion between light, shadow, and color. In the bottom right-hand corner, in the white area above the mat, was Dylan Presley's signature written in pencil. Next to the signature were the symbols 2/2, designating that the photograph was the second of two copies.

Feeling sad, Liz put the fresh towels on the upholstered chair near the entrance to the sitting room and left the suite. Susannah Shay was certainly a busybody, she thought as she walked down the hallway. Tom had lied about his past, but maybe that was because he was Gregory Grayson's brother and didn't want the others in the theater to disrespect his directorial authority because of nepotism. As owner of the theater, Gregory had total control over who he chose to be director. But it still made Liz wonder what Susannah would do with the information. Perhaps blackmail Tom for more lines in *The Bat*?

Liz wouldn't put it past her.

Chapter 15

"I can't believe what's happening to Minna," Aunt Amelia said, taking a cream pitcher from one of the shelves in the pantry and placing it on a sterling tray. Dinner had already been served in the dining room "Is she sure nothing was stolen? Why would someone start a fire and break in the next day but not have taken anything?"

"We think maybe one of his cameras is missing," Liz said as she unplugged the silver coffee urn. "I don't have an answer. But I know it has something to do with Dylan. His room was in worse shape than all the others; someone even used a knife to stab the mattress. I've never seen so much destruction. The good news is, Ryan said Barrier Island Fire and Rescue told him that except for Minna's bedroom and hallway, the rest of the cottage was undamaged from the fire."

"Is there something you, Ryan, and your father are keeping from me about Dylan's death? You three weren't exactly transparent last April." She added packets of sugar and noncalorie sweetener to a Lalique crystal bowl and placed it next to the cream pitcher.

Liz looked over at Aunt Amelia. For years she'd protected and nurtured Liz. Was it time to do the same by not letting her know what her father had learned from Charlotte about the Rohypnol? Last spring, Liz had left Aunt Amelia out of the loop when someone at the Indialantic was murdered. Six months later, Liz was still hearing about it. "I'm not a hothouse flower," her great-aunt had said.

"Come on, spill," Aunt Amelia demanded, her unwavering emerald-green eyes fixed on Liz's face.

Liz gave in and spilled. Afterward, Barnacle Bob, who spent most of his daylight hours in the pantry, not allowed inside the kitchen in case a

Brevard County health inspector stopped by, squawked, "Gash on the head. Gash on the head," then repeated an old Alka-Seltzer television commercial jingle: "Plop, plop, fizz-fizz, oh, what a relief it is."

"Silence," Aunt Amelia said as they walked into the kitchen, she carrying the silver tray and Liz the coffee urn.

"Pretty boy, pretty boy," the parrot repeated from the pantry.

When Liz turned her head to look at him, he flashed her his tail feathers. Liz paused until Aunt Amelia exited the kitchen, then whispered, "I haven't seen Killer today, have you, BB?"

"Meow, meow," the parrot parroted.

Dinner had been served and cleared by Greta. Liz and Aunt Amelia set up dessert, coffee, and tea on the long sideboard in the dining room. Chef Pierre and Liz had put together a meal of simple pan-fried grouper, haricots verts with slivers of almonds and goat cheese, and lemon polenta. It had been a while since Liz had cooked alongside Pierre and it felt like old times. Everything she'd learned, she learned from the Cordon Bleu chef, but now that Greta was here, she'd taken over some of the responsibility of watching over and helping Pierre with the hotel meals, while Liz focused on her novel. Greta always took Pierre's sporadic episodes of memory loss and confusion in stride, never becoming impatient with the eighty-one-year-old chef. Also, if Liz wasn't mistaken, there might be a love affair blooming. If not a love affair, then a deep affection and friendship. Liz even caught Greta reading one of Pierre's Agatha Christies.

Before Susannah came to the hotel, dinner at the Indialantic was a casual affair. Betty and Captain Netherton, along with Greta, had become more like family and needed little fanfare at mealtime, taking most of their meals in the kitchen. Susannah was another story. But now that Minna was staying with them, Liz had been happy to offer her a special meal, especially after what she'd gone through lately.

Liz helped herself to coffee and dessert, not knowing which of the two to choose. She compromised and took half a slice of coconut praline layer cake and half of a bar of blueberry-lemon cheesecake. Then she went back to the table and sat with her father and Minna. Aunt Amelia, who usually ate with Pierre and Greta, was seated with Susannah. Liz had a feeling Susannah had told her friend that eating with the help was a faux pas. Liz had seen the Amy Vanderbilt etiquette book on Susannah's nightstand when she'd delivered towels to the Windward Shores Suite—Susannah's version of the Bible.

While everyone had already served themselves dessert from the sideboard, Susannah sat stiffly with an empty space in front of her.

Finally, Aunt Amelia noticed. Liz heard her great-aunt say, "Help yourself to dessert, Susannah."

Susannah grunted. Then she got up with much fanfare and headed across the room and made loud, clattering noises as she filled her plate. Suddenly, it came to Liz. Susannah Shay wasn't paying for her suite. She would bet anything Aunt Amelia, kindhearted to all strays, was letting Susannah stay free of charge. *Good*, Liz thought. Now she planned to be more herself in front of the stuffy woman.

Fenton led the conversation, steering away from everything that had recently happened to Minna. He talked about the progress in the library and his hopes of getting the Indialantic deemed a national landmark. Earlier, when Minna was serving herself at the buffet, Liz had asked her father if he'd heard anything new from his girlfriend and was surprised when he said he had. She'd told him specifically that Ryan and Liz needed to stay out of the investigation. Which, of course, made Liz want to get involved even more, and she decided she wouldn't pass the warning on to Ryan. She was surprised Charlotte Pearson didn't trust her and Ryan after they'd been instrumental in uncovering a murder plot last spring.

Liz noticed Minna hadn't taken dessert. "Minna, can I bring you a piece of cheesecake or pie?"

"I don't have much of an appetite."

Fenton said, "You have to try Pierre's cheesecake. You won't regret it."

Minna smiled. "I'm sure I won't," she replied.

Liz stood. "Dad, how about you? Seconds?"

"No. I'm fine, Lizzie. But I could go for another cup of coffee."

He handed Liz his cup and she returned to the sideboard, where she took a plate of cheesecake and filled her father's cup from the coffee urn. She turned to head back to the table, reconsidered, then grabbed the remaining halves of the two desserts she'd taken earlier. She still couldn't decide which she liked better.

When she returned to the table, she sat down quietly, surprised at the discussion going on between her father and Minna, especially after the warning from his cop girlfriend to stay out of the investigation. "I've talked to Agent Pearson," Fenton said. "After the break-in at your cottage, she's decided to treat your nephew's death as a homicide."

Liz thought back to this afternoon. Someone was looking for something, and they'd looked the hardest in Dylan's room. If the underwater camera had been in plain sight, as Minna had said, why had they gone to all the trouble of slashing the mattress and tossing drawers? Liz couldn't help herself; she blurted out, "What about Jake? He's beyond suspicious."

"Jake? Dylan's friend? I don't see why he would murder Dylan." Minna's voice cracked. "They were friends. Jake helped Dylan learn everything there was to know about fishing. They even hung out at Squidly's with the rest of crew, telling stories about life on the open sea. It's not easy for a newbie, especially when his pay is dependent on how much fish the boat takes in. The pay is divided up equally, no matter who does what."

"Minna, did Dylan ever complain about anyone on the boat? Someone he had a problem with?" Fenton asked.

"Not that I ever heard. Dylan wasn't a complainer." She dabbed her linen napkin to the inside corners of her eyes. "It was a small crew, sometimes just Dylan, Jake, and the captain."

"How about the captain; did he get along with him?" Liz asked, and her father sent her "the look."

"I never heard anything bad or good about him. Although once, Dylan left one of his cameras on board and went back to the boat at nightfall, hours after they'd docked from a full day of fishing. He told me the boat was idling, like it had just pulled in. Jake and some other crew member he'd never met were transferring a load of fish to a waiting refrigerated van. When Dylan went on board to get his camera, he ran into the captain. He told the captain he'd be willing to work at night if needed, and the captain got extremely angry with him."

"What did Jake say when Dylan asked him about the nighttime excursion?" Liz asked.

Minna took a moment before she said, "I think Jake told Dylan that sometimes they went out fishing at night, per the boat owner's instructions, and if they all wanted to keep their jobs, he should keep quiet about it."

They were silent for a minute, until Minna blurted out, "Why does it have to be murder? Couldn't he have fallen on something and hit the back of his head, then fallen into the sea?"

"You're forgetting about the Rohypnol in his system and the unusual wound on the back of his head..." Fenton stopped when he saw Minna's grimace.

She remained still. After a few minutes, she slapped her hand on the table, "I want to know who killed my nephew. I'll do anything I can to find this monster!"

Liz noticed Susannah glancing over, giving Liz, not Minna, a disapproving glare. Before dinner, Liz had overheard Susannah and Minna talking about the piece she'd bought from the Beachside Gallery. After the break-in at her cottage, Liz could tell Minna wasn't in the mood to discuss her art, and Liz had purposely interrupted them with something trivial. Susannah had pouted in a very *un*ladylike manner.

"Minna," Fenton said, "please be assured we'll find out how this happened. Now that we have the police on board and I've had a chat with Ryan, who you know is my part-time investigator..." He looked over at Liz, then back at Minna.

So much for heeding his girlfriend's warning to stay out of it. Liz couldn't be prouder. He continued, "Are you sure there's nothing you can think of that might be missing after the break-in, besides the camera?"

Minna looked up at the dining room's coffered ceiling. Then she lowered her head. "I'm sorry; all I'm sure of is his underwater camera."

"How about the memory cards from his cameras?" Liz asked. "Were they in his room?"

"I have the memory card to the photos he displayed at the gallery," she said, not too convincingly. Minna stood. "I'll be right back. I need to check something."

After she'd gone, Fenton said to Liz, "I wish I could figure out what's going on. Charlotte is being unusually evasive. She's confident they'll find the killer soon. We'll have to trust her."

"I can trust her, but that doesn't mean I'm not going to continue to try to find out what happened. And neither is Ryan." Then Liz filled her father in on Ryan's idea about getting on board the *Poseidon* on Saturday, posing as a deckhand.

"Doesn't he get seasick?" her father asked.

Liz grinned. "Only for the first thirty minutes."

Her father pulled out his phone and tapped a few buttons. "I just sent you my former client's phone number. He owns a fishing trawler. Tell Ryan to call him and have Earl give him a crash course on what being a deckhand constitutes. I also sent the name of Earl's boat and slip number at the harbor. Ryan should get there at five a.m. if he wants hands-on experience."

They waited for Minna to return to the table, but she never did.

* * * *

Later that night, Liz was in the caretaker's cottage, seated next to Ryan on his new sofa. Since moving in six months before, he'd redecorated the cottage to fit his own style, a far cry from the frilly, doily-covered, and knickknack crammed interior left behind by the cottage's former occupant, who'd been another one of Aunt Amelia's strays.

Shopping at Home Arts and Books & Browsery by the Sea, he had chosen a few decorative items that were on the masculine side. Everything was sparse and clean, in neutrals, the only splotches of bright color were the few select pieces of art he'd hung on the walls. Granted, the sofa was a double recliner and the flat-screen TV covered most of the wall. But other than that, she barely recognized the home she and her father had lived in before she'd taken off to attend Columbia University. The kitchen was another story. It was the same as it had been when Liz was five years old. Like Liz, Ryan prided himself on being a "damn good cook," and he was. Recently, most of his cooking took place in Liz's gourmet kitchen, which Pierre had designed for her as a homecoming surprise when she'd moved back to the island after ten years of living in Manhattan. Her beach house had also been a homecoming surprise. Her father had turned the Indialantic's ancient beach pavilion into her new home sweet home.

"I love where you hung Dylan's photo. That's the perfect spot. I haven't hung mine yet. I'm afraid it will be too sad a reminder of his murder. As soon as we find his killer, I'll place it somewhere special."

"*We?*"

"Yes, partner," she said, then gave him a peck on his rough cheek that once again reminded her of a pirate's. She filled him in on dinner with Minna and her father's former client who owned a fishing trawler. She got out her phone and texted Ryan the info her dad had given her, including Earl's name and phone number. "I just sent you a text with the particulars. You have to be at the harbor at five."

"Five a.m.? No problemo," Ryan said.

"Really?"

"You forget. Just like in the song 'New York, New York,' not only does the city never sleep, the same can be said for the FDNY."

"Aww. You're my hero." She leaned forward and nuzzled his chin, like Bronte did to her. Ryan reciprocated with a kiss on the top of her head.

There was a rapping at the door. They looked at each other, then Ryan got up and answered. "Minna? Is everything okay? Come inside."

Minna looked over at Liz. "Sorry to interrupt, but your father said you were here and I should tell you..."

"Tell us what?" Ryan asked, guiding her to his vacant spot on the love seat.

"My handbag has been stolen."

Liz remembered Minna hadn't had it with her when they went to her cottage after Ryan's phone call. Minna had said she'd left it at Home Arts by the Sea.

"Are you sure?" Ryan asked.

"Yes. We always put our bags in a certain place. Out of sight, in the back room."

"Maybe Ashley saw that you'd left it behind and put it somewhere safe?" Liz looked over Minna's head and connected with Ryan, who was still standing.

After a short pause, Minna said, "I suppose you could be right."

Liz remembered Minna rushing out of the hotel's dining room and asked, "Was there something important in your handbag relating to Dylan?"

"Yes, the memory card with all the photos from the gallery opening. Dylan's and mine."

Liz knew, as Ryan and Minna did, that it was a long shot she'd misplaced her handbag. Odds-on, the same person who'd set the fire and trashed Minna and Francie's cottage had also stolen it.

But was that person Dylan's killer?

Chapter 16

Friday morning, Liz sat on her deck, gazing out at the gentle waves lapping the shoreline as Bronte purred contentedly on her lap. Valiantly, the sun made an appearance as it eased its way above the horizon, occasionally getting erased by a few dusty gray clouds. Storm clouds. But the wind was calm. Her father had called while she was on her first cup of coffee to tell her that a handyman—or, in this case, a handywoman—would be coming tomorrow to secure the storm shutters. Most of the squiggly-lined hurricane models on The Weather Channel showed Hurricane Roberta hitting the Gulf of Mexico, but there were a few showing her heading up the East Coast. Last night before bed, Liz had turned on the television, deciding not to stick her head in the sand anymore about the possibility the hurricane might clobber the island. Living with hurricanes was part of island life, but it didn't mean anyone liked them.

Since she'd moved back to Melbourne Beach the weather had been on its best behavior, but she could remember in her youth the fear and anxiety of past hurricanes—the roaring of the wind and the waterspouts over the Atlantic, along with the floodwaters rising from the Indian River Lagoon. Nine times out of ten, the barrier island would be evacuated. The narrow piece of the island where the Indialantic sat was accessed by two bridges, one fifteen miles north, the other fifteen miles south—one of the reasons mandatory evacuations were so frequent. You didn't want to get caught on a bridge during a hurricane. After the governor made his decree, she, her father, Aunt Amelia, Pierre, and Betty would take off for points north or west, depending on the hurricane's projected path.

Aunt Amelia had always made their fleeing the wrath of Mother Nature an exciting adventure. They would take the side roads of Georgia, South

Carolina, and North Carolina, a menagerie of the Indialantic's pets secure in the back of her father's SUV. She remembered Barnacle Bob sitting on her great-aunt's shoulder, swearing out the window at passing cars who dared to cut them off—his version of the middle finger.

She knew satellite surveillance, water temperature, wind speeds, other storms in the vicinity, and the storm chasers' data from inside the eye wall were only a few of the factors forecasters looked at. The most important in the mix was the human being who had to combine all the variables and go with who they trusted. She remembered watching the models for Hurricane Irma, the largest hurricane ever recorded in the Atlantic, while glued to her television in her SoHo apartment, worrying about her family and friends because its path could go east or west. Thankfully, it had gone west.

In the grand scheme of things, if they had to cancel Pirates' Weekend it would just be a tiny ripple in the sea compared to the possible destruction of their beloved island and the Indialantic by the Sea Hotel and Emporium. Aunt Amelia, along with the emporium shopkeepers, decided if there was a chance the hurricane was headed in their direction, they would postpone the festivities on Saturday and reschedule the entire weekend. Her great-aunt promised to make the decision as soon as the island was put on a tropical storm or hurricane watch.

Tiny Bronte mewed at a seagull perched on the railing, breaking Liz out of her musings. She scooped the petite furball into her arms and went inside the beach house. Aunt Amelia, Susannah, and a group of high-paying ticket holders were scheduled to leave port on their treasure-seeking voyage aboard Gregory Grayson's *Visions of Gold* in an hour, and Liz had promised to see them off. For now, the seas were calm, and if Liz didn't get going, she'd be late for wishing her great-aunt a bon voyage.

After feeding Bronte, Liz took a shower and dressed in cool white cotton shorts and an aqua tank top, simple gold hoops at her ears. In the bathroom, she put a quick dab of concealer on her scar, peach lip gloss on her lips, and a swipe of black mascara on her pale lashes. Her long strawberry-blond hair, usually a harbinger of stormy, humid weather, remained sleek.

Thirty minutes later, Liz walked toward *Visions of Gold*. Because of its size, it was parked parallel to the dock, its bow facing the river, too large to fit in any of the Indialantic's slips. As she got closer, she heard someone singing. Someone named Amelia Eden Holt. Her great-aunt stood in profile at the bow of the boat, her hands on the gold railing. Liz couldn't make out what song her great-aunt was singing, though she strained to hear snippets of the lyrics. It could be "Don't Rain on My Parade," one of Aunt Amelia's favs from the musical *Funny Girl* or..."My Heart Will Go On" from *Titanic*.

When she reached the gangway to the yacht, a white-gloved server stood with a tray of mimosas. He said, "We're leaving port in ten minutes, kindly present your ticket." He handed her a brochure and a sheet designating what the day's cruise entailed. She quickly scanned it:

10 a.m. – christening of the yacht *Visions of Gold* by owner Gregory Grayson

10:30 a.m. – champagne, blinis, and caviar

11:30 a.m. – diving for treasure

1 p.m. – lunch on the top deck

2:30 – diving for treasure

4:00 – share the bounty

4:30 – cocktails and a tour of the Treasure Coast

The last item on the itinerary surprised her. Captain Netherton, who'd been doing tours of the Treasure Coast ever since moving into the hotel, wouldn't be too happy when he found out *Visions of Gold* was offering the same service. Since the hotel's inception in 1926, the Indialantic's riverboat cruiser had been giving tours on the Indian River Lagoon. *Queen of the Seas* had had many makeovers over the years and spent lots of time in dry-dock but still brought crowds clamoring to hop aboard to view American eagles, manatees, dolphins, and exotic seabirds in season when passing Pelican Island. Commissioned in 1903 by Theodore Roosevelt, Pelican Island National Wildlife Refuge was the oldest nature preserve in the United States—and one of the points of interest held most dear to Captain Netherton and his boss, Amelia Holt.

Liz looked up at her great-aunt. She was gesturing with her arms and hands, explaining something to one of the white-gloved servers. Liz was sure the server already knew what role Aunt Amelia had had on *Dark Shadows* and, naturally, her new role as Liddie in *The Bat*.

"Ticket please?" the waiter with the tray said. "We're leaving port soon."

"Oh, I'm not going out," Liz said. "I've just come to wish everyone a safe trip."

He turned away, his nose in the air as he went up the ramp and onto the yacht.

"Lizzie, Lizzie," Aunt Amelia called. She was dressed in a filmy green and purple caftan, a matching scarf tied around her head, its tails floating up in the air from the breeze, giving her bunny ears—a bad sign that the wind was picking up. "Come on board. I must give you a quick tour."

Susannah came up next to Aunt Amelia, frowning, per usual. She wore a white linen suit with a skirt that hit below the knee. Liz could tell at one time the suit had probably cost her a bundle, but now it seemed out of style. Susannah's headscarf and large sunglasses were very Jackie O. Liz remembered her theory that Aunt Amelia was probably letting Susannah stay at the Indialantic free of charge. She just hoped Susannah really did have a condo being built in Vero Beach.

Through pursed lips, while literally looking down at Liz, Susannah said, "Amelia dear, there is no time for tours, we'll be shoving off soon. You can tell your great-niece all about it when you return."

It seemed even Amelia had her limits. "Gregory Grayson himself gave me permission to give Liz a tour. Come, Liz," she said, motioning with her hands.

Liz walked up the ramp and onto the upper deck of *Visions of Gold*.

So, this is what money can buy you, she thought, stifling the urge to add a whistle. Luxury with a capital "L." She didn't see how the yacht was considered a treasure diving ship. Living on a barrier island, she'd seen plenty of salvage boats docked in the harbor and none of them looked like this one. In her experience, most were bare-bones, attired with cranes and the equipment needed to excavate items from shipwrecks at the bottom of the sea. This yacht looked like it should be lazing off the waters of Monaco, with James Bond and a villain fighting it out on deck, both dressed in tuxedos, while a cool Grace Kelly–type blonde looked on.

There were five male guests sitting on white leather swivel chairs holding drinks. One smoked a cigar, apparently a faux pas in Susannah's book because she held a clenched fist to her mouth and performed a ladylike cough. The smoker didn't even look Susannah's way. Instead, he joined in a conversation about the possible hurricane. Liz overheard him saying that if it did hit the Treasure Coast, the next morning would be the best time to search for treasure on the beach.

Aunt Amelia hurried toward Liz. "Come, darling. You won't believe your eyes." She grabbed Liz's arm with her ring-bejeweled hand, while Susannah tottered behind like a drunken sailor. Judging by the greenish tinge to her face, Liz realized Susannah, like her great-aunt, was more of a landlubber than a sea lover. The ship was so large, Liz barely felt any movement at all.

After a tour of the upper deck, with its salons, two dining rooms, and a full kitchen, they came to the stairs leading to the lower level. Liz grabbed the gold railing and scanned the upper deck before stepping down. She didn't see Gregory or his brother, but she did see Erica. She was dressed in a thong bikini covered with an opaque cover-up, a diamond glinting in her navel. Erica laughed at something one of the men said, caught Liz's stare, then glanced away. Liz still couldn't understand Erica and her ex's relationship. Liz hadn't seen Travis since leaving Manhattan and she hoped she never saw him again.

When they reached the lower level, Liz almost collapsed in amazement. In front of her, on the floor, was a humungous rectangular glass window. On either side of the glass bottom were two rows of seating. The water appeared murky because they were docked in the Indian River Lagoon. Liz could only imagine what the view would be like miles out to sea, and she regretted her earlier posturing about being happy she wasn't invited on board. When she got the go-ahead from her plastic surgeon to go diving, she might just book a day of treasure hunting. Or she could just stowaway and forgo the three-hundred-dollar-an-hour price tag. But of course, if Liz didn't pay to come on board, she wouldn't be able to share in the profits of the ship's treasure haul.

When Tom had told her great-aunt that whatever was found on the ocean floor by the diving guests would be divided up equally between them and Treasure Tours by the Sea, Liz had almost laughed out loud. Growing up on the island, she knew all the rules when it came to claiming treasure. As per federal and Florida state law, if treasure from the 1715 Spanish fleet was found in American waters, the gold and other items recovered had to be placed under the custody of the U.S. District Court. Florida would receive 20 percent of the treasure, to be placed in local museums, and the remaining spoils would be split between 1715 Fleet-Queens Jewels, the salvage company that owned the rights to the wreckage, and the person or persons who found it. It seemed, in this case, the treasure sharing was just a gimmick to sucker in rich guests. Especially, seeing that after all the splitting was done, they'd end up with next to nothing. But looking around, at least for the maiden voyage, the gimmick seemed to be working. It was all about the thrill of the hunt anyway. And if someone had the money to blow, who was Liz to judge? She wondered if they knew anything found on the beach was free to keep.

They completed the tour of the lower deck, which included a room with diving suits hanging next to a locker with each guest's name. There were ten lockers, but only eight had names on them. Gregory Grayson had thought of everything. Speaking of Gregory, Liz was surprised she hadn't run into him on her tour. Then she realized why. The same waiter who had asked her for her ticket rushed up to them and said, "Everyone on deck. It's time to christen the ship." Then he looked at Liz and said, "If you don't have a ticket, I'll have to ask you to leave."

Ah, the golden ticket, she thought. She saw Susannah's eyes light up at Liz's taking-down. Hurriedly, they moved toward the stairs. Once on deck, Liz kissed Aunt Amelia's downy cheek, ignoring Susannah, and exited the yacht.

Tom, Gregory, and a man dressed in white, wearing a captain's hat, were standing on the dock. Gregory held a magnum of Dom Pérignon in his hand. A huge red bow had been attached to the side of *Visions of Gold.*

When Liz passed, Gregory nodded his head in her direction, then spoke to the small crowd above that was leaning over the railings. "Welcome, everyone, to the maiden voyage of *Visions of Gold.* It's my honor to christen this ship in the hopes of many fruitful journeys and discoveries of untold riches that each of you have the chance to share in. Captain Charles will be piloting our maiden voyage, part of my Treasure Tours by the Sea venture." He put his arm around the captain's shoulders. Liz glanced at Tom's stricken face, and she thought she understood why. So far, Gregory hadn't mentioned a word of his brother's role.

The small crowd above clapped their hands. The man with the cigar started chanting, "Treasure! Treasure! Treasure!" A few other men joined in. The only female guest gave the men a look similar to the one on Susannah's face. Just because someone had money didn't mean they had class, the expression said.

Liz waited until Gregory smashed the champagne bottle against the ship's bow, then she waved good-bye to Aunt Amelia. As she turned to head back to the Indialantic, Gregory moved toward her. He said, "I invited Minna to come on the maiden voyage, but she didn't feel the timing was right, which is totally understandable."

Unlike Ryan, Liz sometimes spoke without thinking. "This isn't the maiden voyage."

He stiffened his stance. Even though he kept his smile, his pale blue eyes remained cold. "Why would you say that?"

"Oh, nothing, really. It's just that yesterday, I noticed she was missing from the dock."

"Now I remember," he said, glancing in Tom's direction. "The harbormaster had to take her out to make sure she was seaworthy."

Liz knew he was lying. "That makes sense," she said. "Well, hope you find lots of treasure. Take care of my great-aunt; she isn't the best on the open sea."

Gregory didn't hear the last thing she'd said; he had moved next to Tom and was whispering something in his ear. Tom looked like he'd been slapped, then they both walked toward the gangway. Gregory taking the lead, Tom bringing up the rear.

Interesting. Gregory had no idea *Visions of Gold* had already left port. And it appeared he was blaming his brother. If Tom had taken out the ship, what could have been his reason? If Tom had lied to Gregory about being in community theater and owning a travel agency and had really been just an accountant all his life, as Susannah's investigator had said, perhaps Gregory had found out.

She couldn't wait to tell Ryan, though she had no idea what it all meant.

Chapter 17

"You wouldn't believe what hard work fishing is," Ryan said over the phone, as she made her way back to the Indialantic. He yawned. "Getting up at four a.m. was the easiest part of it. The good news is, I feel I'll be able to fake it pretty well when I show up for my shift on the *Poseidon* tomorrow."

"Wow. You're a fast learner."

"Earl's a great teacher. He knows the captain of the *Poseidon*. He's called Captain Ahab. I was afraid to ask way. But because of the threatening weather pattern heading our way, it'll be a short trip. Saved by the threat of a hurricane," he said, adding another yawn. "Hey, do you want me to swing by? I have one more stop to make: the harbormaster. I want to find out who owns *Poseidon*."

"A good idea. I'm sure Charlotte knows, but as of now, she's not even sharing info with her boyfriend. My father seems pretty sure she's close to finding Dylan's killer."

"I'll give her a call later, see if I can glean anything new. It's okay to share some things we know to get reciprocal info, right?"

"Of course, if Charlotte does reciprocate." Jealousy reared its green head, and Liz stomped it out with her next words. "The more we know, the better. I'm headed to the Indialantic. Jake is scheduled to stop by, and I plan to grill him like Grand-Pierre did yesterday's grouper."

"Speaking of grouper, did you know that a goliath grouper can weigh up to four hundred pounds?"

"No, I didn't," she said. "You sound excited. Am I going to lose you to a life on the open sea?"

"I didn't know you had me."

There was a moment of silence, which Ryan broke. "Sure you don't want me to swing by to pick you up? I can tell you more fish tales."

"I'd love that, but I don't think you want to run into Jake, especially if you're planning on going on *Poseidon* tomorrow incognito."

"True. I'll see you later, then. Text me when the coast is clear."

"Will do. And text me when you find out who owns *Poseidon*." She'd almost added a "Love you," at the end of the conversation. Not a *love* you; more of a you-mean-a-lot-to-me, let's-see-where-we're-going type of endearment. She was a writer, but she couldn't think of another word to convey her feelings for Ryan. She pocketed her phone and took the path at the back of the hotel that swung around to the south-side kitchen entrance and walked inside.

"Lizzie," Pierre said. "You just missed Dylan's friend. A nice-enough young lad, but he brought all the wrong things for Amelia's pirate picnic. Shall I go to Honest John's to see what I can find?"

She went to the table where the chef was sitting with his feet up on a chair, *The A.B.C. Murders* splayed open and facedown in front of him. "No need to, Grand-Pierre, I have a feeling Pirates' Weekend will be postponed because of the approaching storm. We can worry about the food tomorrow."

Pierre didn't own a car, but he did own a vintage motorcycle with an attached sidecar that he kept in a shed behind the caretaker's cottage. If Pierre wasn't cooking or reading mysteries, he could usually be found tinkering with it. He'd shipped it from France thirty years ago. Liz had had many fun rides in that sidecar as a child, and suddenly she felt nostalgic for the good ol' days, when Pierre's mental state was as sharp as his hero, Hercule Poirot's.

Liz went to the refrigerator and opened the door. Inside was one small package wrapped in wax paper. She took it out and brought it to the center island, then unwrapped it. Inside was the poorest excuse for seafood she'd ever seen. She couldn't even determine what type of fish it was. Not only were the filets a mess, with scales sticking to the paper, but she also saw bones crisscrossing every which way. "Did Jake tell you what kind of fish this is, Grand-Pierre?"

He looked over at her. "I seem to recall it's grouper."

Liz rewrapped the fish and put the whole package inside a plastic bag, then sealed it. She would throw it away later. "Come, Grand-Pierre, let's go help Kate rehearse for her part in *The Bat*. She needs help with one of her scenes before Auntie and the others return from their outing. It's the first time I've seen Kate scared of anything."

"Ah, my little Katie. What a splendid idea. I loved Mary Roberts Rinehart's *The Circular Staircase* when I first read it decades ago. Quite the surprise ending. Ç'est magnifique."

Pierre put his feet down on the floor and stood. His posture had started to slump more with each passing year, but he was still physically fit from swimming in the Indialantic's Olympic pool every morning. The same pool where movie stars and other celebrities had swum during the hotel's glory years.

"Let's bring her some lemon raspberry bars to keep her motivated," he said.

"Great idea. I'll grab a few water bottles."

They met at the swinging doors to the dining room and Liz held them open, then followed him through. Greta had cleared away the breakfast dishes and the room was neat and tidy. They headed to the opposite side of the room, and Liz noticed movement outside the floor-to-ceiling arched window that faced the front of the hotel. She went to the window and saw a motorcycle peeling out of the circular drive, sooty exhaust escaping from the tailpipe. She turned back to Pierre and asked, "When did you say Jake stopped by with the seafood?"

Pierre scratched his head, then looked down at his watch. "Nine thirty. I know because Greta gave me my pills. Always the same time every morning, along with a glass of green juice."

So why was Jake just leaving the property now? She'd wanted to ask Pierre, but she kept her questions to herself, filing it away until she could talk to Ryan or her father.

When they reached the open door to Aunt Amelia's screening room they heard Kate's strong voice reciting lines. They walked inside. Liz flipped a few switches, turning on two more spotlights for the stage, along with the runway lights on either side of the aisle.

Kate looked up, her glossy dark bangs covering her eyes. "Hallelujah! The troops have arrived."

Over the past week, Liz and Kate had been rehearsing Kate's lines for *The Bat* in between dealing with customers at Books & Browsery. Liz thought she'd gotten them down perfectly, but Kate demanded of herself that she not miss a single word, maybe because she'd been involved in competitive sports all her life. Plus, she had Susannah to contend with. The decision hadn't been made yet whether Kate would pile her long brown hair under a derby hat and play a male or play Detective Anderson as a strong female. The time period was the late thirties to early forties. Susannah had a point when she said there weren't many actresses playing female detectives then. The only one Liz could think of was Myrna Loy, who played Nora Charles in *The Thin Man* movies, but she would probably be considered more of an amateur sleuth than a detective.

Liz and Pierre went down the aisle, then climbed the three steps to the stage. Pierre set down the plate of lemon bars on the top of a speaker, and Liz added the three water bottles.

While Kate filled Pierre in on her character, Detective Anderson, Liz went behind the huge projection screen and retrieved two folding chairs that were leaning against the back wall, then brought them back to where Kate and Pierre stood.

Liz settled Pierre first, then took a seat. "Roll. Action!"

"First, let me set the scene," Kate said. "Imagine we're in an isolated mansion on a large estate. I picture one of the old robber baron estates in Newport."

"Pierre and I have seen both movie versions of *The Bat*," Liz interjected.

"Good. Good," Kate said, but continued to fill them in on the plot. "The scene I want to rehearse is right before the intermission. Elderly spinster Cornelia Van Gorder rents the mansion for the summer. According to newspaper reports, a criminal known as 'the Bat' has been terrorizing the neighborhood. All the servants in the house swear the mansion is haunted."

"Got it," Liz said, a tad impatiently. She couldn't keep her mind off Jake hanging around the Indialantic an hour after he'd supposedly left the kitchen.

"This scene is in the second act, when Detective Anderson gets knocked on the head and dragged to the other room. I need you to tell me if my physicality is on point. The scene takes place in a small room with a fireplace."

They watched as Kate bent down, then craned her neck, looking up the imaginary chimney for something with her imaginary flashlight. All of a sudden, with surprising finesse, she jerked forward and fell splat on the stage.

Pierre clapped his hands. "Bravo, Katie."

Liz saw Kate's eyelashes flutter, and there was an almost imperceptible upward twitch to the corners of her mouth.

"Okay, Kate. You can get up now. Are you supposed to be dead or wounded?" Liz asked with a grin.

Kate stood and brushed off her jeans. "I'm not telling. It will ruin the surprise of my performance. You'll have to wait and see."

It looked like they had another Aunt Amelia on their hands.

"I think the scene might be more convincing if one of you pretended to hit me on the head." Kate took a water bottle off the speaker and handed it to Liz. "Bash away, bestie!"

Liz smiled. "My pleasure."

After six different fake wallops on the head, Kate seem satisfied that she'd nailed the scene. "Now," she said. "Let's rehearse a few of my lines from act one. Liz, you can play Cornelia Van Gorder, Susannah's part. And Pierre, if you don't mind, you can read along and prompt me if I forget a word or two." She handed Pierre and Liz a copy of the play. "Page seven, if you please." Then she took her mark on the stage. "Okay, Cornelia, your line, top of the page."

Kate read her lines flawlessly until the end of the scene. She said, "'That was a figure of…'"

"Speech," Pierre prompted Kate.

"'That was a figure of speech,'" Kate said, continuing as Detective Anderson. "'The newspapers named him the Bat because he moved with incredible rapidity, always at night, and by signing his name' I mean, 'he leaves the symbol of his identity—the Bat, which can see in the dark.'"

Liz read Cornelia's part. "'I wish I could. These country lights are always going out.'"

"'Sometimes he draws the outline of a bat at the scene of the crime. Once, in some way he got hold of a real bat and nailed it to the wall.'

"End scene," Kate announced. "And I only missed one word!"

All they needed was some melodramatic organ music.

"Perfection," Pierre said.

"Thanks, Chef," Kate said. "Did you two know that Rinehart's villain, the Bat, was the prototype for the superhero Batman of DC Comics fame? Bob Kane, the creator of Batman, mentioned in his autobiography, *Batman and Me*, that the character in the 1930 movie *The Bat Whispers* was the inspiration for his Batman."

"No, I didn't, know that," Pierre said.

Liz handed Kate her copy of the play. "Neither did I. And I never saw *The Bat Whispers*, only the two midcentury teleplays."

"I just watched it on YouTube," Kate said. "The UCLA film school had the original movie reformatted and restored."

"Oh, how wonderful. I don't think Aunt Amelia has seen that one," Liz said. "I'll have to tell her when she gets back. You did an excellent job."

"Thanks, Liz. Remember, there are still some parts open. Tom told me he's holding open auditions after Pirates' Weekend."

Immediately after Kate said the words "Pirates' Weekend," a deafening alarm rang on their cell phones—either an Amber Alert or a weather warning. Liz was betting on the latter.

A hurricane watch had been issued for Melbourne Beach.

"I'm sorry for Aunt Amelia," Kate said after looking at her phone. "She was so looking forward to Pirates' Weekend."

"You can't stop Mother Nature or Hurricane Roberta, it seems," Liz said. "Auntie will rally; she always does."

Pierre stood and folded up his chair.

Liz rushed over to him. "I've got it, Grand-Pierre!"

"Lizzie, I am more than capable of carrying a folding chair, *ma petite.*"

She realized she was doing it again: swooping in to try to fix things when nothing was broken. "Of course you can. Let's reconvene in the kitchen at around six. Susannah and Aunt Amelia should be back by then. Kate, come for dinner. I saw the recipe for Mediterranean grilled shrimp with garlic-cilantro sauce on the counter."

"One of my favs," she said, looking at Pierre. "However, every dish you make, Chef, seems to be my favorite—except those fried smelts in anchovy sauce you made once for fish Friday."

"Ah, an old recipe of my mother's. A comforting dish that reminds me of home."

"Kate, do you mind telling Minna about our plans for dinner when you go back to the emporium?" Liz asked.

"No problem. Should I start telling everyone Pirates' Weekend will be postponed?"

There was another loud sound coming from their phones. Liz looked at hers and said, "Yep. The watch is now a warning. Time to batten down the hatches."

Chapter 18

Even after a few protests from Susannah, Kate, Aunt Amelia, Minna, Greta, Pierre, Susannah, and Liz sat together for dinner at the long farm table in the Indialantic's kitchen. They discussed the maiden voyage of *Visions of Gold,* while supping on Mediterranean shrimp over homemade linguine with an avocado Greek salad and crusty Kalamata olive bread.

"You'll never believe who found treasure!" Aunt Amelia said. "Tom."

Liz added a little more salad to her plate. "Wow. How fortunate. What did he find?"

"A piece of silver. Just like the one I found years ago. Tom decided to share the spoils with the guests, seeing he's the proprietor of Treasure Tours." Amelia looked over at Liz. "You remember, Lizzie, when I found the coin, we were pretending we were shipwrecked on *Gilligan's Island.*"

Susannah interrupted. "Yes. Yes. We all know about your one-episode role on *Gilligan's Island*, and how you came up with the Tina Louise red hair color you're still copying decades later. Personally, I think the whole treasure-diving part of the voyage was the least interesting, although watching everything through the glass bottom had its merits, and the white-glove service was quite exceptional; reminded me of years ago, when I'd visit relatives on Boston's Beacon Hill. Servants wearing white gloves make your guests feel special. Like on *Downton Abbey.*" Susannah's eyes darted to Greta.

Greta gave it back to her with a look that said, *Yes, that would be happening about the twelfth of never.*

"Did anyone else find treasure?" Minna asked.

"A cannonball," Susannah answered. "One of those obnoxious males found it. I sure wouldn't call that treasure."

Minna said, "Cannonballs from the 1715 fleet are very valuable for historians; also, if they find the cannon nearby, it gives an indication of what part of the sunken ship you've discovered, along with the time when the vessel sank. Of course, the best part of the galleon to find would be the cargo area, which held the queen's gold and jewels."

"I thought it was a magical experience," Amelia said. "Did you know there was even a white baby grand piano on board? I was willing to sing a few lines from one of my musicals, but unfortunately, not one person knew how to play the piano. Too bad your father wasn't on board, Lizzie."

"Yes, what a shame," Susannah said.

Liz couldn't tell if Susannah was being facetious or sincere. "Sounds wonderful, Auntie. Who's ready for dessert?"

Greta and Liz prepared dessert in the pantry. Greta said, "I just wanted to tell you something that happened the other day when Minna told me to tell Mr. Grayson she'd been called away. When I went into the lobby, he was coming down the stairway in a hurry. He seemed flustered when he saw me but didn't give an explanation. I didn't question him because I don't know what relationship Mr. Grayson has with the hotel. I just thought you should know."

"Did he have anything in his hands?"

Greta gave her a double look. "Not that I saw. Why? Do you think he was up to no good?"

"No," Liz replied, laughing. "He seems very interested in the hotel. Asked if Auntie was thinking of selling."

"She isn't, is she?"

"No. And I told him that."

"Good. Just let me know whatever you need from me to help keep the Indialantic afloat. I wish I had savings to invest, but old age has been a little costlier than I thought it would be."

Liz patted her arm, "Greta, you've been invaluable to everyone here, especially Aunt Amelia. In fact, I would say you're priceless. No need to worry about our finances. We're doing well. And perhaps after we get historical status, things will become less stressful for Auntie."

"Then that's what I'll pray for," Greta said.

When their meal was finished and everyone left the kitchen, Liz mused that it had been a productive day, especially considering everything going on around her, including Hurricane Roberta. She'd even managed to get in a few hours' writing. She'd volunteered to do the clean-up. When she was finished, she left the dish towel on the counter, dimmed the kitchen lights, then tiptoed quietly into the butler's pantry, afraid of waking the bald-headed parrot. She untied her apron. As she reached to hang it on the peg next to Grand-Pierre's, she heard the door from the dining room slam against the kitchen wall. Susannah charged inside. "Elizabeth! Where is my photograph that was hanging on the wall in my sitting room?"

Liz turned and looked at Susannah standing in the middle of the kitchen. Susannah's face was mottled with red blotches, her hands clenched in fists. Liz said, "I have no idea."

"It was there this morning. Now there's an empty space on the wall."

"Is anything else missing?"

"No. Not even my signed first edition Amy Vanderbilt, thank the Lord! I want you to summon Mrs. Kimball immediately. And after that, the authorities."

"Slow down, Susannah."

Susannah put her hands on her bony hips and narrowed her eyes. "Don't tell me to slow down. What kind of hotel are you running here? Your great-aunt told me just a smidgeon about what happened last spring. I had to do my own investigating to find out the real story."

Liz remembered the dossier she'd found under the printer in Susannah's suite and didn't question her sleuthing abilities. She stepped out of the pantry and said, "Let's find Greta. Not to accuse her of anything, but to find out if she was in the Windward Shores Suite today."

Barnacle Bob jerked awake, "Snap, crackle, pop. Snap, crackle, pop."

"Can't you keep that infernal creature quiet?" Susannah asked. "I feel like I'm staying in a dysfunctional zoo instead of a former highly rated hotel."

For the first time, Liz didn't tell BB to behave; let him squawk to his tiny heart's content.

She met Susannah at the swinging doors leading into the dining room. Susannah pushed against one of the doors, then strode through, not bothering to hold it for Liz. *Where oh where could Susannah's manners have gone?* she thought as she narrowly avoided getting hit in the face when the door catapulted back. On its outward swing, she scurried through the doorway and entered the dining room. As she tried to catch up to Susannah, she glanced out one of the dining room's windows, recalling this morning, when she'd seen Jake pulling away on his motorcycle, a whole hour after he'd delivered mutilated seafood to Grand-Pierre. Then she remembered Susannah saying that on the night of Minna's show, she and Jake had fought over the now-missing photograph.

When they reached Susannah's suite, it was as she'd said: the framed photograph was missing from the wall. They'd first stopped at Greta's suite, where she told Susannah that she hadn't been inside the suite since early morning, and the photo had most definitely been on the wall then.

Dylan's murder had something to do with his photography. Something he saw on the fishing trawler that was illegal, most likely exposed in one of his shots. It seemed all roads led to Jake.

* * * *

It was twilight, and Liz and Ryan sat in the Indialantic's gazebo, away from anyone who might overhear their conversation. There hadn't been a sunset over the lagoon and the wind was picking up. Dried palm fronds cartwheeled over the lawn like tumbleweed. It was still too early to gauge the hurricane's path as it moved slowly through the Caribbean, so far avoiding any populated land masses. Most forecasters thought it would hit the United States somewhere near Everglades National Park, then move either toward Miami or the Keys.

Luckily, she'd brought a thermos of coffee with her in case Ryan was too tired from his morning on the fishing trawler to fill her in on every last detail of the day's discoveries. Even with a cup of java under his belt, he kept nodding off, missing half of what she was telling him about her morning on *Visions of Gold*. She made sure he was alert when she told him that Jake had hung around the hotel long after he'd delivered the mutilated grouper. Then she filled him in on the missing photograph from Susannah's suite.

"And here I thought *I* had a busy day," he said, taking another gulp of coffee.

"One other thing. My father's guy got back to him about the gold coin I found on the beach under Dylan's body. It is indeed a gold doubloon from the 1715 Spanish fleet. After it was cleaned, it had all the proper markings for the time period."

"Congratulations!" he said with a burst of energy and pulled her in for a kiss. Halfway through, his eyes closed. Liz guessed it wasn't because he was in the throes of ecstasy.

She gently pushed him back against the decorative iron spires that followed the perimeter of the structure. Her great-aunt had built the gazebo to replicate the one in *The Sound of Music* movie. There couldn't be a more romantic spot on the grounds of the Indialantic. "You need to get some sleep. You have another day of fishing and snooping ahead of you, matey. But first, I want to hear about everything you discovered at town hall."

"Are you using me for my investigative skills, Elizabeth Amelia Holt?"

"Of course. That and other things," she said, smiling. "Now, on with it! What did you find out, Mr. Investigator?"

"I got some information from the harbormaster on who owns *Poseidon*. When I talked to Charlotte, she said she already knew the name of the company that owned it. In fact, she wanted me to let it go. I think from now on we'll have to keep things between ourselves."

"Did you tell her that you were going undercover on *Poseidon*?"

"No."

"Good. So, who owns the boat?"

"A company called Central Coast Boatworks. It doesn't tell me much, I'm sure it's what's referred to as a shill corporation, but I'm calling in a favor down at town hall. She should get back to me later today." He yawned.

She? "You need to get to bed." Liz screwed the cup on the top of the thermos and got up from the bench. "I know we're keeping my dad's girlfriend out of the loop, but I promised I'd tell him everything we learned going forward. Are you okay with that?"

"Of course. I just don't want him to think I'm putting his daughter at risk."

"Don't you worry. I learned all my digging skills from dear ol' Dad."

Liz looked over at Ryan. He'd fallen asleep in a standing position and jerked awake whenever he swayed too far to the left or right. She pushed away the dark hair covering his eyes with her hand. He looked so peaceful, but she had to do it. "Okay, big boy. Time for bed!" Then she pinched his biceps, barely finding loose skin.

"I'm awake. I'm awake."

"I just had a great idea. I've been texting Betty everything that's going on while she's in London at her Sherlock Holmes convention. We need to enlist her aid. You know her snooping skills are rock solid."

"Snoopiest eighty-three-year-old teenage mystery writer I know," he said.

Liz missed Betty and couldn't wait until she was home in only a few short, or, at the rate things were going, two *long* weeks.

"She have any insight into Dylan's death?"

"Like us, she thinks we need to do a background check on Jake and follow him around."

"I checked his background," Ryan said as he stood. "He had a couple of run-ins with the law before he was eighteen, but the files are sealed. Also, I saw something online about him being involved in a fraternity incident that involved a female student. The case was dismissed because she dropped the charges and recanted her story. As for following Jake around, I hope to do that tomorrow on *Poseidon*."

Darkness had fallen and the two iron filigree streetlamps in front of the gazebo switched on. He put his arm around Liz as they walked down the gazebo steps, each thinking their own thoughts, the only sound the crashing of the waves in the near distance. She glanced at him. His nose and cheeks were a brownish-red from too much sun exposure, adding another dimension of handsomeness to his already dark good looks. She reached up and pressed her finger to the top of his nose.

"Ouch!"

"You need to wear sunscreen tomorrow, buster. I can loan you some." Because of the skin grafts and still-healing skin on her right cheek, Liz wasn't allowed much sun.

"Yes, bossy pants."

She grinned but thought back to her relationship with Travis. Even though he'd been much older than Liz, she had played mother, nurturer, not to mention enabler, on more than one occasion. Ryan was the opposite of Travis, more than able to handle his own needs, while at the same time being supportive and encouraging to others. "Your morning trip might be canceled because of the weather," she said. "Are you sure you'll still be heading out to sea?"

"Whether they cancel or not, I plan to be on that boat."

"Do you need a lift home?" She nodded in the direction of one of the hotel's golf carts parked outside the gazebo. The most popular mode of transportation on the island.

Ryan laughed. "No. If I have to, I think I'm able to crawl the thousand feet it takes to reach the caretaker's cottage." Before leaving, he pulled her into an embrace. He'd recently showered, and his hair was still damp when she ran her fingers through it. She inhaled the fresh scent of soap on his neck. After a long kiss, she looked up at him and said, "Please be careful. Maybe we're making a mistake and we should listen to Charlotte. After all, she's a homicide detective."

He placed his pointer finger on her lip. "Don't worry about me. I can take care of myself."

For some reason she shivered, even though it was seventy degrees.

Were they getting in over their heads?

Only time would tell…

Chapter 19

Saturday morning, Liz found Aunt Amelia, Greta, and Minna battening the hatches in the Indialantic's center courtyard. All the umbrellas on the tables had been taken down and stored, and the heavy iron furniture was stacked against the wall.

"I take it we're canceling Pirates' Weekend," Liz said, helping Minna roll one of the potted palms to the corner alcove.

"I think we have to, Lizzie." Aunt Amelia put her hands on her wide hips and surveyed the cleared area. "It's still too early to say if Roberta will hit or go out to sea, but I can't take a chance. If it does hit, it will only be a category one. And this old lady has survived many of those without a care."

They all said at the same time, "You're not an old lady!"

"I know that, my dears. I'm talking about the Indialantic by the Sea," she said, patting the stucco wall.

They laughed.

"Auntie. I assume you talked to Susannah this morning?" Liz asked.

"Oh yes. She's in such a tizzy about the missing photograph, she's taken to bed."

Liz wondered if Susannah really was upset, or if she just didn't want to help in the hurricane preparations.

"Susannah talked to me about the photo at breakfast," Minna said as she wheeled another tree across the terrace to shelter. "She wanted to know if I had the first print in the series. I couldn't help her because I have no idea which one she bought. She tried to describe it but did a poor job of it, only telling me the main colors."

Liz described the photo to Minna, remembering it from when she'd seen it on Thursday, when she'd delivered towels to the Windward Shores Suite.

"Oh, that's one of my favorites. I think Alyse has the first numbered print. And as unbelievable as it may seem, I got a call last night from Beachside Gallery, telling me every piece of Dylan's had sold."

"Every single one?"

"Yes," Minna answered.

"That's wonderful!" Greta said as she rolled up a small area rug.

It seemed too coincidental that every photograph had sold. Liz had tossed and turned all night, not able to sleep much later that six. Most of her worries centered on Ryan, who was shoving off to sea with a potential murderer. During the night, there'd been a text message from Betty, who was still in London. What Betty had suggested was something so simple Liz felt embarrassed she hadn't thought of it herself. If there was a clue in Dylan's photographs that would incriminate his killer, why weren't they looking at them with a Sherlockian magnifying glass or, better yet, getting hold of the memory card where they were stored? Liz was a fanatic about backing up all her writing. She even kept different USB drives of the same manuscript in her father's office, Betty's blue bomber's glove compartment, and her handbag, not to mention all the copies she kept sending off to her clouds in cyberspace. Liz looked over at Minna, wanting to get her alone to see if her handbag had turned up. From Minna's reaction at dinner last night, Liz had assumed the memory card was in Minna's handbag.

Liz joined her and said in a whisper, "Ryan and I were in the gallery on Thursday and there were still at least ten or twelve of Dylan's works on the wall. Do you know if there was one buyer or several?"

"I didn't think to ask. Does it make a difference? I'm so thrilled that all the money from the sales will go to Dylan's pet project, getting work for vets. Do you suspect the purchase of his photos is linked to his death?"

"It might be. Do you have any idea where Dylan might have stored the backup for his digital photos? A laptop, external hard drive, or memory card?"

"Yes. He gave me a portable drive of everything he'd chosen to go to Beachside Gallery."

"Did you ever find your handbag?"

"Just as you and Ryan said last night, it was in Home Arts, but not where I usually put it. Ashley said she hadn't moved it. I'm pretty sure I wouldn't have put it in Francie's cubby drawer. Unless I'm completely losing it."

Before Liz could ask if the drive with the photos was in Minna's handbag, Aunt Amelia came up behind them. "You're not losing it, Minna dear. You've been under a lot of stress. After we're finished here, I'll make you a soothing cup of tea. Rose hip, I think."

"Thanks, Amelia," Minna said. When Aunt Amelia wasn't looking, she mouthed, "Later" to Liz.

Liz didn't want to involve her great-aunt in the conversation, so she waited until she walked away before asking, "Minna, was the memory stick with Dylan's photos in your handbag?"

"You know, in all the excitement of finding it this morning, I forgot to look. My handbag's in my suite. I'll let you know when I go upstairs."

"Thanks. I don't know if it means anything, but the photos are worth checking out," Liz said.

Greta, who had gone poolside to secure everything small enough to store in the pool house, came into the courtyard and announced, "Amelia, the landscape crew is outside to help secure the Indialantic. They told me they have many more stops because of the hurricane and want to know where they should start."

The next few hours were spent overseeing the crew whose job was to remove every piece of furniture from the suites' terraces, then store everything in the large building next to the caretaker's cottage that had once been a ten-car garage. After being away for ten years, Liz had forgotten how much work went into preparing for a hurricane.

She kept looking at her phone, waiting to hear from Ryan. It was almost noon and he'd told her it would be a short trip, depending on the hurricane. The latest forecast had Roberta heading up the East Coast, with possible landfall in Port St. Lucie, a town seventy miles south of Melbourne Beach. Thankfully, it still had a category-one status.

After the crew left the grounds, Liz strolled over to the caretaker's cottage, hoping to find Ryan. The wind was whipping at forty to fifty miles per hour, but it was partly sunny, with only puffy white clouds moving briskly against the afternoon sky. Finding no sign of Ryan, she went to the emporium to see if Pops had heard from his grandson. He hadn't. The amount of worry she had for Ryan's safety showed how strong her feelings for him were. She was still conflicted whether that was a good thing or bad based on her former relationship with Travis. She took out her phone to text him and noticed that today's date was the same as the release of her ex's novel, *Blood and Glass*. With everything going on with Dylan, Pirates' Weekend, and now the hurricane, she'd completely forgotten. She was only mildly curious what the reviewers would say when they read the fictitious account of Travis and Liz's relationship. She knew what a talented writer Travis was, hence his winning a Pulitzer Prize for *The McAvoy Brothers*, but she also knew that in every argument or speed bump in their relationship, he'd blamed her. There was nothing she could do about it now, so she texted Ryan for the sixth time.

Seconds later, she received his text: *It's all a bust.* Poseidon *has an entirely new crew from when Dylan went overboard.* Jake hasn't worked on the boat since the day Dylan was found on the beach. One interesting thing: I saw Victor on the dock, near Poseidon. Going to follow up on things. See you soon.

That was disappointing. Unless they could find the original crew and interview them, how could they learn anything about the day Dylan died? And Jake—what kind of game was he playing? Showing up yesterday morning, pretending to bring seafood from *Poseidon.* And what connection did Victor have with the boat Dylan had disappeared from? Liz had to let it go for now; she had her own things to check out.

She answered Ryan, *Come to my beach house when you get back. Key's under the cement mermaid by the steps to my deck.*

Instead of waiting around to hear from Ryan again, Liz decided to do some sleuthing of her own and cruised south on A1A toward the Sebastian Inlet. The beach was known for its surfing competitions and was home to generations of world-class surfers, both male and female. Having grown up on the island, she knew all about the lure of a pre-hurricane surf.

When she pulled into the parking lot, she saw five warning flags. Posted on a chalkboard was a hazardous riptide statement. She glanced toward the jetty where the biggest swells formed and saw at least a dozen surfers. She hoped one of them was Jake, Dylan's so-called friend, who might have also been his murderer.

She searched the parking lot for Jake's motorcycle. It wasn't there, so she grabbed a blanket from the trunk of the car and headed toward the wide sandy beach that butted up to the long jetty. The incoming waves against the jetty caused the swells to be larger than normal—part of the Inlet's appeal to surfers nationwide.

After she identified every surfer in the water, Liz saw none of them was Jake. She went up to one of the surfers who'd just emerged from the ocean, who looked to be the big kahuna of the bunch; he was older than most of the others, probably in his midthirties. He reminded her of Cliff Robertson, who'd played The Big Kahuna in one of her and her great-aunt's favorite movies, *Gidget.* Amelia Eden Holt hadn't had a part in it, but she had auditioned for one of Sandra Dee, aka Gidget's, beach-buddy girlfriends. Her great-aunt didn't have a narcissistic personality, so when she'd told Liz the director had said she hadn't gotten the part because she was too pretty, Liz totally believed her.

When Liz reached him, she said, "Excuse me. Can you tell me if you've seen Jake? His family is looking for him. It's very important."

Liz was five-foot-eight and the big kahuna towered over her. He was even taller than Ryan's six-foot-three. He took his time to answer as he towel dried his hair. "Jake Marshal? I didn't think Jake had family."

"Um...well, not exactly ...blood relatives," she stuttered, "but concerned friends."

"Are you one of them?" he asked.

She smiled. Let him believe what he may. "Yes."

"Haven't seen him since yesterday afternoon. Actually, I'm surprised he's not here to enjoy the pre-Roberta surf."

Liz reached into her handbag and took out a piece of paper and a pen. She scribbled her phone number, then handed it to him. "My name's Liz. Please call or text if you see Jake. It's imperative that I reach him."

He looked down at the paper, then extended his hand. "I'm Alex."

She shook his hand. "Thank you."

"I didn't say I would give this to him. You aren't a bill collector, are you?"

"No."

"Just curious. I know the surfboard he just bought was a Ferrari Challenge Stradale. Cost at least five thou, a lot for a fisherman's salary. He's one hell of a surfer, though. I'll pass this on if I see him."

"Thanks, Alex."

He took his towel and wiped away the sand clinging to his legs. There was a large scar near his left knee. He must have noticed her stare because he said, "Blacktip shark, from when I was twelve."

Liz couldn't believe she'd so obtrusively stared at his leg. But, as she'd begun learning from her own scar, it was human nature to be curious, and usually after the curiosity followed concern and caring. "And you still surf?"

"Of course. It's just a scar."

Indeed.

"Plus, this is October. Springtime is shark time in Florida, not fall."

"Your wife must worry about you surfing in shark-infested waters."

"No wife, and the chance of getting another shark bite is slim. I'm not worried."

Good, he wasn't married. And he seemed fearless. Something about him made Liz think he and Kate would make the perfect match. Kate had dated while Liz had been living in New York. But since Liz had moved back to Melbourne Beach, it seemed Kate had forgone the dating scene in lieu of watching over Liz. Now that Liz and Ryan had a blossoming relationship in the works, she wanted the same thing for her best friend. "Well, thanks, Alex. Be safe," she said, walking back to the car.

On her way back to the beach house, Liz thought about Jake. There was no feasible way he could be the head of a drug-smuggling operation. He was too young and immature. There had to be records of the former captain and crew of *Poseidon*. If there were, she hoped Ryan would find them.

It wasn't until three o'clock that Ryan showed up on her doorstep.

"It's about time you got here!" Liz said. "I was worried. I almost called Charlotte Pearson and had her put out an APB."

He stood silent, his dark eyes glaring in her direction. His arms were held straight to his sides, like it took all his control to keep them there. In his left hand was a shopping bag.

"What's wrong?" she asked. "Pops? A dead end in our investigation, partner?"

He snarled his lip like an evil character in a *Harry Potter* movie, and she thought she heard him sarcastically repeat the word, "Partner" under his breath.

"Come inside. The wind is really picking up; I can tell by the chimes. Did you notice they're playing our song?" Ryan had bought her the Woodstock wind chimes as a gift after her old set took flight during a wicked thunderstorm. They played the melody "Bells of Paradise," and every time they sang, she thought of Ryan.

He didn't come inside. Instead he said, "Why didn't you tell me?"

"Tell you what?"

"About the book."

"What book?" *Oh-h, Travis's book.* "Uh-h-h…"

"It was in the window of Beachside Books for all the world to see. I thought we were close enough that you might've mentioned that your ex-boyfriend was writing a book based on your relationship." He opened the bag and took out a flyer with the Beachside Books logo on top, then flashed it in front of her. "And you also might have mentioned that your boyfriend plans to make a stop in Melbourne Beach on his book tour."

"He what? I had no idea about that. I think you'd better rein in your anger a little before I have to ask you to leave. The book is a work of fiction."

He reached into the bag and pulled out a thick hardcover with a white book jacket. Pictured on front was a large shard of glass with blood on it. "Shall I read the back cover?" He didn't wait for her to answer. "'When Pulitzer Prize–winning author Marcus Peterson meets…'"

"Stop!"

"Don't worry, I'm leaving. Hey, you want my copy? Or are you going to wait until Travis Osterman blows into town so he can autograph it?" It seemed brooding, arrogant Ryan had reared his not-so-ugly head, just as he had last April, when he'd assumed things about her that weren't true.

"Oh no, you don't. I apologize for not telling you about the book, but I never even read the proofs his agent sent a while ago. They're locked in my father's filing cabinet."

"How long have they been there, Liz? Might be something you would bring up in one of our many conversations. Something we could tackle together?"

Liz's cell phone ironically rang to the tune of "What a Wonderful World." She took it out of her pocket, looked down, and saw a local number. She tapped the phone and answered, "Liz Holt."

"Elizabeth, it's Sally Beaman, your old friend from Melbourne Beach High. Any chance you'd like to come on Channel 12 for an interview about Travis Osterman's newly released book, *Blood and Glass*? I'd love to get your take on it."

"My take? I haven't read it and don't plan to. Gotta go." Liz glanced in Ryan's direction. Was Sally crazy? She hadn't talked to her in years and barely talked to her in high school. She didn't owe the woman anything but a "No, thank you," which she'd said into the phone, then pressed the End button.

Ryan remained in the open doorway, a sardonic smirk on his face. "Mr. Osterman?"

"Uh. No. Maybe we should meet later, after you've cooled down. You don't own me!" She regretted the words as soon as she'd said them. They sounded so juvenile.

"You're right, Elizabeth Holt. I don't own you." Then he turned and walked across the deck and down the steps.

She went out on the deck and called after him, "Big jerk! What about Dylan's murder?"

"We'll meet in your father's office," she heard him say. "I'll text you when."

"Yes, sir, bossy pants."

Ryan ignored her and disappeared from view. She turned, picked up the flyer from Beachside Books that he'd tossed to the ground, and went inside. She slammed the French door and looked down at the flyer, breathing a sigh of relief when she saw next to the line "Travis Osterman Author Visit—To Be Announced."

If there was one thing she knew about her ex, he was the complete opposite of dependable, and she wondered if he'd found someone else to make sure he made all his scheduled appointments and book signings. Not her worry. But something that *was* her worry was when she thought of the card she'd found on the floor of Ryan's Jeep. The one with the lingerie-clad woman photographed in sexy poses. She should have thrown it at him, but that would be childish. She wasn't a child. Then she sat next to Bronte on the window seat and cried like a baby.

Chapter 20

An hour later, Liz was in Kate's cottage, eating a fish taco at her tiny kitchenette's table. A beach shack on stilts would be a better description of Kate's cozy home. It had a pale aqua clapboard exterior and faded peach shutters with cutouts of mermaids. The cottage's square footage was only slightly larger than those featured on tiny house television shows. The best thing about the cottage was its roomy sleeping porch with a view of the Atlantic and a porch swing the size of a queen-size bed. Kate had sacrificed half of her great room to extend the depth of the porch.

The interior of the cottage was crammed with vintage books and eclectic items from Books & Browsery. Things she borrowed, then returned to the shop, depending on the season or the urge to spend a little more time with them before finding them a good home. Each time Liz stepped inside the décor would be different from her previous visit. Most items still wore their price tags, and on more than one occasion, Liz would find the perfect gift for someone at the Indialantic or something to go into her own beach house. Only last month, she'd brought Ryan home a vintage, locally published cookbook entitled *Firehouse Fare*, a collection of recipes from a firehouse in Cocoa Beach. He'd made firehouse sweet potato hash, and instead of using regular butter and sugar, he'd substituted coconut butter and coconut sugar for a healthier spin. It had been delicious.

Why must her thoughts always circle back to Ryan?

Liz looked over at Kate, then pointed to the corner of her own mouth in mirror image, to show Kate where a tiny cube of mango clung. Before coming to Kate's, Liz had stopped at Pete's Food Truck. Even though a hurricane was on its way, the truck had still been parked in the Fifth Avenue Beach parking lot, where she'd procured two of her favorite meals that weren't prepared by someone at the Indialantic by the Sea. Pete's fish tacos with mango-cilantro salsa had just the right ingredients to make the freshly caught fish of the day he marinated in lime juice and honey: a gastronomic delight.

"I understand how Ryan might feel betrayed," Liz said. "But honestly, I just wanted to push Travis and his supposedly fictitious novel out of my mind. That was my old life and, as I've learned in therapy, I can't control people, places, or things, only my reaction to them."

"Wisely stated," Kate said, wiping her mouth with a napkin. "You didn't even tell me about Osterman's novel. I'm your best bud, and I have no problem with that."

"That's what I'm saying." Liz slapped her hand on the table. "He's such a big jerk!"

"I don't know about that," Kate said. "I can see his side too. But I know something for sure; I won't be looking into those book pages anytime soon."

Liz smiled at her friend's loyalty to both her and Ryan. Then frowned at the thought of Ryan's ire.

"So, change of subject," Kate said. "You've filled me in on all the latest, so what's your next step in catching Dylan's killer?"

"I kind of hoped Ryan would be the one to steer us in that direction after we shared everything we'd learned today. But I don't think that will be happening too soon."

"What's with the Charlie-Brown face? I have an idea," Kate said, getting up and grabbing the pitcher of ice tea from the counter, then pouring some into Liz's empty glass.

"Is it dangerous?" Liz asked. Kate's ideas in the past had gotten them into plenty of trouble. Like the time they snuck onto the property of one of the nearby oceanfront estates on a cool winter night to use the Jacuzzi, only to find themselves in the back of a sheriff's car and the recipients of a stern talking-to from Fenton Holt, who at the time was Brevard County's lead defense lawyer. Or the time…

"Let's head over to Squidly's. You said Jake and the original crew from *Poseidon* hung out there? I know Kevin, the barkeep. If anyone knows anything, he will."

"Won't they be preparing for Roberta?"

"Hell no. They stayed open during Irma. Everyone had a great time. Me and Skylar included."

"How is Sky?" Skylar was Kate's older brother, who ran the Barrier Island Sanctuary Education Center, just ten miles south of the Indialantic. "I've barely seen him since I've been back."

"Oh, you know him. He's always flying to DC to try to get money to keep the center afloat. He has a new girlfriend. I think you'll like her. Very down to earth. Nothing like Brittany."

"I can't wait to meet her." Skylar was like a brother to Liz. In high school, Skylar and Brittany, the owner of Sirens by the Sea, had dated briefly. Things hadn't turned out too well after Skylar spied one of his mother's missing bracelets in plain view atop Brittany's handbag. Liz had her own issues with Brittany and her kleptomania, dating all the way back to middle school. "Speaking of dating. I think I might have found the perfect guy for you. The big kahuna." She told Kate how she'd met the handsome surfer, Alex, at the Sebastian Inlet. "If I wasn't involved with Ryan, I think I'd snatch him for myself." Was *she involved with Ryan?*

"I'm game," Kate said.

"Also, Alex told me Jake just bought an expensive surfboard, a Ferrari Challenge Straddle or Stradale? You're a surfer; have any idea where he would buy it? Maybe we could find out where he lives if we visit the surf shop."

"Wow. That's a nice board. It's Stradale, and there's only one place within sixty miles you could buy one: Ziggy's Surf Shack. It's within walking distance from here. Let's go."

She was always game for anything, one of the qualities Liz loved most about her friend. "I'll do the dishes," Liz said. "You go get ready for Ziggy's and Squidly's."

Kate got up from the table. "Do you mean our Tweety and Sylvester glasses?"

"Exactly," Liz said. "I'm lucky I didn't bring over one of Grand-Pierre's meals, seeing you don't have a dishwasher. Have you ever made a big meal in this kitchen?"

"Oh, you'd be surprised. Once, I had my entire family over for Thanksgiving. We set up tables outside and ate under the stars and candlelight, with the sound of the crashing waves in the background for ambience."

"Sounds heavenly. Now get going. I want to find Jake before someone else we care about gets murdered."

Chapter 21

As they approached the slatted wooden structure with its thatched tiki roof, Liz worried that this might be the first and last time she saw Ziggy's Surf Shack. It seemed it wouldn't take a hurricane to level it, just a wolf, huffing and puffing and blowing it down, like the house of sticks in the fairy tale *The Three Little Pigs*.

The bell on the flimsy screen door tinkled when they walked inside. Reggae music played in the background, and there was the definite scent of sandalwood incense in the clouded air. The perimeter of the small space had at least a hundred surfboards stacked against one another in all shapes and colors. "Ziggy even sells vintage wooden boards," Kate told Liz. "Before they were made of polystyrene foam at their core, covered with fiberglass cloth, then finished with epoxy resin. I've sold Zig a few from some of my major scores at garage sales and flea markets."

"And what awesome boards they were, Kate Fields," Ziggy said, emerging from the back room through a doorway of hanging beads. He was on the short side, anywhere from his mid- to late-seventies, with a dark tan and numerous wrinkles on his long, weathered face. His thinning gray hair was pulled back in a ponytail that swung back and forth like the beaded curtain he'd just parted.

"Zig, I'd like you meet my friend, Liz Holt."

"Aloha, Liz," he said, bowing at the waist. "What do I owe the pleasure, ladies? You have a prize for me, Kate? As you can see, I'm running low on stock." He gestured with his arm to encompass the surfboard-packed room. The same arm that was layered with leather and puka-shell bracelets.

Kate laughed. "No. Sorry; nothing new, I mean vintage, this time, Ziggy."

"Well, an old surfer dude can dream, can't he? All the special boards you've found for me, Kate, aren't for sale at any price, even though there have been many beggars and promises of loads of greenbacks. The babies you find go right in my quiver." He pointed to the ceiling, where a collection of unusual-looking boards lay atop thin wooden beams.

"They belong in a museum," Kate said. "Speaking of price: We're wondering if you sold a Ferrari Challenge Stradale to someone named Jake."

Instead of answering, he went to the front of the shop, climbed on a step stool, and reached up for a red lacquered surfboard with an iconic gold Ferrari crest and rearing stallion logo. He brought it over to them, "This one is mine. Number 23 out of 425. Limited edition."

Kate stroked the surface of the board as if it was a living creature. "What a beaut!"

"Isn't she?" Ziggy said. "As to your question, why do you ask?"

"Jake supplies weekly orders of seafood to my great-aunt's hotel, the Indialantic by the Sea," Liz said. "He didn't show up this week and we're concerned. Alex at the Inlet told me he'd hasn't seen him in a while." A white lie.

"How is Amelia? Haven't seen her since her last production at the Melbourne Beach Theatre. She made a wonderful Lady Macbeth."

"She's great," Liz said. "She's in rehearsals for a mystery, *The Bat*."

"Kudos to her. Has your great-aunt ever shared any of her old surfing tales with you? Did you know Amelia was one of the few Bettys who could really ride a wave in her youth? The wave heights were out of this world back then. But that was before they screwed around with the jetty. Just not the same. Like everything else in this day and age, I suppose."

"Wow," Kate said. "I didn't know Aunt Amelia ever surfed. Did you, Liz?"

"No. I just knew about the few television shows in which she played a surfer. And here I thought I knew everything about Auntie."

Ziggy hung the board back on the wall over the window. "Please send her my regards, and tell her if she ever wants me to pick her up to ride the rails, it would be my pleasure."

Liz knew she wouldn't be passing that invitation along. An eighty-year-old surfing? Then she remembered who she was talking about and stifled her protective nature. "I'll pass it on, Ziggy." One of Aunt Amelia's often-used phrases resounded in Liz's memory: *The only thing that limits someone is their limiting beliefs.*

"As for your question about young Jake," he said, "he bought my Ferrari number 343 out of 425 only last week."

"Do you happen to know where he lives?" Liz asked.

"Maybe he paid with a credit card?" Kate interjected.

Ziggy scratched his head, "No, he definitely paid cash. Although he did have the board on layaway for a month; might have his address on an index card in my file box."

Liz tried to keep the excitement out of her voice. "That would be great. We just want to make sure he's okay."

Ziggy moved toward the curtain at the back of the shop, then went behind a counter that looked more like a bar. It was made of bamboo and faced in dried palm leaves, reminding Liz of one she'd seen in old photos of the interior of the Indialantic by the Sea's Beach Pavilion.

"Can't blame you for checking up on him, especially after that awful story of the young man everyone thought was lost at sea off a fishing boat but now might have been murdered. Didn't the body show up on the Indialantic's beach?"

"Yes, it did," Liz said.

Ziggy looked at Kate. "Young Jake works on *Poseidon*. Wasn't that the same boat?"

Kate hesitated. Liz could see her wheels turning, deciding whether to keep the charade going or come clean. She chose the latter. "You caught us, Zig. It's true we want to make sure he's okay, but we also want to ask him some questions."

"I need to 'fess up," Ziggy said. "Jake's a scoundrel, and I'm pretty sure he's involved in some bad things."

"Drugs?" Liz asked.

"The motto 'Drugs, no thank you, I'm a surfer' is something drilled into most wave riders. Surfers get high off a good day in the water and need to be steady on their feet. But there's something squirrelly about Jake, especially recently," he said, reaching under the counter and retrieving a metal index-card box. He flipped open the top and after about thirty seconds said, "Got it. He lives in Palm Bay. Let me copy the address." He transferred the address to the back of his business card, then handed it to Kate.

"Thanks, Zig. I owe you one."

"No, we're square. Just keep on the lookout for that 1950 balsa-wood board signed by Hobie Alter. It's in the number-one slot on my bucket list. And good luck. Hope the kid's all right. There's always hope for redemption, I always say. Look at me." He grinned.

"Thanks, Ziggy," Kate said. "I promise to put out feelers for the Hobie."

"Nice meeting you, Ziggy," Liz added.

"You too, Liz. And don't forget to say aloha to Amelia."

"Promise." Liz had a feeling Ziggy had been a player back in the day. Maybe he and Captain Netherton could compete for Aunt Amelia's attentions. Or Amelia and her eighty-three-year-old bestie, Betty, could each pick one of the two. Liz wondered what old-time television actor Ziggy would remind Aunt Amelia of. And would it be the way he looked now, or when she'd known him as a teen? Just take away his ponytail and Liz thought Ziggy was the spitting image of Ray Walston, who played Uncle Martin on one of her great-aunt's '60s television shows, *My Favorite Martian.* Liz would ask Aunt Amelia who she thought Ziggy looked like right after she passed on his invitation to go surfing.

It was no wonder Liz had become a writer; there was so much interesting material and so many characters to choose from on their own little island. Unfortunately, one of those characters was a cold-blooded killer. Liz didn't believe in omens, but she couldn't help recalling her premonition of gloom and doom on the morning she'd found Dylan's body. She looked over at Kate's sunny smile and tried to shake the bad vibes causing goose bumps at the back of her neck. She realized part of the reason for her morose thoughts had to do with Ryan. Why hadn't she told him about Travis's book? She knew why; she was a pro at compartmentalizing her pain and locking it away, just like she'd done with the *Blood and Glass* manuscript she'd locked in her father's filing cabinet.

As they walked out of Ziggy's, Liz looked up at a sign over the door, ENJOY LIFE, ONE WAVE AT A TIME. Sounded like a plan.

If only a hurricane wasn't headed their way.

Chapter 22

Squidly's was surprisingly crowded pre-hurricane. Liz and Kate had taken a seat at the bar, each ordering a glass of rosé. After Molly, Squidly's only female bartender, delivered their wine and a basket of homemade Cajun-spiced plantain chips, they discussed their next move.

Kate took a sip and gave Molly a thumbs-up. Then she said to Liz, "After we talk to my guy Kevin when he gets back from his break, should we head to Palm Bay to find Jake?"

Liz wasn't sure if that was a wise idea without cluing someone in on where they were going. If only Ryan hadn't gotten so mad about Travis's book, he'd be here with them and they could check out Jake's place together. "Maybe we should call my dad before we go any further. But I don't think it would hurt to drive by Jake's house to see if any lights are on or his motorcycle is parked out front. My father told me Charlotte is already on Jake as a suspect; she probably knows where he lives."

"Call Ryan instead," Kate said, crunching on a chip that left Cajun dust on her lips. "He's a professional. You guys should be able to put aside your petty differences."

"I don't know how petty they are. But you could be right."

"Well, never mind, because look over at that corner table." Kate pointed to an alcove under a shark's jaw filled with pearly whites that was straight out of the movie *Jaws*. Ryan was sitting with Charlotte.

Liz lost it.

She stormed over to them but didn't know what to say once she arrived. She opened her mouth, but nothing came out.

"Liz. What are you doing here?" Charlotte asked.

"Yes, Liz, what are you doing here?" Ryan looked tired, his eyes bloodshot, but he was still able to send daggers to her heart. Had he decided to share what he'd learned with Charlotte instead of her?

Her worries were quelled with Charlotte's next words. "Good; I'm glad I've got you together. Ryan, who I assume is trying to help find Dylan's killer, is interfering in my investigation. And now that I see you, I'm sure you didn't take to heart the warning I gave your father about leaving things alone. The fact that you're both at Squidly's must mean you know that the former crew on *Poseidon* hung out here. Well, I can put both your minds at ease. They haven't been seen since Dylan's body washed up on shore. I can also tell you that I'm not saying you can't share any information you find about his death. But that's all it can be. It's not going to be a two-way street."

Liz caught Ryan's gaze and he gave her a slight nod.

"Of course," Liz said. "I'd better get back to Kate."

When Liz reached the bar, Kate was gone, Liz assumed to the ladies' room. She sat on the barstool and took a long slug of her wine. She was happy Ryan hadn't arranged to meet Charlotte, but she still felt unsure how to proceed in their investigation. She was reminded about Minna's loss and everything she'd learned today. She had to bite the bullet and get Ryan alone to fill him in on the latest developments; then they could decide together whether to share the information with the Brevard Sheriff's Department.

Fifteen minutes later, Kate returned. "Worried about me?" she asked. "When I saw you talking to Ryan and Agent Pearson, I decided to search for Kevin."

"Why, Kate Fields, you're blushing."

She adjusted her short sundress on the stool, then looked shyly at Liz. "We've had a flirtation going on for about a decade. Whenever Kevin's in a relationship, I'm not. Or when I am, he's not. He's a good guy. Just not bring-home-to-momma material." Kate's mother lived in Arizona; she'd moved there around the same time Liz had gone off to Columbia when she was eighteen. Kate's father had passed away when she was ten, his death being one of their bonds, because Liz had also lost her mother at an early age. It must have been lonely for Kate with both her mother and Liz leaving her behind, but then Liz remembered that Aunt Amelia and her father had filled in as Kate's surrogate family and still held that role. "So, did you learn anything about Jake or the crew from Kevin?" Liz asked.

"He had a lot of wonderful things to say about Dylan. Jake and the former crew of *Poseidon*, not so much. He said most of the crew were drifters, not from this area."

"Another dead end."

"Not completely. Kevin told me Jake dated one of Squidly's waitstaff. In fact, here she comes now."

A petite brunette who barely looked of drinking age took a seat on the barstool next to Kate. "You wanted to talk about Jake? The kid with an angelic face and the soul of the devil?" She turned and said to Molly, "Mol, a shot of Patrón, please?"

Molly took the bottle from the holster on her hip and poured it into a shot glass, then set it on the bar. The girl grabbed it, chugged it back, and slammed the shot glass onto the bar. She said, "Okay. I guess I'm ready. What do you want to know?"

Liz leaned forward and extended her hand in front of Kate. "Hi, I'm Liz." The girl shook just the tips of Liz's fingers and said, "Felicia."

Kate turned to her. "Hi, Felicia. I'm Kate. We just wanted to know if you've seen Jake recently."

"Yes. Like a bad penny, my mom says, Jake always shows up. But also like a penny, whose worth is next to zero, I send him away."

"When did you see him last?" Liz asked.

"Yesterday, down at the harbor. I like to help my uncle when he brings in his catch for the day, a way to earn extra cash because there aren't many big tippers in Squidly's. He wanted some of Uncle Fred's bluefish but wasn't willing to pay for it, so I gave him some grouper for free. Just to get rid of him."

That explained the seafood Jake had brought to Pierre, Liz thought. "Did Jake ever talk about when the guy on his boat fell overboard during the storm?"

"You mean that sweet thing, Dylan, who everyone is saying might have been murdered? No, Jake wouldn't talk about Dylan. He was superjealous of my friendship with Dylan." She smiled, and it transformed her face. "That was one of the reasons I dumped Jake. Too clingy. Who needs that?"

"Who indeed," Kate answered.

"You aren't suggesting Jake had something to do with Dylan's death, are you?"

"Not necessarily," Liz said. "But we and the police have a few questions for him."

"I'm sorry, but that's just one reason to stay as far away as I can from him."

"Do you know if Jake does drugs?" Kate asked, motioning to Molly to pour another tequila shot for Felicia.

She downed the shot before answering. "Jake is into uppers, says he needs them for his job. He never knew when he'd be called to go fishing. He claims to just take prescription Adderall, but I've seen white powder in his nose on a few occasions. Another reason I want that loser out of my life." She got up from the barstool and said, "My shift is over. If you and the police really think Jake was involved, let me know. I'll get another restraining order against him."

Liz rooted in her handbag and took out one of the Indialantic's business cards and a pen. She wrote her name and cell phone number on the back, then handed it to Felicia. "Thanks for the info. Call if you hear from Jake?"

She took the card and looked at it. "My great-grandmother used to work at the Indialantic by the Sea. My gran still tells me great stories of when she went there as a kid. Let me give you my cell number."

Felicia recited her number as Liz added it to her cell phone contacts, then said, "Better run."

"Please be careful around Jake," Kate said. "I've told Kevin about everything, so talk to him if you need to."

"Will do." Then she walked toward the kitchen and disappeared through the swinging doors.

Liz leaned into Kate. "Well, that went better than expected."

Someone tapped Liz on the shoulder. She turned and saw a scowling Ryan.

"What went better than expected?"

Liz was torn between telling Ryan to take a hike and filling him in on what they'd learned. He took the dilemma out of her hands by saying, "Charlotte's gone. Both of you come over to my table in the corner."

Liz bristled at his command but kept her mouth shut. She did it for Minna and her sister-in-law, Alyse, and she did it for Dylan.

After they were seated, Ryan said, "I only told her one thing: what I suspect the murder weapon was. A goliath grouper fishhook. The thing is huge! If you fell or are pushed on it, the wound would resemble what I saw on the back of Dylan's head."

"Gross," Kate moaned.

"But get this. It wasn't on the deck of the boat, it was below deck. So, if the hook was the cause of the wound, that means Dylan didn't lose his footing during the storm, then bash his head and fall overboard, as Jake said."

Liz noticed someone looking over at their table, probably listening to Ryan's passionate retelling of his morning. She moved her chair closer to his and said in a low voice, "We know he was murdered because of the Rohypnol. I know, and you know, Dylan wouldn't take a date rape drug on his own. Slipping someone a Roofie doesn't make them a murderer; however, now that you say the murder weapon wasn't on deck, we have more evidence to say he was murdered."

"By Jake?" Kate asked.

"He would be my number-one guess," Ryan said.

"Did you tell Charlotte all this?" Liz asked.

"I had to. They need a forensic team down there to see if they can find any trace of Dylan's blood."

Liz's stomach churned at the thought. "Even if they do find blood, that just proves he was murdered. But is that enough to say Jake did it? And if he did, why? And why would the whole crew disappear? That would have to make them all involved."

"Wait," Kate said. "Let me re-cap: The entire crew from when Dylan supposedly fell off *Poseidon* disappeared and they've been replaced with an entirely new crew and captain?"

"You got it," Ryan said, taking a long pull on his mug of beer. Squidly's had twenty beers on tap, eighteen of them were microbrewed in Florida. "There was only a small crew on the boat, four men and the captain. This morning there was the same number. They bring in enough fish, but I wouldn't call it a big-time operation. So, to kill Dylan because of something he saw, it must have been drugs."

"Then Dylan's photos must show something," Liz said. "I'll talk to Minna. She said she has the memory card with the photos from the gallery opening."

"Let's reconvene in the library tomorrow morning," Ryan said. "Liz, you should have your father join us."

"Aren't we forgetting something?" Kate looked at Ryan, then Liz. "A little old thing called Hurricane Roberta." She took out her phone and tapped the screen.

"First things first. Let's go find Jake." Then Liz told Ryan how they'd gotten hold of Jake's address from Ziggy, and about Felicia and her dealings with Jake. "Felicia said she saw Jake Friday morning before he delivered seafood to the Indialantic. So hopefully, he's still around. I went down to the Inlet earlier and talked to a surfer who said he was surprised Jake hadn't shown up today because he'd been hyped all week because of the huge pre-hurricane waves they were forecasting."

"Speaking of showing up," Ryan said, "do you have any idea why Victor was lurking around the harbor near *Poseidon*?"

"That seems strange," Kate mused. "Did you ask him?"

"No," Ryan answered. "I didn't, but I followed him. As soon as he saw Captain Mark, he slunk off into the shadows. By the way, Liz, the new captain on *Poseidon* is really a nice guy."

"You mean Captain Ahab?"

"He got his nickname because he has a prosthetic leg and likes to quote from *Moby-Dick*. Captain Mark is basically as scary as kitty Bronte."

"Well, that's a relief," Liz said. Ryan shot her a look, like he doubted she cared about him. And things had been going so well. "I did see Charlotte talking to Victor at the Indialantic. Maybe we *should* stay out of it. She seems to be on top of things." Liz filled Ryan in on the email from the private investigator Susannah had hired to look in to Tom's background. "He's been an accountant in Jacksonville for fifteen years. Why would he lie about directing theater and owning a travel agency? And why insert himself in his brother's life after all this time? Apparently, they hadn't met before he came to the island."

The three of them remained silent for a few moments while the bar buzzed with laughter and loud conversation. A four-person band called Shark Attack did their requisite cover of "Margaritaville" by Jimmy Buffett. The crowd joined in while Molly strolled around with her tequila holster, pouring shots for the many takers.

Kate got up from the table. "It's been real, folks, but I need to get home. Liz, as you know, I have some rehearsing to do." She looked at Ryan. "Because of the cancellation of Pirates' Weekend and the coming hurricane, Tom, with lots of prodding from Aunt Amelia, has scheduled a rehearsal of *The Bat* tomorrow. Everyone with parts will be there."

Liz interjected, "Auntie has assured everyone that the Indialantic is the safest place for miles if the hurricane does hit. A mandatory evacuation has been issued for anyone living in mobile homes and low-lying areas, but so far it's voluntary for the rest of us." She thought of Ziggy's Surf Shack's flimsy walls. "The main thing I heard is they're worried about flooding. Luckily, the hotel was built on a higher elevation than its neighbors."

"Well, I need you both there for moral support," Kate said. "Maybe you two will see how much fun it is and try out for a role. Minna's coming, I might have talked her in to trying out for one of the other roles."

Ryan smiled, seemingly letting go of his earlier anger. "Okay, but only if I can play the Bat."

"Oh, didn't you know? The person who's the Bat won't know about it until a few weeks before dress rehearsal. Plus, we have a few other slots to fill. Ryan, pick one and maybe you'll end up being the Bat."

He grinned and shook his head. "No thanks, Kate. I've already promised Aunt Amelia and Liz I'll play Henry Jennings at Pirates' Weekend."

Liz looked surprised.

He added, "That's enough role-playing for me."

"Kate," Liz said, "I thought you were going with me to check out Jake's address."

She looked over at Ryan. "I'll let you two do that. I need to practice my lines." When Ryan looked away, Kate winked at Liz.

Chapter 23

Ryan programed Jake's address into the GPS. They didn't speak until they'd turned off Highway 1 and Ryan pulled through the two fifty-foot stone pillars that read Palm Bay.

Palm Bay was a small community on the Indian River, just south of Melbourne and north of Sebastian. Liz glanced out the window at the numerous mobile home communities. The voice on the GPS announced, "You have arrived."

Ryan pulled to the side of the road and put the Jeep in Park. It was dark, and there weren't any silhouettes of houses or even sheds.

Then Liz said, "Look." She pointed to her right, where there was a rutted trail that led into a small forest of Florida pines whose needles and branches pushed upward like candles on a menorah. Ryan turned. It was only seven o'clock, but the sky was inky black and the wind rocked the Jeep from side to side. Ahead, a small brick house stood with its storm shutters secured. The once-steel shutters were rusty and corroded; it appeared they hadn't been taken down in years. Jake's bike wasn't parked outside.

Ryan parked the Jeep and they got out, walking the perimeter of the house. There were storm shutters on the back windows too, but the screened porch opened to a sliding glass door. It took Ryan a second to open the locked screen door.

"You've done this before, I assume?"

"Every firefighter worth their salt knows how to gain entry into a burning house."

She glanced at his profile. It seemed his tirade about *Blood and Glass* had been forgotten. At least she hoped that was the case.

They stepped through the open door and onto the porch.

After peering inside, Ryan said, "No one's here. If we go inside, we could be charged with breaking and entering."

Liz elbowed him, "Aren't you a firefighter? Didn't we just see smoke coming from inside?"

"Always thinking, Ms. Holt." He picked up the stationary side of the sliding glass door and lifted it out of its flimsy track.

"Wow. That was amazing."

He wiped his hands on his jeans and smiled down at her. "Let's make it snappy. I'd like to come out of this without anyone knowing."

There was only one huge bedroom, a common room, a small kitchen, and one bath. If Liz hadn't seen the outside, she would never have believed the inside. It was as if a fairy godmother—or a fairy godfather, in Jake's case—had transformed the place into a high-tech, luxury Manhattan apartment. There were three flat-screen TVs on one wall in the main living area, and every piece of furniture looked like it had been recently bought.

Liz walked over to a panel on the wall near the front door, "What's this?" she asked.

"Uh-oh. That's not good. We'd better be quick."

She gave him a questioning glance.

"It's a top-of-the-line security system. I have a feeling Jake might be on his way as we speak."

"And how about the police? Are they on their way too?"

"By the looks of things, I don't think Jake would want to involve the authorities. This isn't the home of a twentysomething fisherman."

"More like a drug smuggler," Liz said as she walked into Jake's bedroom closet, Ryan following behind. She separated a line of T-shirts hanging in the closet, seeming consistent with a surfer. On the wall at the back of the closet was a small safe. "Can you break into that, Mr. Investigator Firefighter?"

"No. That's where I draw the line. Safecracking wasn't part of the job. We'd better leave before Jake gets back. We have to somehow have Charlotte get inside and check it out in a legitimate way."

Liz was disappointed. As she backed out of the closet, something on the upper shelf caught her eye. It was a camera, possibly an underwater camera. "Quick," she said. "Give me your cell phone."

He hesitated.

"Don't worry; I won't look at your female contacts." Oops, that didn't seem to be the right thing to say.

"Where's your phone?" he said, a slight irritation in his voice.

"In my handbag in the Jeep."

He handed her his phone, and she took a picture of what she thought was the underwater camera Minna had said was stolen from her cottage.

Ryan pointed to the wall adjacent to Jake's king-size bed. "Look at that display."

On the wall was a nasty-looking collection of knifes. There were twelve in total, all with black handles and gleaming silver blades. "Are those fishing knives?" she asked.

"Deep-sea diving knives. A lot fancier than any I've seen in my two days aboard a fishing trawler. Those serrated blades look lethal."

She handed him back his phone. They looked around a little more and found a room with mounted surfboards, more in keeping with Jake's surfer boy image than the rest of the house. Ryan replaced the sliding glass door and they left. They hadn't found Jake, but they'd both agreed he was up to his eyeballs in something illegal, perhaps something that might even bring the death penalty.

The subject of Travis's book didn't come up on the way back to Squidly's, yet there was something not right between them. Liz was exhausted and couldn't wait till she was drinking tea with her feet up, reading a Sherlock Holmes story with Bronte sitting on her lap. She gave Ryan a peck on the cheek. He pecked back; then they said good night. She promised him that she'd fill her father in on what they'd learned before heading home. A task she didn't relish, especially if she decided to tell him about their illegal activities.

She parked the Caddy at the back of the hotel. Just as she reached for her handbag, "What a Wonderful World" trilled from her cell phone. She hoped it wasn't Sally asking for an interview about *Blood and Glass*. It wasn't. It was Betty calling from London. *Please don't be something bad*, Liz thought the moment she heard her voice. Betty was very tech savvy for an octogenarian, and they usually communicated via text to save on overseas charges. Betty was also a wiz with electronics and had been instrumental in solving a murder at the Indialantic last spring. Liz missed her partner in crime. "Betty. You all right?"

Then Betty dropped a bombshell so explosive, if Liz wasn't already sitting down, she would have fallen to the ground in a dead faint. She told Liz Central Coast Boatworks was owned by Gregory Grayson, making him the owner of *Poseidon*.

Liz was torn between telling Ryan or her father first. She chose to tell her father in person and Ryan by text.

The winds howled and palms swayed as she made her way up the walkway to her father's office. Liz knocked, then turned the handle, surprised the door was unlocked. When she walked inside she saw Minna sitting across from her father at his desk.

"Sorry; I didn't mean to interrupt. I can come back later."

"No reason to; I was just leaving," Minna said. "I asked your father if he'd mind looking into Dylan's death. I'm not too happy with what the police have done so far. And after what you said about Jake, Liz, I'm beginning to wonder if he isn't culpable in my nephew's death. I also just told your father the memory card for Dylan's photos wasn't in my handbag. I think someone stole it, and it must be related to the fire and the missing camera from Dylan's room."

"So, it was stolen while your handbag was in the emporium?" Liz asked.

"I'm not sure," Minna said, running her fingers through her short, spiky hair. I only checked a little while ago, per your suggestion."

Fenton gave Liz a chastising look. It must be hard for him to balance what he learned from Charlotte with what she and Ryan were doing. But wasn't he the one who'd said they should come to him with anything they found? Well, here she was.

"Gregory Grayson is the owner of *Poseidon*," she blurted out.

Minna gasped. "Are you sure? Why wouldn't he mention that?" Minna stood up and charged to the door. "I'm going to ask him myself." Then she flew outside faster than the forecasted windspeeds for the hurricane.

"Daughter, what have you done?"

What had she done? "I think Minna had a right to know. Ryan found the name of the corporation that owns the fishing fleet, and Betty just confirmed that Gregory Grayson was the owner."

"Betty? Is she back from London?"

"No. You know Betty; uncovering anything on the web that's discoverable is her forte. But in retrospect, I probably shouldn't have told Minna about Gregory."

"You got that one right. What does Ryan say about it?"

"I just texted him. If you don't mind, Daddy, don't tell Ryan I told you in person. He seems to think I keep leaving him out of things."

"Trouble in paradise?"

Liz told her father about Ryan finding out about Travis's book. Her father had a way of extracting secrets from her, then setting her on the straight and narrow when she strayed off the path.

"I know I told you that Charlotte said to stay out of things," he said. "But if she only knows the name of the company who owns *Poseidon* but isn't privy to the fact that Mr. Grayson owns it, I think I should tell her."

"Don't say it came from me. Blame it on Betty. Betty's bulletproof and doesn't care about anyone's opinion."

He laughed. "That's because Betty is eighty-three."

"Now that we know Gregory owns *Poseidon*, do you think he might be involved in drug smuggling? Maybe that's how he got all his money."

"Have you ever seen Jake and Mr. Grayson together? It seems a stretch to think he could be involved in Dylan's death. Before we crucify him—which is probably what Minna is doing right now—we have to give him the benefit of the doubt on his involvement."

"Innocent till proven guilty. Got it. You could be right. It could explain why he's been courting Minna. He feels guilty that her nephew fell off one of his boats and is trying to make it up to her. We know he wasn't on *Poseidon* that night. Don't we? When the Coast Guard answered the distress call, I assume they documented everyone on board. And I think if Gregory Grayson was there, Charlotte would've told you."

"All she's confided is that Jake is a person of interest," he said. "How did Ryan's morning go on *Poseidon*?"

Liz shared the news that Victor Normand had been snooping around the harbor, along with the fact that the entire crew on the fishing trawler had disappeared, including Jake. "I don't know how it's all related. Jake didn't leave town, but he pretended to still be working on the fishing boat as a cover. And with a photo of Dylan's missing from Susannah's suite, there has to be something incriminating in it. Susannah told me that she and Jake fought over it at the gallery on Minna's opening night."

"Let's not speculate. I'll talk to Charlotte in the morning. You leave the rest of the investigating to her and her department."

"I'll try, if you promise me that you'll let me know what Charlotte says. One more thing, which your girlfriend already knows about." She thought she saw his face flush at the word *girlfriend*. "There was a goliath grouper hook on *Poseidon* that Ryan thinks was the cause of the wound on the back of Dylan's head. He showed me a photo. I've never seen anything so gruesome. He's already told Charlotte about it. Her CSIs are checking it out."

He took off his reading glasses and rubbed the space between his eyes. "Just be careful. I hope you've shared everything with me."

Liz got up, walked to the door, and opened it. Guilt keep her from going through. "Ryan and I may have done something illegal, but until I talk to him, I want to keep it on the down low."

"Illegal? Quick, give me a dollar."

It was an old routine of theirs. She reached into her pocket and pulled something out. "Sorry. Only have a quarter." She tossed it onto his desk.

"I'm now under retainer as your attorney. Just in case. In the future, let Ryan do all the dangerous stuff."

She put her hands on her hips and stuck out her lower lip. "Why? Because he's a guy?"

"No. Because he's a professional, has a private investigator's license, and I can't afford to lose you."

"You won't, Dad." She couldn't help but think of her mother, who'd died twenty-three years before. "Since when does Ryan have a PI license?"

"Since today. It just came in the mail."

"Interesting. He never told me he'd applied."

Her father gave her a knowing look.

She stepped through the open doorway, then turned. "It's starting to blow pretty hard out there. Greta stocked up on water and nonperishable food, and the gardeners have secured the buildings. Now we just wait."

"I don't think it's going to be a big one. But I've been wrong before," he said.

"Hope you're right. Love you." Then she shut the door.

Secretly, Liz was thrilled Ryan had gotten his license. It made his move to the barrier island a more permanent one. Originally, he'd been on leave from the FDNY to help his grandfather at Deli-casies after he had his knee operation. Then Ryan had assisted her father in winning a case for one of his clients. Afterward, Ryan had decided to stay in Florida and work for Fenton and his grandfather.

Liz knew their relationship was another reason he'd chosen to stay in Melbourne Beach, which made her smile as she walked to the Caddy. She hadn't locked the door; who in their right mind would want to steal it? Well, maybe a vintage car collector. When she opened the door and looked down at the seat, she was surprised to see a handwritten note there.

Had to go follow up on something I've just learned. Sweet dreams. And I'm sorry for my surly attitude earlier. I don't own you, but I sure love being with you. I'll bring you breakfast in the morning. XO, R

On top of the note was a single gardenia. Her favorite flower.

Chapter 24

Liz had fallen asleep to The Weather Channel. Bronte woke her with a soft meow and a chin nuzzle. "Oh, you sweet thing," Liz whispered. "I think we might have to go over to the Indialantic for a couple of days. Hurricane Roberta is getting too close for comfort."

After feeding Bronte and getting dressed, Liz had her second cup of coffee. She'd made a full pot, expecting Ryan to show up any second with his promised breakfast. He'd better hurry, because during the night, the weather had taken a turn for the worse. She checked her phone and saw that the hurricane warning remained. Fortunately, there wasn't a mandatory evacuation of the island. She texted Ryan: *Coffee's made.* No response. She waited an hour, packed a few things, including Bronte, and drove over to the Indialantic.

When Liz walked into the kitchen holding a basket with Bronte snuggled inside, Aunt Amelia was on her hands and knees looking for something under the farm table. Liz put the basket on the floor and Bronte peeked out but stayed inside. Aunt Amelia stood up and looked down at the basket. "She's such a darling little thing."

"She surely is," Liz said as she grabbed a French pastry from under the glass dome. "Auntie, you haven't seen Ryan this morning, have you?"

"No. I called Pops last night and told him that we were closing the emporium for a couple of days. The wind is fierce, and there are high tide and flood warnings out. I think people on the island will be busy stocking up in case we lose power, which, as you know, happens pretty frequently." Amelia turned toward the pantry. "BB, where oh where did I put it?"

"Lassie, come home. Lassie home," he crooned. A palm branch hit the kitchen window, and Barnacle Bob fluttered his wings and squawked, "Batten the hatches, matey."

Aunt Amelia walked toward him. "Don't worry, BB, we're safe as a bug in a rug. Don't even ruffle a pretty feather."

There was something comforting in her great-aunt's words, even though they were meant for Barnacle Bob. Liz felt the security of being in the bosom of her family, especially with a hurricane approaching. Manhattan was vibrant and exciting, and she missed Broadway and concerts in Central Park. But she didn't miss the aloneness she'd felt at times there. She'd tried to get Travis to visit Melbourne Beach, but he never could fit it into his schedule, even though their life revolved around his. In the writing award hierarchy, a Pulitzer Prize trumped a PEN/Faulkner every time. In all fairness, she hadn't made it back to the island either, expecting her family and friends to come see her in New York.

"What did you lose, Auntie?"

"Oh, Lizzie, I can't find my lines for today's rehearsal. I know I put them on the table. If I didn't know Susannah is allergic to the kitchen, I'd suspect her of purposely hiding them. I hope not, because today is the first day the five of us are rehearsing a scene together, and I want to try out a little tweaking I did to my lines. Kate said you'd be there. We decided it will keep our minds off the approaching hurricane. Erica invited her ex to come watch. I hope he approves of my performance."

Liz walked over to her great-aunt. "Gregory Grayson is coming here?"

"Yes, darling. Isn't it wonderful? Maybe he'll override his brother and make me Cornelia and have Susannah play the maid after he witnesses my performance."

Should she tell her or not? Last spring, Liz had left her out of the loop and she'd been hearing about it ever since. "Auntie, there's something I have to tell you, but you have to promise to keep quiet about it until Dad talks to Charlotte."

"Of course, dear. You can trust me. I won't breathe a word. Even when I learned *Dark Shadows* had been canceled by overhearing one of the producers telling the director, I never told a soul. Instead, I made my role that last season the best I could."

"Gregory Grayson is the owner of *Poseidon*," Liz blurted out.

"Dylan's boat? Why didn't he tell anyone? Do you think Gregory is involved in Dylan's death?"

"All I know is, he's the owner of the parent company that owns a slew of fishing trawlers. I still think Jake is involved." Then Liz gave her great-aunt a short synopsis of what they knew so far about Jake, leaving out last night's breaking and entering for obvious reasons.

"Lordy, what a tangled web. Does your father know all this?"

"Yes, he knows everything." *Well, almost everything.*

"How about Minna? Does she know about Mr. Grayson?"

"I told her last night. By the way, have you seen her this morning? She ran out of Dad's office when she heard the news. Gregory's been courting her since the night of her gallery opening, I'm sure she feels deceived."

"As she should. Perhaps it's Mr. Grayson's way of assuaging his guilt for not coming forward about owning *Poseidon*."

"Perhaps. He could also be involved somehow, trying to keep her close so he's privy to the investigation into her nephew's death."

Pierre entered the kitchen from the dining room, his toque on straight and his usually slumped posture erect. "Lizzie, *chérie*. Are you ready for the hurricane? It's been a while since we've ridden out a storm together. Just in case we lose power, I have batteries in all my torches and the next Agatha on your list." He shuffled over to the table, took a seat, and placed his long-fingered chef's hands on the table. Liz loved his hands. They were healing hands that had come to the aid of every boo-boo and scraped knee she'd had as child. He would go out to his garden, pluck a few herbs, and then make her a poultice. Her tummy aches and fevers would disappear like magic. Now she wished she could find the magical elixir to cure him of his memory loss.

"Pierre," Aunt Amelia said, "have you seen a copy of my script for *The Bat*? I thought I left it on the table."

"*Non.* But I do have today's dinner menu." He removed his white chef's hat and reached inside. *"Voilà!"*

Liz went to him and took it out of his hands. When she looked down, she saw it was a copy of her great-aunt's script.

"Thank you, Grand-Pierre. I'll show it to Greta."

When Pierre turned away, Liz quickly handed the script to her great-aunt, who lost it the pockets of her long, flowing chiffon skirt. "Pierre, are you coming to the screening room later to watch an old broad in action?"

He put his toque back on his head. "Who would that be, Amelia? There are no old broads around here. Only you, Mademoiselle Holt."

"Pshaw, you charmer, you," Amelia answered.

Liz looked out the window. The wind was fierce, and so was her worry about Ryan. Had she gotten it wrong about their breakfast date? She took out her phone to see if he'd texted. Nope.

Aunt Amelia and Pierre started talking plants, a hobby and passion they both shared. Pierre's kitchen garden was one of his great loves, that, and his cooking, along with reading one of his endless supplies of Agatha Christies.

Pierre got up from the table and said, "I am off to do some reading in the lobby, ladies, until it's time to reconvene in the screening room. I look forward to another magnifique performance, Amelia. Au revoir, mademoiselles."

At Pierre's mention of her eighty-year-old great-aunt as a mademoiselle, which translated to *miss* in English, Liz felt a tug at her heart. Aunt Amelia had never married, but during her television days, when she lived in beautiful downtown Burbank, she'd been engaged three times. All three men had been actors and all three, according to her great-aunt, had egos the size of the Hollywood sign that towered over Los Angeles. Liz often asked her great-aunt if she was sad that she'd never had a husband or children. She always answered the same way: "Who needs a husband to clip your wings, and who needs children when I have you, Lizzie dear?"

She remembered Ziggy from the Surf Shack and his mention of Aunt Amelia as a teen surfer. Maybe she could fix them up on a date. "Auntie, guess who I met yesterday? Ziggy from the Surf Shack. He said you used to be quite the little surfer, back in the day."

"I was little back then," she said, adding a giggle. "Now look at me. At least I'm building muscle, thanks to Paolo." She flexed her upper arms, and a dozen bracelets slipped to her elbows, jangling against one another. "How is Ziggy? I haven't seen or thought of him in ages. Has he been on the island all this time?"

"Yes. You never told me you knew how to surf."

"It was so long ago. I tried to keep up with it when I moved to California, but my career had to come first."

"Well, he said he'd pick you up if you ever want to go with him down to the beach at the Inlet."

"Really? After all this time? I'll ask Paolo if he thinks I could give it a try and make it to the age of eighty-one."

"You still boogie board. It might be fun. It might also be enjoyable to go out on a date with Ziggy. Maybe cocktails beachside?" Aunt Amelia rarely drank. But when she did, it was always a Mai Tai.

Aunt Amelia smiled and looked off into the near distance.

All this waxing romantic reminded Liz of Ryan. She glanced at her phone again. Nothing. Just as she started to text, *Are you...* Susannah blew through the swinging kitchen doors dressed in her Cornelia garb, minus the wig.

"Amelia, Amelia. I must talk to you at once! I've just learned something about a few of our cast members that bears repeating." She grabbed Amelia's arm and pulled her into the pantry. Barnacle Bob squawked and flapped his wings. It seemed he felt the same way about Susannah as she did about him.

Liz went to follow them inside the pantry, but Susannah said, "Not for young ears; this is a private conversation." Then she closed the door in Liz's face.

Not about to give up, especially knowing Susannah's snooping prowess and the PI she had on retainer who had looked in to Tom's background, Liz grabbed a juice glass from the cupboard and placed it against the pantry door, leaning in to listen.

"Victor Normand is a fraud," she said. "The man does not exist, which might explain his poor acting skills. He told me he'd trained at the Lee Strasberg school in New York City. I know someone who works there; she checked her records and can find no Victor Normand. And he wasn't born in North Carolina, or a myriad of other lies he's told me. My mind is like a steel trap. I don't forget anything. I thought you should know. Amelia, do you think we should confront him together?"

"No, Susannah, I don't think we should. It isn't up to us to pick the cast for *The Bat*. Plus, it was Erica who had him join our little troupe. She's a wonderful actress. We might lose her if we make trouble about Victor."

"I don't know if Erica is such a great actress," Susannah snapped. "Her diction is all wrong. She needs to speak from lower in her diaphragm, so she can project to the audience in the back row. Did you know, I just found out she's not only part owner of *Visions of Gold* but also the Beachside Gallery? No wonder she was cast in the ingénue role. Nepotism at its finest. Gregory Grayson must have had a subpar divorce lawyer to have given her so much."

"Thanks for the information," Amelia said, "but I don't see how it affects us."

"I think it's imperative that you keep abreast of the things going on in your establishment. Next time I'll keep my news to myself."

"Please do," Amelia answered.

Snap! Go, Auntie.

Liz stepped away from the pantry door when she heard Susannah's 1940s' shoes click-clacking toward her. She pretended she was busy stacking already stacked pastry on the glass pedestal cake plate.

As Susannah passed, she said, "Elizabeth, bring two pastries to the dining room and a hot cup of water for my tea."

Liz looked over at Aunt Amelia.

Aunt Amelia beat Susannah to the swinging doors. "Please serve yourself, Susannah. Liz is not an employee. Greta is busy setting up the screening room to be our safe room during the hurricane because it's the centermost room in the hotel and has no windows."

Susannah stomped over to the pastries, took three instead of two, *with her fingers*, and tossed them onto a china dessert plate.

Liz couldn't help herself. "*Miss* Shay, there are silver tongs next to the pastries; they keep your fingers from getting sticky."

Susannah didn't know what to say. Miss Decorum, with her pretentious bag of tricks, seemed at a loss for words.

Aunt Amelia stood next to Susannah. "If you require a napkin, we keep the table linens in the pantry. Also, if you don't mind, please tidy up after you're finished, and put your plate in the dishwasher. It would be such a great help on a day like today."

Susannah looked toward the pantry. "I'm not going anywhere near that macaw. He's always giving me evil looks." She grabbed a roll of paper towel, stowed it under her arm, grabbed the plate, then carried them into the dining room.

When Susannah was out of earshot, Liz said, "She's not paying to stay in the Windward Shores Suite, is she, Auntie?"

"Not a dime."

"You're too tenderhearted," Liz said, kissing her great-aunt on her velvety cheek.

"I'll take that as a compliment, Lizzie. I know a few things about Susannah you don't, and I think you might see things differently if you knew what she'd recently been through. Never judge a person till you've walked in their shoes. I won't break her confidence. However, I won't allow her to take advantage of me. From now on this kitten is turning into a tiger where Susannah is concerned!" She pounded her ample chest and roared, causing the numerous strands of violet and red beads on her necklace to clash against each other.

"Roar away, Auntie. Roar, away."

"Put a tiger in your tank," Barnacle Bob added from the pantry.

Liz raised an eyebrow and Aunt Amelia said, "An old Esso gasoline commercial."

"Ah. And?"

"I played a mother in a woody station wagon filled with towheaded children getting gassed up at an Esso station from an attendant dressed all in white. Not a speaking part, but I did get a month's worth of free fill-ups for my little red roadster."

"Of course you did, Auntie." Liz glanced at the clock. "I'm starting to get worried about Ryan. I think I'll go over to the caretaker's cottage to see if maybe he slept in. But with the sound of the wind, I doubt he'd be able to sleep."

"Don't get blown away, dear. We're meeting in the screening room at noon. See you then."

Chapter 25

The wind gusts had increased, and misty rain swirled around her. She hadn't worn a rain slicker and an umbrella would be useless. When she reached the cottage, she peered through the window and saw no sign of life. She knew where Ryan kept an extra key and lifted the small stone ibis statue by the front door to retrieve it. She knocked, then put the key in the lock and opened the door. The force of the wind pushed her inside.

"Ryan? You here? Hey, sleepyhead, where's my breakfast?"

She went into his bedroom, her former bedroom, and smiled. There wasn't a trace of femininity left; the room was clean, classic, and all male. Ryan's bed hadn't been slept in. So where had he gone? Had he slept on the sofa?

After searching the other bedroom, Liz left the cottage and replaced the key. She took the path that led to the Indialantic's dock and saw Victor hurrying in her direction, fighting the wind with his head down. He didn't notice Liz until he was almost upon her.

"Victor," she said, "are you on your way to the Indialantic for rehearsals?" She thought about what Susannah had said about him—that he was a ghost. Maybe he had an assumed name? Liz made a point to talk to Charlotte via her father and have his background checked. Especially if he'd been hanging around *Poseidon*. If Gregory Grayson was involved in Dylan's death, maybe his chauffeur was too.

He glanced behind him and looked in the direction of the dock, as if he was searching for someone. Erica? Liz took a step closer. He said, "Yes. Amelia insisted. She says the Indialantic is the safest place on the island."

She could barely hear his words over the howling of the wind. "It is the safest. There's even a cellar under the kitchen," she shouted. "Although we haven't been down there in ages." She had no idea why she'd just told him that. If he was involved in Dylan's murder, the Indialantic's cellar would be the perfect place to hide a body.

A rootless palmetto bush went breezing by them. Victor said, "I'd better get to shelter, and you should too. You haven't seen Mr. Grayson, have you? I dropped him off a while ago."

"No. Maybe he's inside. I know Auntie is excited he's coming."

They said their good-byes, and Liz went to the dock to check that her father's vintage Chris-Craft motorboat was secured safely. As if her father would ever forget to take care of his baby, *Serendipity*. She continued along the dock, glancing ahead at *Visions of Gold*, and saw that it was also locked up and tied tight to the dock in anticipation of the Indian River Lagoon's rising.

A turkey vulture stood on the piling next to the yacht. Even as she got closer, it refused to leave. It sent her an eerie stare, its black, unblinking eye in sharp contrast to its bald head, the color of diluted blood. The vulture didn't ruffle a feather as Liz approached. She ducked her head and flailed her arms. Finally, the huge thing left its perch. It took flight, uttering its signature guttural cry. The same cry she'd heard the day she'd found Dylan on the beach.

A feeling of dread overcame her. She glanced behind to make sure no one was around, then climbed on board *Visions of Gold*.

The cabin was locked, and tarped awnings covered the windows. All the deck furniture had been removed. There were white caps on the river and the yacht rocked back and forth. Instinctively, Liz held on to the gold railing and fought the wind until she reached the back of the boat.

Tendrils of wet hair covered her eyes. She swiped them away and looked ahead. Lying on the teak deck was Gregory Grayson. Blood oozed in a wet circle on his gauzy white tunic. In the center of the circle, the blood was a deeper red, resembling a dartboard. Liz crouched and put two fingers to Gregory's neck to find a pulse. There wasn't one. His right cheek was bruised and there was a scratch in the center of the bruise. She took out her phone and dialed 911, then she called her father and told him to meet her at *Visions of Gold*. Lastly, she called Ryan; he didn't pick up, so she left a message.

She waited next to the body with the wind and rain buffeting her face, the swaying of the boat adding to the nausea in her gut. Acid rose in her chest and she leaned over the railing just in time.

After emptying her stomach, she came back to the body and forced herself to look at it again. At first, she thought he'd been shot, but now she could see the tear in the fabric of his shirt. A tear made by a knife.

Chapter 26

Her father, the first responders, CSIs, and the authorities, including Agent Charlotte Pearson arrived ten minutes later. Liz gave Charlotte a brief statement, while her father held tight to Liz's trembling hand. As she was talking, an officer came up to them holding something in a clear plastic bag. He said, "Found the murder weapon, boss."

Liz looked at the bag and gasped. The diving knife with the serrated edge and black hilt looked identical to the ones she and Ryan saw last night displayed on Jake's bedroom wall.

"What's wrong, Lizzie?" her father asked.

She pointed to the knife. "It has to be Jake who killed Gregory. The knife is similar to the ones he has displayed at his house."

"His house? When were you at his house?" Charlotte screeched.

Oops. "We'll talk later," Liz said to Charlotte. "I'll see you at the Indialantic. I can't stand in the wind and rain anymore."

"Oh no, you don't!" Charlotte said, loud enough that her team turned their heads and looked their way.

She'd never heard Charlotte raise her voice before. She was always coolheaded. Liz took a step backward on the dock. Her sneaker got wedged between the planks of wood and she teetered, then fell back on her rear end, unharmed but superembarrassed.

Instead of Charlotte rushing over to ask if Liz was okay, she said, "I want Jake's address. Pronto." Then she tugged on the sleeve of the patrolwoman holding the knife "Take down the address this young lady is going to give you, then ask Judge Cranston to give me a call for a warrant to search the premises. When you get the warrant, treat it as a crime scene until we know differently. I'll come by later."

"Our resources are spread pretty thin because of the hurricane," the officer said, sheepishly. "Are you sure the judge will be in?"

"Speak louder! I can't hear you over this wind," Charlotte shouted. "Do as I say. You're wasting time."

Whoa, Liz thought as she stood up, minus one sneaker. She felt proud that she'd recognized the knife as being similar to the ones they'd seen at Jake's. Then she had a horrible thought. If she and Ryan had told Charlotte last night about finding Jake's house, maybe the knife would still be in its slot on the wall and Gregory Grayson would be alive.

After giving her statement, Liz told the detective that everyone involved in the play were meeting in the screening room. Charlotte instructed—more like demanded—that Liz make sure to keep everyone inside the Indialantic until the CSIs were done with the crime scene.

Liz knew who Gregory's killer was, so she didn't understand what Charlotte wanted with anyone else at the hotel. Gregory was stabbed by the same person who'd murdered Dylan—Jake.

Before leaving, Liz asked Charlotte, "You haven't heard from Ryan, have you?"

"We met this morning for breakfast. It seems the two of you have been quite busy."

Say what! Now who was keeping things from the other? Regardless, she was relieved Ryan was okay.

Charlotte looked over at Fenton, who was talking to one of the first responders. "Your father also filled me in on a few things this morning. I can't say I'm happy you didn't heed my warning about not getting involved."

"Did you already know Gregory Grayson was the owner of *Poseidon*?" Liz asked.

She didn't answer.

"Does my dad get brownie points for sharing that information?"

"You and Ryan sure don't for not telling me that you'd found Jake's house."

Liz tried to look chastised, but inside, she was proud of Kate, Ryan, and her sleuthing.

Fenton came up to them. "Everything all right?" he asked, first looking at Charlotte, then Liz.

They answered, "Yes," both at the same time."

He said, "Charlotte, one of your first responders had to leave. A tree knocked over a utility pole in town. It's lying in the middle of Fifth Avenue, blocking bridge traffic."

Charlotte turned to Fenton. "Thanks. I'll call headquarters and have them send a few patrol cars."

"The island isn't under mandatory evacuation, is it?" Liz asked, looking at the detective while she held on to her father's arm and slipped on her sneaker.

"No. Still voluntary. The worst of the hurricane will be in the next few hours. It seems we're lucky; most of Roberta will be offshore. However, we could still catch the edge of the eyewall, and winds are forecasted to be seventy to seventy-five miles an hour."

"Well, Charlotte, if your guys," Liz said, pointing to the CSI team, "need shelter, please send them over. The more the merrier, especially seeing Jake is on the loose. We could use the protection. Any hypotheses on why Jake would kill Gregory?"

Charlotte ignored Liz and turned to Fenton. "I need to get back to work. You go on ahead and I'll be there shortly."

Liz watched her father; he stepped toward Charlotte as if he wanted to kiss her, then stepped back, realizing they were being watched. "Okay. See you inside."

Fenton put his arm through his daughter's and they set off for the Indialantic, helping to steady each other through the miasma of swirling plant life, projectile branches, and palm fronds. One step forward, three steps back.

Liz attempted conversation but was drowned out by the wind. When they arrived safely, she suggested she'd collect Bronte and meet her father in the screening room.

"I'll meet you there after I change into dry clothes," he said. "Charlotte was very clear that she wanted to tell the group herself about Gregory's murder. We'll have to play along until she arrives."

Liz agreed, then dripped her way to the laundry room, where she'd stowed her overnight bag and Bronte's necessities. As she reached down to pick up her bag, she saw the pile of clothing she'd thrown in the back of the golf cart when she'd found Turtle nesting on them on the day of the fire. She opened the door to the industrial washing machine. Washing Dylan's clothes was the least she could do for Minna; later she would ask if she wanted to give them to her sister-in-law or donate them to the vets.

As she emptied the basket into the washer, something dinged against the wall of the washer. Reaching in, her hand clasped something. She pulled it out. A memory card! After she changed, she set off to find where her great-aunt had put Bronte. Then she'd try to find a place to view the photos on the card.

Liz not only found Bronte napping in the hotel's lobby, but also Venus, Caro, Turtle, and Killer. Each had found a cushion or corner to curl up in, or, in Bronte's case, her basket. The wind rattled the hurricane shutters, but none of the animals seemed to notice. The revolving door had been boarded up with sheets of plywood and hurricane shutters covered the windows, casting the lobby into semidarkness. The only light source was a brass banker's lamp with a green-glass shade on the check-in counter. Between the howling wind and the sound of the now-horizontal rain pelting the hurricane shutters, Liz felt spooked. What if Jake was crouched between the counter and the mail cabinet, ready to spring, holding another knife from his collection.

She realized that even though Killer wasn't an attack dog by any stretch of the imagination, he would at least bark and try to lick the face of any intruder lurking in the darkness. Relieved, she went to the center of the Persian rug, under the unlit Baccarat chandelier, and clapped her hands. "Okay, everyone. Time to move to a safer place." Killer opened one large eye, then closed it. "Yes, Killer, time to herd your posse into Auntie's screening room. There'll be treats." At the word "treats," all the pets opened their eyes and looked at her. Bronte yawned and stretched, and Liz went to pick up her basket. "Let's go."

She stepped through the large arched doorway and into the hallway. Behind her, Venus, Caro, Turtle, and Killer followed, until they came to the door to the screening room. Liz whispered, "Keep quiet. We don't want to disturb the rehearsal." Then she opened the door and reached under the cushion in Bronte's basket for a handful of treats and passed them out as the pet parade filed inside. Killer never had a problem eating cat treats, only instead of one treat, as she'd given the felines, she gave him five. She was sure, if she called a button a treat, Killer would lap it out of her hand with his big tongue and down his gullet it would go.

The screening room was in shadow except for a single spotlight on stage. Liz turned on the flashlight function of her phone and directed the animals toward the back wall, under the projection booth. Aunt Amelia had lined up three cat beds and one huge cushion for Killer. His cushion was so large, it must have come from the Enlightenment Parlor. Venus settled on cat bed one, and Turtle slunk under the last seat of the back row, preferring his privacy. Killer and Caro chose to snuggle together on the only place that would fit Killer's large body: the cushion.

Liz took a seat in the center of the last aisle, then placed Bronte's basket on the seat next to her. Pierre, Minna, and Greta sat in the front row. The room was windowless and all the sounds from the hurricane were drowned out by the ongoing dialogue on stage between Erica and Victor.

They were wearing their costumes. Liz barely recognized Erica in her sweet, mild-mannered ingénue role. Victor was perhaps the worst actor Liz had ever seen, and she'd seen plenty over the years in some of Aunt Amelia's productions. He was stiff and had no clue what to do with his arms. The end of Victor's sentences trailed off, making her lean forward to catch each word. Liz remembered overhearing Susannah's tête-á-tête with her great-aunt in the pantry, Susannah saying Victor wasn't who he said he was. Liz hoped Victor didn't quit his day job as Gregory Grayson's chauffeur.

Her heart beat out of her chest when she realized Victor had already lost his day job; his boss was dead.

The scene they were rehearsing dealt with a blueprint that might reveal in which room in the rambling mansion a large sum of money was hidden. Just after Erica/Dale delivered a spellbinding monologue, Victor/Dr. Wells received a cell phone call. Tom, who was in the wings, called, "Stop!"

Victor put the phone to his ear, ignoring Tom, who charged toward him. Tom's mouth was in an irritated frown, giving him a bulldog appearance. Victor sideswiped him and disappeared behind the curtain. Liz felt panic rise. Where was her father? He was supposed to help keep all the parties inside the screening room until Charlotte arrived. If Victor planned to leave the room, how would she stop him? Then she remembered meeting Victor on her way to the dock. How long had Gregory been dead? She was sure Jake was Gregory's killer, but he could have an accomplice. As they'd all postulated, Jake didn't fit the drug kingpin mold.

Erica and Tom might have a lot to gain from Gregory's death. Victor could have killed Gregory to help Erica. Oh no. Minna! Liz had told her last night about Gregory owning the ship her nephew had died on. Had she taken the law into her own hands? Impossible. How could the knife from Jake's house be the murder weapon if Minna killed Gregory in a fit of anger? And where was Ryan? He'd met with Charlotte for breakfast and Liz still hadn't heard from him.

Victor reappeared on stage. In a loud voice, with clear diction, he said, "I apologize, Erica. I have some business to attend to. I'll be back shortly."

Erica unbuttoned the top button on her blouse. "Why is it so damn hot in here? So, what is it now, Victor? My ex needs you constantly at his beck and call? Tell him you'll be there when you're done with your scene."

"I can't do that. He pays my salary and, as a matter of fact, the whole cast's." He leapt off the stage. "I'll be back soon."

He came up the aisle, and Liz hurried to meet him before he reached the door. "Victor, you really shouldn't be going out in this weather. We're all sequestered for the next few hours at least. My auntie would be really upset if something happened to you on the Indialantic's grounds."

"Don't worry about me. I can handle rough weather. I'd better get to Mr. Grayson before I get fired."

That was impossible, Liz thought. How could a dead man fire him? Who had been on the other end of the phone? Because it surely wasn't Gregory Grayson. Jake? Liz put her arm out to stop him, but he barreled by, opened the door, and stepped into the hallway. Liz should have sicced Killer on him. Even though the Great Dane was called Killer, petite Bronte had a better chance of stopping Victor.

Defeated, Liz went back to her seat and took out her phone. She texted her father about Victor leaving the screening room, ending with a *Where are you?!* The door opened from the hallway and her father stepped inside. He came to sit beside her and Bronte.

She leaned in and whispered, "Read your text."

Fenton took out his phone and looked down at the screen. She watched him copy and paste her text onto another text with the heading "Char." Then shrugged his shoulders, as if it was all he could do.

The lights dimmed, and Liz heard Tom say, "Take your places." A spotlight illuminated the center of the stage. Haloed beneath was Aunt Amelia. At least Liz thought it was Aunt Amelia. Instead of waiting for expert seamstress Francie, part owner of Home Arts by the Sea, to return from abroad to make her great-aunt's costume, it appeared Aunt Amelia had taken a trip to the Halloween Store. Liz knew immediately which costume her great-aunt had chosen: the freaky maid's costume from *The Rocky Horror Picture Show.* Fortunately, instead of boy shorts and fishnet stockings, Aunt Amelia had added a skirt. Susannah as Cornelia and Kate as Detective Anderson entered from stage left.

Susannah stumbled when she caught sight of Aunt Amelia. The toe of her sensible shoes caught on the corner of the tapestry rug. She immediately went flying into her great-aunt's arms. Aunt Amelia kept her balance, and they twirled around like they were performing on a 1940s' version of *Dancing with the Stars.* Liz had to give Susannah credit; she turned to the audience and said, "I hope that took your mind off the Bat, Liddie dear."

Pierre thought the scene was part of the play and applauded. Kate hurried to Susannah and Aunt Amelia, her Sherlockian deerstalker hat falling off on the way and her long hair cascaded down, covering her face.

Liz heard Greta giggle after she ascertained everyone was unharmed.

"Well, that didn't go too well," she whispered to her father. "But it was quite entertaining all the same." She looked toward the door. "I hope Charlotte comes soon. I think it would be prudent to let everyone know there's a killer on the loose."

"I'm sure she'll be here shortly," he whispered.

The door opened, and instead of Charlotte, Ryan walked in. Liz felt immediate relief when she saw his attractive, unshaven face. His black FDNY T-shirt was soaking wet, along with his dark, almost black hair. He really looked like a pirate. Not a gentleman pirate like Henry Jennings, but a rogue one, like Captain Kidd.

Ryan saw them and sat in the seat next to Fenton. "What did I miss?"

Liz reached over her father and punched Ryan on the arm. Hard.

"Ouch."

"Where were you?" she hissed.

"Had to make sure my grandfather was safe."

"Is he?"

"Yes. His condo's community center was built last year and can withstand whatever Mother Nature throws at it. In fact, he invited everyone here to go there if we need shelter."

"Hush!" Susannah called from the stage. She'd positioned herself in front of Aunt Amelia, blocking her from the audience. Then Susannah performed a soliloquy that even the Bard himself would have been proud of.

Then it was Amelia Eden Holt's turn.

Liz had to say Aunt Amelia flourished under the pressure of playing Cornelia/Susannah's flighty, terrified maid. Her comedic timing was on point, with her high-pitched "The Bat. The Bat. The Bat is out to get us!" dialogue, as she jumped around the stage with the agility of a woman half her age. Aunt Amelia had everyone laughing. When she finished, Liz heard Barnacle Bob call out from the shadows, *"Bravissimo! Bravissimo!"*

Liz, Fenton, and Ryan gave her a standing ovation, which Aunt Amelia soaked up like the orange Bain de Soleil gelée she liked to slather on her body while tanning by the Indialantic's pool. In the past, after Liz applied Bain de Soleil to her great-aunt's freckled shoulders, she, Aunt Amelia, and Barnacle Bob would break out in song: "Bain de Soleil...For the San Tropez tan."

If Liz closed her eyes, she could almost smell the suntan lotion's distinctive perfumed scent. Her great-aunt had received a truckload of the stuff in the early '70s, after doing a commercial in which she played a sunbather pretending to soak up the rays on the French Riviera. Even though it had been decades since Aunt Amelia's last free tube had run out, Bain de Soleil was still sold today and remained a staple in Aunt Amelia's beach bag.

During the applause, Charlotte walked into the screening room. She flipped on the lights and made her announcement about Gregory Grayson's murder.

Erica swooned. Tom took a seat on a prop table, his face ashen at the news that his brother was dead. Susannah paced back and forth across the stage, muttering under her breath. Aunt Amelia came down the steps and hurried up the aisle toward her nephew and great-niece. Then they went into a Holt family huddle, which included Ryan.

After Charlotte had one of her officers write down everyone's name and contact info, she told them they were free to go, warning that the worst of Hurricane Roberta was upon them and they might want to stay put for their own safety.

Liz pulled Charlotte aside and asked if she'd read her father's text about Victor receiving a phone call from a dead man. Charlotte didn't seem concerned; she just shrugged her shoulders and turned away to answer a phone call. All Liz heard was, "Yes, Judge. That is correct." She assumed Charlotte was still trying to get a warrant to search Jake's house.

Pierre and Greta left for the kitchen. Pierre had prepared a light luncheon they were going to bring into the screening room.

Erica and Tom said they were passing on lunch and left the room together. Liz and Ryan followed them out, then went to the lobby to catch up but couldn't hear each other over the wind. It sounded like a jet's turbine was parked outside the lobby's doors. The lights flickered, and Liz held her breath. The power went out, then the emergency generator kicked in. The generator hadn't been upgraded in decades; it was next on her aunt's mile-long Indialantic improvement list.

"Come," Liz said to Ryan. "I know where we can go." She took Ryan's hand and led him into the Enlightenment Parlor. They left their shoes by the door. Liz lit some candles and turned on a lamp covered with one of Aunt Amelia's scarlet chiffon scarves, then they sat together on a round cushion the size of a double bed, where Liz told him about the memory card she'd found in Dylan's clothing. "Now your turn. Why did you meet with Charlotte for breakfast without me?" She stuck out her lower lip.

"Well, Ms. Nosy Pants, last night I emailed Betty and asked her where she found the information about Gregory owning *Poseidon*, which sent me through an interesting maze of cyber twists and turns. And what do you think?"

"How should I know? Spit it out!" she said with a grin.

"I found a court document stating that Thomas Grayson had contested Philip Grayson's will."

"Let me guess. Philip was Gregory and Tom's father?"

"You got it."

"Did you find out the outcome?"

"No. But your father's on it."

"Good."

"So why did you meet with Charlotte for breakfast?"

"She called me because she wanted to tell me that the goliath grouper fishhook on *Poseidon* had been partially to blame for Dylan's death. It had his blood on it."

"When you say 'partially,' does that mean he was thrown into the sea while he was still alive?"

"It's very possible."

"I pray he'd passed out from the Rohypnol before he was hurt and thrown overboard. The vision of his death is too ghastly to conceive any other way."

"Charlotte also reiterated that we needed to keep out of things. They're very close to solving Dylan's murder and we'd better not screw it up. That's why I didn't tell her about our trip to Jake's last night. I assumed she already knew about it and didn't want to jeopardize any evidence she'd found."

"That's understandable. But I had a horrible thought: If we did tell her about last night, Gregory might be alive today."

"We had no way of knowing."

"I guess you're right. We'll soon find out. I overheard Charlotte trying to get a warrant for Jake's premises. Obviously, she hadn't known it existed. She owes us now."

"I don't think that's how it works," he said, pulling her closer.

She felt comforted by his tight embrace and relaxed into him. "I just remembered something you didn't see earlier," she said, jerking forward. "Victor was on stage attempting to act. He's bad. Really, really bad. Anyway, he got a call on his cell phone, then ran off the stage, saying it was Gregory calling him, which was impossible because Gregory was already dead. Victor's a big fat liar. Also, I saw him near the dock, right before I went on *Visions of Gold* and found Gregory. I bet Victor and Jake are in this together." Then Liz went on to tell him about Susannah's latest prying into Victor's life before *The Bat*. "He's not who he says he is. Or at least using an assumed name."

"Maybe a stage name?"

"The way he just acted, I doubt he would need a stage name."

"I'll look in to that one with some of my ties in New York."

"Great," Liz said. "I think Jake seems the type to place the blame on someone else. If we or the police find him, I bet he squeals after five seconds of Charlotte interrogating him. And I wouldn't be surprised if Victor was in on whatever is going on too."

"Or Tom," Ryan added.

"Or Erica," Liz added. "We need to look at the photos on Dylan's memory card."

"Quick question, snoopy pants: Why didn't you turn over the memory card to Charlotte a few minutes ago?"

"Honestly, I forgot all about it. Let's let things go in the meantime," she said snuggling up to him. "We've done as much as we can. How about a truce from now on? No secrets?"

"Done."

"Pinkie swear," she said, holding out her pinkie finger.

He intertwined his finger with hers.

"Congrats on getting your PI license. Dad told me."

"I wanted to keep it a secret so we could go out and celebrate," he said.

"Anything else you're holding back, Mr. Stone?" She thought about the picture of the lingerie-clad woman she'd found.

"Nope. And you?"

"Nope. Unless you want to read the *Blood and Glass* manuscript in my father's office. Because I don't plan to."

"Nope. Not necessary."

Liz tried to leave behind the teensy-tiny seed of doubt that lingered.

Ryan put two fingers under her chin and turned her to face him. Then he leaned in for a kiss.

Just as their lips met, they heard a crash.

"What the heck was that?" Liz asked.

Ryan jumped up and pulled Liz to her feet. "I don't know, but we'd better check it out. Fires can start from downed electrical poles. Only takes a single spark."

Chapter 27

The loud boom they'd heard turned out to be the felling of one of the tallest palm trees on the grounds, the tree pictured on all the brochures and postcards since the Indialantic's inception. On top of that, the tree had landed on the old fountain in front of the hotel's entrance, decapitating the statue of Hercules.

"The poor guy needed a facelift anyway. He only had half a nose and one ear," optimistic Aunt Amelia said as they helped themselves from a long table filled with food on the screening-room stage. Aunt Amelia helped serve, reminiscing about the delicious meals provided by craft services on the set of *Dark Shadows*.

Naturally, Susannah contradicted her. "*Dark Shadows* had the worst food I've ever eaten in my long career."

"Maybe Hilda was off for those *few* days you were there," Amelia said in retaliation. "Because I know the food was heavenly."

Go, Auntie!

When Liz saw Tom and Erica had joined the line for food, she elbowed Ryan and whispered, "I thought they'd left."

Ryan, Liz, Kate, and Fenton brought their plates and drinks to the back row of the theater.

"Kate," Liz said," when did Tom and Erica show up?"

"A few minutes ago," Kate said. "They had to turn back because A1A had turned into a river. I still can't believe Gregory Grayson was murdered. Liz, you must be traumatized; first you find Dylan, now Mr. Grayson."

"It all seems surreal."

"Do you think it was Jake?" Kate asked.

"Yes."

Liz saw her father looking at his phone. She asked, "Was Charlotte able to get a warrant to search Jake's?"

"She's there now," he said.

Kate stuffed a prosciutto and cheese pinwheel into her mouth. "You know who else returned to the hotel? Victor. I saw him on the phone in the lobby. By the way, Liz and Ryan, where did you guys slip off to? *Enlighten me*," she said with a wink.

"Dad, eat something," Liz said, noticing him looking down again at his phone, his plate untouched.

"Just heard something else, Liz. I'm sorry to say the diving knives you saw on the wall at Jake's are all accounted for."

"Are they sure?" Liz was stunned.

"Yes. But there's been another very interesting development. Someone called in a tip a few minutes ago on Jake's whereabouts. Charlotte's on her way now to pick him up. They also opened a safe at Jake's. Charlotte can't tell me what's inside. Frankly, I'm surprised she shared this much."

Ryan looked at Liz, and they high-fived each other. Then Liz told her father about the memory card she'd found in Dylan's clothing. "While your girlfriend is arresting a killer, maybe we can find more evidence to put him away for life."

Fenton gave Liz "the look."

"I know. I know," she said. "Innocent till proven guilty. Even if he's not guilty of Gregory Grayson's death, at least he can come clean about what happened on *Poseidon*."

He said, "Let's bring our food to my office. We can view what's on the memory card on my laptop."

Fifteen minutes later, they were at her father's kitchen table, huddled together in front of his laptop. The wind speeds from the hurricane seemed to have lessened, but it would be a while before it was safe to venture out. Fenton inserted the memory card into an external reader and a grid of about a hundred photos popped up on the screen. Her father hit the Slide Show button and they watched an amazing display of underwater shots pass before them. About thirty photos paraded by, but there didn't seem to be anything that would help them find a killer.

All of a sudden, Ryan called out, "Stop!"

Fenton pressed the Pause button.

"Look there." Ryan pointed to the bottom left-hand corner of the screen. Covered in silt and muck on the ocean's floor was a section of a ship. It looked as if a giant saw had split a Spanish galleon in half.

"Is it one of the missing 1715 Spanish fleet ships?" Liz asked, her heart pounding in her chest.

Fenton wrote the photo's number on a piece of paper. "It could be." Then he started the slide show again.

There were a few shots of the underside of *Poseidon* facing up toward the surface of the ocean. Dylan's camera had a powerful light, and in the next shot they saw a close-up of a diver in a wet suit, pointing to the surface with his left arm. Near the diver's wrist Liz saw something familiar.

"Stop!" Liz shouted. "Can you blow it up? I know that tattoo. I think it's Jake's."

Fenton expanded the shot. Sure enough, there was a partial tattoo of a Kraken, the tips of its tentacles extending from the sleeve of the wet suit. The same tattoo Liz had seen on Jake's arm the day after the gallery opening, when Jake was supposedly returning Dylan's camera.

They continued through the rest of the photos at a faster pace because the laptop's battery was draining. They wouldn't be able to send any of the photos to the police because the power was still out and there was no Wi-Fi. They were forced to sit tight until they heard from Charlotte that Jake had been arrested. The very last shot showed Dylan's open-faced palm. In his hand was the crusted gold coin Liz had found under his dead body.

Poseidon wasn't smuggling drugs; it was diving illegally for treasure from the doomed 1715 Spanish fleet. And, Liz would bet, Gregory Grayson was the brains behind the operation. Until Jake killed him.

Chapter 28

Liz, Ryan, and Fenton spent the rest of the afternoon in the game parlor, which had been the hotel's original card room. Aunt Amelia had built a large walk-in closet at the back of the room that was filled with shelves holding card decks and board games. Some of the games were vintage, dating all the way back to the 1940s. Liz, Ryan, Amelia, Kate, and Fenton started a marathon game of Monopoly. The old game had its original metal game pieces. Liz's favorite was the dog, Kate the car, Aunt Amelia the iron. Fenton couldn't decide between the cannon or the ship and chose the cannon. When Liz asked Ryan which piece was his favorite, he said he never cared which game piece he used, as long as it landed on Boardwalk and Park Place before anyone else, and grabbed the top hat.

Minna sat with Tom at the next table. There was an unopened deck of cards between them. Of all the people mourning Gregory's death, Minna seemed the saddest. Tom had looked stunned when Charlotte told the group about the murder, but he hadn't cried or shown any emotion.

Fenton reached over, putting his hand on Tom's shoulder, and said, "I'm so sorry for your loss."

Tom looked back and said, "It seems impossible. Who would want to kill him? And why on *Visions of Gold*? Do you know how he was killed?"

Agent Pearson hadn't imparted the cause of Gregory's death when she'd addressed everyone in the screening room, only that he'd been murdered.

Even though he knew, Fenton said, "No; I'm sorry."

Erica and Susannah sat at a table for two, next to the billiards table, a Ouija board between them. Susannah's fingertips were on the pointer and she was swiping left and right, from letter to letter, at a frantic pace. When she stopped, Erica let out a little sob. Liz couldn't believe sensible

Susannah was in to the occult, even if it was a harmless game of distraction, one Liz and Kate had played with Aunt Amelia many times when they were children.

Pierre, Greta, and Victor were in the middle of a game of Clue. The game had been Liz and Kate's favorite. They always got excited when one of them guessed whodunnit, along with the what and where, especially because the other game players had advantages: Fenton was a lawyer, Pierre an Agatha Christie addict, and Betty a teenage mystery writer.

Victor acted like everything was normal, even though he must have known Gregory had already been dead when he'd received his earlier phone call. Liz wasn't about to confront him; she'd leave it to Brevard County Sheriff's Department to do that. But she wouldn't take her eyes off him and she doubted Ryan or her father would either.

Periodically, during the late afternoon and early evening, Aunt Amelia gave a weather report. Not from the new phone her nephew and great-niece had given her, but from the battery-operated radio she'd used during every past hurricane on the barrier island. "Winds down to sixty miles an hour," she called out. The last report had gusts to seventy, so things were looking up, even though it still sounded like Armageddon outside the game parlor's metal-shuttered windows.

Ryan won Monopoly. It had been neck and neck between him and competitive Kate. The good thing about Kate was that she wasn't a sore loser, but of course, Liz could count on one hand the times she'd lost at anything.

Liz saw Tom had left Minna alone at the table. She went over and took a seat. "Do you believe this latest turn of events?"

"I never wished him dead," Minna said. "But I can tell you this: Dead or not, I blame him for my nephew's death. A man shouldn't own so many things that he isn't in touch with the day-to-day operations of his businesses."

Maybe Gregory did know what was going on, as in pirating and illegal salvaging.

"He feigned closeness to me," Minna said. "Because of guilt, no doubt. How could he?" She took a sip of water. "Liz, do you think Jake killed him?"

"That would be my guess. This isn't for public consumption, but I think Jake will be arrested real soon."

Minna's shoulders relaxed.

"I have to ask," Liz said. "When you ran out last night after I saw you in Dad's office, did you go to see Gregory?"

Minna looked around furtively, making sure they weren't overheard. "Yes. I saw the Maybach at the Beachside Gallery and went inside. I'm not proud to say I slapped him across the face. And I wasn't gentle. I regret it now, obviously. But I was so angry."

"Did anyone witness it?" Liz asked.

"Why, yes, Mr. Ruskin was there. Gregory even had the nerve to bring me into his little safe room for some champagne, so we could discuss the situation in private. What situation? I've asked myself over and over again. The one where he pretended to be a caring friend about my nephew's death, then held back that he owned the boat Dylan was murdered on? Still. I wasn't mad enough to kill him."

"Well, someone was," Liz said. "Do you know if Gregory planned to come to the hotel to watch rehearsals today? Or do you think he wouldn't dare show his face after your little skirmish?"

"Oh, Liz, I don't know. I ran out of there like a maniac. With the winds picking up and driving A1A at night, I'm surprised I made it back here in one piece. There's something you or your father might be interested in. I don't know if it has any bearing on the murder, but when I was in Gregory's safe room or hurricane room or whatever you call it, I saw a thick packet from the IRS with both Gregory and Erica's name on it. And I looked around for any illegal drugs but didn't see anything."

"Good job," Liz said. Now that they'd found the memory card and had reviewed the photos, Liz felt it might be better to keep it from Minna until Charlotte had a chance to go over it. She did ask, "Did you find the memory card you said was in your handbag?"

"No. It wasn't there. It must have been stolen. And my keys to the drawer at the gallery where I keep some of Dylan's prints are missing. They must have been stolen too."

Liz remembered the keys she'd found on the floor of Minna's BMW. "Two small keys?" Liz asked.

"Yes. Why, have you seen them?"

Liz told her that she'd put them in Minna's drink holder the morning she'd returned the BMW.

"Oh, Liz. That's wonderful. I can't wait to show Alyse some of her son's prints."

"Did you ever learn who the buyer was who bought all of Dylan's remaining prints yesterday?"

"When I was at the gallery last night, confronting Gregory, I asked Mr. Ruskin if he knew who'd bought the photos so I could thank them. He said the photos were missing when he'd come into work, but there was a cashier's check in the till. When he asked Mr. Grayson if he knew who bought them, he said the person wanted to remain anonymous."

Gregory himself must have been the anonymous buyer, not wanting anyone to know *Poseidon* was being used for illegal treasure salvaging. Liz took out her phone and opened the photo app. "Can you tell me if this is Dylan's underwater camera?" She showed Minna the photo she'd taken from Ryan's phone.

"Yes! Where was this taken?"

"Jake's closet. I think we're very close to getting retribution and closure for you and your sister-in-law. Keep the faith."

"I will, Liz. Thanks for being a true friend."

Aunt Amelia had tried to get everyone involved in a game of charades, but the natives were getting restless, so after a quick supper of soup and sandwiches, she pestered everyone to move upstairs to the music room for a little entertainment. The worst of the hurricane was over, but it had been decided, mostly by Aunt Amelia, that everyone should stay the night until Roberta was safely away. No one complained; they knew leaving at night would be treacherous. Even if the storm had passed, there was always the possibility that not just one but both bridges to the mainland could be closed and they already knew A1A was flooded.

Aunt Amelia and Susannah sang a few show tunes with Fenton at the piano. Susannah had a good set of lungs on her, especially when she and Aunt Amelia did "Something Stupid," Susannah with the Frank Sinatra part, Amelia with Nancy.

At one point in the evening, Fenton called Ryan and Liz out of the music room to tell them that Jake had been arrested. "According to Charlotte, Jake admitted to killing Dylan, but he claims it was an accident. Jake swears he didn't have anything to do with Gregory Grayson's death. He panicked when he saw Dylan snapping a few underwater shots of the submerged schooner. When Dylan and Jake surfaced, they went below deck, where Jake slipped a Roofie into Dylan's coffee, hoping he'd pass out and have no memory of his discovery. Jake didn't expect Dylan to fall back and hit his head on the giant hook used to bring in four-hundred-pound goliath groupers. When he saw the damage the hook had done, he carried Dylan up on deck and threw him overboard. Then Jake told the captain Dylan was missing, and the captain called the Coast Guard. It seems the captain and crew were involved with the salvaging but didn't have anything to do with Dylan's death."

"Wow," Liz said. "What does Jake say about Gregory's involvement?"

"Gregory was upset when Jake told him what had happened to Dylan. He had Jake set the fire at Minna's as a distraction to get any film that would show *Poseidon* was a salvager. Gregory paid off the captain and crew and sent them out of the country but kept Jake around so he could keep close to Minna. Apparently, even though Gregory owned the gallery, he had no idea Dylan's photos would be on display alongside Minna's art. It was a decision made by his gallery manager and Minna."

"Does Charlotte believe Jake about not killing Gregory?" Liz asked.

"Not now, she doesn't. But she can't charge him with Gregory's death until she gathers more evidence. However, she can charge Jake with Dylan's death. I just don't know if it will be a murder charge."

"Fenton," Ryan said, "do they know the location of the person who called in the anonymous tip on where to find Jake?"

"That I don't know. We're lucky she shared this much. We'll have to wait and see how things unfold. At least we know what happened to Dylan. So tragic."

Chapter 29

Monday morning dawned dark and dreary, but at least Hurricane Roberta was spewing her madness over the Atlantic, not threatening landfall. They'd learned late last night from their cell phones that Roberta had come within fifty miles of Melbourne Beach but never touched sand. With any luck, she would be the last of the hurricanes that season and they could take a sigh of relief until May. Liz had to prod Bronte awake, while Aunt Amelia snored in the other room, sounding like a lawn mower needing repair.

Last night, her great-aunt had assigned suites to everyone stranded at the Indialantic. Liz and Bronte stayed with Aunt Amelia. Kate slept with Minna in the Oceana Suite. Susannah refused to share the Windward Shores Suite with Erica after the ominous message she received on the Ouija board, so she stayed with Greta in the Swaying Palms Suite. Ryan went to the caretaker's cottage, taking Victor and Tom with him. Liz had been happy they wouldn't be staying in the hotel. There was a slim chance Jake was telling the truth when he said he hadn't murdered Gregory.

Liz showered and dressed, happy the power had returned. She went to the kitchen and was surprised Pierre wasn't in the pantry writing out the day's menu. But understandably, they'd all had a rough time of it. After Liz fed Bronte, she went directly to her father's apartment via the back hallway by the hotel's service elevator.

She rapped on the door and heard him say, "Come in."

Liz opened the door and stepped inside. Her jaw dropped when she saw Charlotte sitting with her father at the kitchen table with a mug of coffee in her hand. On the table in front of the sofa was a copy of the *Melbourne Beach Times*. The top headline read, **Farewell, Roberta. Hurricane Skirts Island**. Below was another headline: **Suspect Arrested**

in Murder of Local Fisherman; Also Questioned in Stabbing Death of Local Billionaire Gregory Grayson. It seemed even in the throes of a hurricane, the media didn't sleep.

Liz stepped closer to the table. "Sorry to interrupt. I just wanted to hear the latest."

"Have a seat," her father said.

Liz sat next to Charlotte, who looked fresh and perky and, as usual, was dressed impeccably. The light scent of her perfume filled the room. Liz assumed the detective had pulled an all-nighter but still managed to look like she'd gotten a full eight hours of sleep.

For a minute, no one spoke. Then Fenton said, "I gave Charlotte the memory card after I showed her the photos. Last night, I asked Minna to ask her sister-in-law to send the photo that was a duplicate of the one stolen from Ms. Shay's suite. Would you like to see it?"

"I remember seeing it, but I'd love to see what was so important that Jake or Gregory had to steal it."

Fenton got up from the table and went to the kitchen counter. He grabbed his open laptop, then placed it in front of Liz.

She admired the composition and vibrancy of the colors, as she had when she'd seen it in the Windward Shores Suite. At first, she couldn't find a reason why the photo had been stolen. Nothing looked amiss. Then she zoomed in on the fish laying on ice chips and saw it. The camera's flash had caught not only the iridescent glow of fish scales but also some green glass peeking out from under the shaved ice. Not green glass but emeralds. Emeralds from the 1715 Spanish fleet shipwreck. The outer circumference of the emeralds was crusted with debris from being buried at the bottom of the ocean for over three hundred years, but the center of some of the stones still shone in all their brilliance. "Amazing," Liz said, adding a whistle. She turned to Charlotte. "What did you find in the safe at Jake's house? Pieces of eight?"

Charlotte remained stone-faced.

"Come on," Liz said. "Throw me a bone. If it wasn't for Ryan and me, you wouldn't have found Jake's house."

Liz saw a slight upturn to Charlotte's perfect lips.

"Nailed it," Liz said. "There was treasure in the safe? Right? So what's your theory? Gregory found out Jake was stealing his booty, confronted him, and Jake stabbed him?"

"We're still in the beginning stages of our investigation," Charlotte said, standing up from the table. "I'd better get back to the office. We're trying to get a feed on the high-tech security cameras Jake had installed in his house. Maybe we'll get a shot of you, Liz?" She winked, as if it was a joke, but Liz didn't laugh. And why hadn't Charlotte mentioned Ryan's name?

Charlotte moved toward the door and said to Fenton, "Please remember to tell Minna Presley to come down to the station."

The police must have heard about Minna and Gregory's skirmish at the Beachside Gallery the night before his death.

Just as Charlotte put her hand on the door to her father's office, Liz's phone rang. The caller ID read Felicia: the bartender at Squidly's who'd dated Jake.

"Hello," Liz said into the phone.

"Hi. I just saw the paper, and I know Jake is a deadbeat and a loser, but the time frame they put in the paper about that billionaire's death..."

"Yes?"

"Jake was with me. Well, not actually with me. But I called the cops on him yesterday morning when I saw him lurking around my front yard. We were kind of hoping a palm tree might fall on him from the hurricane."

"Did they arrest him?" Liz asked as she motioned for Charlotte to come back. "Can you hold on one minute, Felicia? I'll be right back." Liz put the call on hold and told her father and Charlotte who had called, then got back on. "Okay, sorry. Did they arrest Jake?"

"No," Felicia said, "they just gave him the usual warning. But I know he was there all morning; my mom even videoed it in case there was trouble. Like we've had in the past."

"Thanks for calling. Do you mind if I pass the phone to Agent Pearson from the Brevard County Sheriff's Department. I'm sure she'll want to talk to you." Liz didn't give her a chance to answer and shoved the phone into Charlotte's hand.

You're welcome, Liz said to herself.

After Charlotte arranged to meet Felicia at the station, Liz said good-bye to her father. He'd been as stunned as she that Jake might not be Gregory Grayson's killer. Liz planned to fill Ryan in on what they'd learned. She was also curious about how last night's sleepover had gone with Tom and Victor.

Once outside, she had to sidestep branches and small bushes that littered the walkway on her way to the caretaker's cottage, realizing for the first time the importance of what Felicia had just told them. If it wasn't Jake, who did that leave as Gregory's killer? Victor, Tom, or Erica? Or someone else who had it out for Gregory? Doubtful. Then she thought of Minna. No, Liz wouldn't even entertain that idea. At the top of Liz's list would be Victor, the man with no identity. But then there was the half brother who might have resented the treatment he got and the will in which he received nothing. Erica was an ex-wife. Who knew what resentments she might be harboring or if she benefited in any way from Gregory's death?

The wind was rough, the sky dark, but there was no rain. She'd almost reached Ryan's cottage when she heard an engine whirring. Looking toward the dock, she spied *Visions of Gold* pulling away at full speed with a man and a woman on the bridge. She didn't have time to think; all she knew was that a crime scene was leaving the dock, and she would bet it wasn't the police behind the wheel. She yelled Ryan's name as she bounded toward her dad's Chris-Craft. She charged onto the dock and leapt on board, throwing off the lines. She quickly removed the canvas and found the hidden key. She turned the key and pushed the Start button. It started with barely a sputter. Before she had a chance to pull away in pursuit, she heard a voice behind her.

And it wasn't Ryan's.

"Get out of the way. I'll be piloting this boat. Take a seat; we don't have time for formalities." Victor Normand took the helm of *Serendipity*, nosing her out of the cove at full throttle.

Liz glanced at him and saw a gun sticking out from the waistband of his pants. It was lunacy to be on the open waters in the aftermath of a hurricane. What had she been thinking? At least she knew every nuance of *Serendipity* and was an expert at piloting her. She had no idea about Victor's boating skills.

With each huge wave, Liz's stomach heaved. They were on the lagoon; what if Victor followed *Visions of Gold* onto the ocean? The small powerboat didn't have a chance. All she could do was hold on for dear life. And as she bumped along, she realized how dear her life really was, praying Victor wouldn't kill her.

The spray from the waves blinded her. For about five minutes, Liz couldn't tell where they were headed. Finally, Victor slowed the engine. To their right, she saw *Visions of Gold* run aground on a small island. The one Betty and Liz called Treasure Island, where they'd picnicked over the years—their private oasis. She didn't see any signs of life onboard the yacht or the island.

Victor pulled in close to shore, then dropped anchor. He turned off the ignition, pocketed the key, and jumped in the water. "Stay here. Don't do anything."

"Like I could. You have the key," Liz croaked. If she was in a movie, she would climb on *Visions of Gold*, call the Coast Guard, and have them give her step-by-step instructions on how to pilot a yacht, because in movies, an average Joe could land a commercial airplane. But this wasn't a movie and Gregory's killer wasn't an actor—or maybe he was. A *bad* actor.

Even if she did get onto the yacht, it had run aground; only a tugboat could pull it out.

Only ten minutes passed, but it seemed like hours before she heard shouting and saw three figures coming out of the dense, palmetto-filled forest.

Suddenly, it all made sense.

Chapter 30

Tom and Erica waded toward *Serendipity,* Victor following behind with a gun pointed at Tom's back. Liz remained frozen on the bench. She needed a plan but couldn't think of anything until they got back to the dock. Maybe Ryan had heard her call him and he was waiting with Charlotte and her father? But what if Victor didn't return to the Indialantic? What if he planned on dumping Tom, Erica, and Liz on his escape to the open sea?

Victor helped Erica up the ladder. She stumbled onto the deck. Her face was bleached of color and her lips trembled as she collapsed onto the white cushioned bench on the port side of the cruiser. Tom came up the ladder with Victor right behind him, the gun still pointed at his back.

"Stand still and put your hands behind your back," Victor said to Tom.

Instead of doing as he was told, Tom turned and attempted to punch Victor. Crazy, seeing Victor still held a gun. Victor kicked him hard and Tom fell facedown on the deck.

Before Liz could think of a way to help him, Victor announced, "Thomas Grayson, you are under arrest; anything you say or do will be..." The words of the Miranda warning continued as Victor secured Tom's arms behind his back and slapped on a pair of handcuffs.

Erica started to cry. "Thank you, Evan. I was almost a goner."

Evan?

Victor, or Evan, stepped up to Liz and held out his hand. "Special Agent Evan Winston, IRS Crime Investigator" Then he shook Liz's already trembling hand.

Liz wished there were such a thing as smelling salts, like in Aunt Amelia's day, because she had a feeling she might faint.

Chapter 31

Liz stood ankle deep in the shallow water off the small uninhabited island in the Indian River that she, her father, Aunt Amelia, and Betty had been visiting ever since Liz was a small child— Treasure Island. Liz, Ryan, Fenton, and Charlotte were celebrating Tom's and Jake's arrests with a gourmet picnic basket from Pierre and wine and cheese from Deli-casies by the Sea. Fenton's Chris-Craft bobbed in the water in the same location *Visions of Gold* had run aground by an inexperienced pilot. The luxury yacht had been towed away from the island and would be sold at auction, along with most of Gregory Grayson's other assets.

"So, Charlotte, tell me if I've got this right," Liz said. "Victor's real name is Evan Winston and he's an IRS-Crime Investigation agent. And you and the Sheriff's Department have been working with him this whole time, trying to catch Gregory Grayson in what you thought was a drug money-laundering operation involving *Poseidon* and other boats he owned? But it turned out to be illegal treasure salvaging instead of drugs. Gregory was selling the recovered treasure to buyers in other countries, including Spain, where the 1715 fleet originated?"

Charlotte smiled. "Yes. You said a mouthful, Liz." She wore a sundress over her bathing suit and sat on a blanket next to Fenton, sipping wine from a paper cup. She wasn't wearing makeup and her usually perfect hair stuck out as if she'd borrowed one of Aunt Amelia's Phyllis Diller wigs.

When Aunt Amelia had first shown Liz her impression of the comedienne's cackling laugh, wearing a crazy wig and pretending to smoke a cigarette from a long black cigarette holder, Liz hadn't seen the humor. But then her great-aunt had showed her some old television clips of Diller on *The Tonight Show Starring Johnny Carson* and Liz hadn't been able to stop laughing.

"Charlotte, how long have you been investigating Gregory Grayson?" Liz asked.

"Mr. Grayson's been under the IRS's radar for quite some time, but it wasn't until his brother came to town that we were able to piece together a little of the puzzle. Apparently, Tom had been cooking Gregory's books for years." There was a piece of cilantro stuck between Charlotte's two front teeth. Liz didn't have the heart to tell her—just in case she reverted to the old, reserved Agent Pearson.

"Tom really was an accountant all his life. Not a director or a travel agent?" Ryan asked as he passed Fenton one of Pierre's mini duck confit sandwiches.

"After Tom and Gregory's father died, and Tom saw he was left out of the will," Charlotte said, "he contacted Gregory to say he'd better set him up or he'd go to the authorities with all he knew about the illegal treasure salvaging and money laundering."

"Crazy," Liz said, sitting next to Ryan on the blanket, keeping her wet feet on the sand. "Susannah Shay found out Tom was an accountant, not what he said he was. She might be an asset on your team, Charlotte."

Charlotte laughed; it was almost a giggle. Who was this new and improved woman?

"So how does Jake fit in to all this?" Ryan asked.

Charlotte stole Fenton's sandwich from his hand, took a bite, then passed it back to him. After she swallowed, she said, "I think Jake is exactly who we thought he was, just one of the crew on *Poseidon* who would go out and salvage treasure from the 1715 fleet with the rest of the crooked crew after normal fishing hours. Dylan was hired as a day worker to keep things legit. He was never supposed to know about their clandestine treasure looting. Jake's going to be charged with murder, because even if he thought Dylan was dead when he tossed him overboard, forensics determined he was still alive. Jake was also accused of adding a Roofie to a young woman's beer back at the University of Central Florida a few years ago. The girl recanted, not wanting to be stigmatized by the notoriety."

Liz could understand the woman's stance.

Everyone was silent for a few minutes, then Ryan said, "Liz, you're getting a sunburn on your back. Hand me the lotion."

She went into her beach bag and handed him the Bain de Soleil.

"This has a sunblock filter of four. What's the point of using it on your fair skin? You'll be toast in a half hour."

"That's okay. The sun feels good. It's been a while." Liz still wore a big floppy straw hat and had makeup on her scar with a sunblock factor of 40, but it was the first time since coming back home that she felt happy to be in the sun. "How does Erica Grayson fit in to all this?"

"Ms. Grayson knew about the money laundering; she just didn't know where the money was coming from," Fenton said. "The four years she was married to Gregory they filed a joint tax return. Erica's name was on some of the property and assets that were under scrutiny. If Gregory went down, so would Erica. So the IRS offered her a deal, if she would cooperate. Evan became her supposed boyfriend, Gregory's chauffeur, and one of the actors in the Melbourne Beach Theatre so he'd have an inside track on where the money was coming from."

"A sting operation," Liz said.

"Exactly," her father answered.

Ryan wiped his greasy hands on a napkin, then said, "Charlotte, why were you involved in the whole IRS operation?"

"We've been close to catching drug smugglers in the harbor. I'm involved in trying to get a murder conviction for a dealer who was part of the ring. We've been spending a lot of time trying to find the dealer's supplier. When the IRS contacted us about Gregory and we found out he was the owner of *Poseidon*, and then Dylan went missing, we offered our assistance."

"What!" Liz said. "You knew Gregory was the owner of *Poseidon* all this time?"

"Yes. But even Evan couldn't get enough to charge him, especially after the entire crew and captain disappeared. Jake was the only one who'd hung around. And even he was hard to keep tabs on."

"So you didn't know where he lived until I told you?" Liz asked.

Charlotte took a bunch of grapes from the picnic basket Pierre had packed and popped one in her mouth. "No. Jake was staying in a motel in Sebastian. We assume Gregory told him not to go to back to his house in Palm Bay until everything regarding Dylan's death was cleared up. Gregory had Jake set the fire, steal the camera, and search for any photo drives that might point to treasure salvaging. Gregory's the one who bought all Dylan's remaining photos from the gallery, in case they showed treasure salvaging was going on."

"What were Tom's plans when he took Erica out on the yacht?"

"Erica told Agent Winston that after Tom admitted to killing Gregory, he planned on killing her by throwing her into the lagoon and making it look like an accident. He knew Erica was privy to the fact that Tom had been manipulating Gregory's books for years."

Liz interrupted Charlotte, "Look! A manatee."

They all stood. Liz said, "Let's wade in slowly. They're so friendly, I bet it'll play with us."

They did as they were told, and sure enough, the gentle manatee swam in between their legs. Every Melbourne Beach elementary student, including Liz, learned about manatees. She knew they were the closest relative to the elephant, were around twelve feet long, and weighed up to fifteen hundred pounds. Ryan dove underwater and Liz heard strange squealing noises. When Ryan emerged, he told Liz he'd had the most interesting conversation with Mr. Manatee. And she believed him.

When they decided they'd had enough fun in the sun, everyone packed up and boarded *Serendipity*. Liz took the wheel, reveling in the feeling of the wind against her face, expertly avoiding the wakes of other boats passing by.

Ryan came up behind her and said, "You sure know how to handle a boat, Skipper."

"My dad let me take the helm when I was thirteen." Liz looked ahead to her father and Charlotte, on the bow of the cruiser. "Charlotte seems like a different person here. What do you think has changed?"

"I think she realizes she's got a good man, someone she trusts and can let her hair down with. Just like you have me," he said.

Chapter 32

"I found it!" Liz heard one of the Pirates' Weekend scavenger hunters shout.

The Indialantic's grounds were dotted with participants broken into teams of four. The rain/hurricane date for Pirates' Weekend had finally arrived. It had been two weeks since Tom and Jake were arrested.

The day couldn't be more perfect. Both the hotel and the emporium's parking lots were full. Yesterday's day of shopping had been a huge success, and even though Tom's shop, Treasure Tours by the Sea, was closed, no one seemed to notice. Liz, Ryan, and Kate had spent all day Saturday leaving items for the scavenger hunt on the hotel's grounds, including the Indialantic's beach. Everything to be found on the scavenger list had a pirate theme: a captain's wheel, an anchor, a sword, a noose, a Jolly Roger flag, a musket, skeleton bones, painted gold rocks, a rum bottle marked with "XX," fishermen nets, a tankard, a wooden plank, and a nautical chart. After a team found one of the items on the list, they would check it off and write down the coordinating point value. Kate had made a copy of the map found in the *Capt. Jeremiah Jennings*'s book. She'd dipped the map in tea and, after it dried, burned the edges for an authentic feel. The team with the most points would be given the rolled up and tied map, then sent on their way to dig up their treasure.

Aunt Amelia had buried her grand prize at the location that had been marked with an "X" on Kate's map, near Snag Harbor Cove on the shore of the Indian River Lagoon, and the grand prize hadn't been divulged to anyone, not even her nephew. Aunt Amelia loved surprises. When asked what she wanted for her birthday or Christmas, she always said the same thing: "Surprise me."

There was a two-hour time limit to find twenty-five items on the list. Liz glanced at her watch; only a half hour to go.

Tables of food were set up in front of the gazebo. Pierre, Ryan, Pops, Greta, and Liz had all contributed to the menu, trying to stick to the pirate theme but turning it up a notch with things like blue crab cannonball cakes, Jamaican jerk chicken Popsicle peg legs, Kraken pasta made with scallops and shrimp over squid ink linguine, and shark bait tuna tartare with mango aioli. Pops even made veggie platters that featured a cauliflower skull and crossbones with red grape tomatoes for eyes. Understandingly, the cauliflower skull was more in keeping with Liz's great-aunt's original menu. Aunt Amelia had been so excited by Pop's vegetable artistry that she'd given him a smooch on his cheek. Ryan said he'd never seen his grandfather blush before.

Aunt Amelia had started the day's festivities with Barnacle Bob on her shoulder, but after a few expletives and wisecracks, he was relegated to his cage and moved next to a pirate skeleton dangling from the branch of a three-hundred-year-old moss-covered oak: a reminder of what could happen if BB didn't behave himself.

There were two large tents set up on the hotel's great lawn. One was a dining tent, because you never knew when the weather could change in Florida. The other housed homemade items for sale made by the artisan members of the Home Arts by the Sea collective. Liz had bought a beautiful raw silk knitted throw in ocean shades of blue, aqua, and sand-white. She'd also purchased a hand-thrown turquoise pottery vase with flecks of copper, planning on putting it away to give to Aunt Amelia for Christmas. It would be perfect for an arrangement of flowers from her great-aunt's cutting garden.

The Barrier Island Historical Society had set up a table displaying brochures of points of interest on the island, of which there were many. Fenton and Liz hoped that soon the Indialantic by the Sea Hotel would be one of those points of interest. The Barrier Island Sanctuary Education Center also had a table. The center was only a few miles away from the Indialantic and had live exhibits and interactive areas that focused mainly on the preservation of the island's large sea turtle population.

The last table was inside the gazebo and seemed the most popular. Aunt Amelia had coordinated with a local no-kill pet shelter to bring in a truckload of pets to be adopted. The last Liz checked, there were only two dogs and one cat left for adoption. She had a feeling if no one chose them, Aunt Amelia would add them to her menagerie.

Ryan, Aunt Amelia, Liz, and Fenton had all dressed in pirates' costumes. Instead of Ryan being gentleman pirate Henry Jennings, Aunt Amelia had given Fenton that role. She'd coerced Ryan into portraying the notorious pirate Blackbeard. Liz had to admit, with his dark looks and five days of not shaving, Ryan fit that part better than Jennings. Ryan had spent the day before memorizing a short monologue he recited while sticking in words like, "Arrr," "Avast," and "Blimey." Then he went on to tell the tale of Blackbeard, an English pirate who sailed the Caribbean on his pirate sloop *Queen Anne's Revenge*, which he had renamed after capturing a French merchant ship. And even though Blackbeard had looked menacing with his long black beard, there was no evidence he was the violent marauder pictured in fiction; he never harmed his crew or murdered anyone he'd captured.

Aunt Amelia and Liz had dressed as the two most notorious female pirates in history. Both had served under the English pirate Calico Jack, the first pirate to fly the iconic flag with a skull and two crossed swords. Liz played Mary Read, an Englishwoman whose mother had passed her off as boy so she could collect money from a paternal grandmother. Years later, when Mary served in the military, still disguised as a male, her ship was captured by Calico Jack and Mary joined the crew. When Liz recited her story to the attendees of the scavenger hunt, she left out the sad end of Mary Read, who supposedly died in prison while pregnant. Calico Jack didn't fare too well, either. He was captured by a pirate hunter and died by hanging in 1720, in Port Royal, Jamaica.

Pirate Anne Bonny, Aunt Amelia's character, couldn't have been more perfect for her. Like Amelia, Anne was a fiery redhead. Anne was Pirate Calico Jack's lover in the Bahamas during the Golden Age of piracy, and even bore him a son. Unlike Mary Read, Anne dressed as a woman. Aunt Amelia had researched her part by watching the 1951 movie *Anne of the Indies*, starring Jean Peters. The pirate princess costumes worn by Peters were certainly more in Aunt Amelia's wheelhouse than dressing like a male.

"How's my favorite pirate?" swashbuckling Ryan asked Liz as he leaned in for a kiss.

"How's *my* favorite pirate?" she asked back, swiping her finger across his lips to remove the black that had transferred from her painted beard.

"I think your great-aunt should be very proud of herself. Does that woman ever rest?"

"She's a powerhouse, isn't she?"

They looked over at Aunt Amelia near the gazebo, wearing a costume made by Francie before she'd left for her trip abroad. The green satin flared dress had a black velvet bustier with two rows of green satin laces and bows. The laces strained against her great-aunt's generous bosom. Beneath the dress was an off-the-shoulder, gauzy peasant top with billowing sleeves affixed with green satin bows. Black lace-up, knee-high boots with two-inch heels completed her ensemble.

Aunt Amelia noticed them looking at her and motioned them over.

Ryan took Liz's hand, and they walked toward the gazebo, passing Fenton, who'd just blown a whistle and announced, "Aye, fifteen minutes left, mateys."

As soon as Liz and Ryan walked up the gazebo steps, Aunt Amelia pushed something furry in Ryan's arms. The ugliest, mangiest, cutest puppy Liz had ever seen. Its coloring was similar to Francie's tortoiseshell cat Turtle, blacks and browns and russets. Its fur was choppy, long and short in patches. It had a pointy black goatee and long black lashes over large dark brown eyes. The puppy's eyes reminded Liz of Ryan's.

"Isn't he the most perfect companion, Ryan?" Aunt Amelia clapped her hands, her large gold hoop earrings swinging from side to side.

"Ugh." He was at a loss for words.

Liz took the dog from Ryan's arms and held him in the air. "Aren't you adorable?"

"Adorable?" Ryan looked at Aunt Amelia.

"I swear, as soon as I saw his cute little mug, I thought of you, Ryan. He needs a home and you have one."

"Aren't his paws a little on the large size?" Ryan asked.

"Pshaw," Aunt Amelia said, "he'll grow into them."

Liz handed the puppy back to Ryan. He glanced down and saw the dog was fast asleep in his arms.

"Come on, Ryan. You have to take him," Liz said. "He's one of a kind."

"That's for sure," he said, laughing. "I'll tell you what, Aunt Amelia; if no one else adopts him before the day is over, I'll consider it."

Aunt Amelia smiled. Liz knew what the smile meant. There wouldn't be any chance of someone else adopting the puppy. She had made up her mind. The dog would be Ryan's.

They heard another whistle and looked toward the center of the lawn, where Fenton stood surrounded by the scavenger hunt teams. Amelia handed the puppy off to one of the shelter's volunteers, then whispered something in her ear—no doubt, "This pup is adopted."

"Hurry, Liz and Ryan, let's go see which team won the treasure!" Aunt Amelia shouted, excitement flushing her cheeks.

A traveling band, all wearing eye patches and bandannas but not looking much like pirates in their jeans and sneakers, performed a drumroll. Liz, Ryan, and Amelia made their way to the edge of the crowd, stopping just in time to hear Fenton announce the winning team. Aunt Amelia had given each team a ship's name, and *Mutiny on the Bounty*, was the winner. Fenton handed the team captain the rolled-up map and a shovel, and the crowd followed behind as the team turned toward the lagoon and followed the shore south.

Kate ran up to Liz, Ryan, and Aunt Amelia. "This is so much fun! Aunt Amelia, I can't wait to see what you buried as the treasure."

When they reached where "X" marked the spot on the map, the team captain started digging.

Aunt Amelia nudged Liz. "I think he's a little too far to the west of where I buried the treasure."

"That's the fun of it," Liz said, "Let him dig around a bit."

"You're right, Lizzie. It's great theater."

The team captain grew weary and handed the shovel off to another member of his team. The woman continued to shovel, throwing piles of dirt high in the air behind her. A few minutes later, they heard her shout, "I hit something!"

Aunt Amelia said, "Uh-oh! That's not where I buried it." She made her way through the crowd and stood on the edge of the hole and looked down. "Stop!"

The woman with the shovel moved back. Aunt Amelia got on her hands and knees and looked in to the hole. Then she turned and called out, "Fenton, can you have someone from the Historical Society come take a look?"

Amelia explained to the winning team that they hadn't found the treasure she'd buried. A third member of the team took the shovel and the map, and he and Aunt Amelia played a game of hot potato.

"Cold. Warmer, cold, burnin' hot," she said.

At the base of a small palm tree, he inserted the shovel. After removing four shovelfuls of dirt, he bent over and reached down, extracting a small treasure chest the size of a jewelry box. Aunt Amelia moved next to him, excitement in her emerald eyes.

The man opened the chest. He said, "Is it real?"

"Indeed it is," Aunt Amelia answered. "From the 1715 Spanish Fleet shipwreck. I've talked to the Barrier Island Treasure Museum and they'd be willing to purchase it from you, so you can divide the spoils four ways. I thought it would be fun to hold a piece of history and then be able to see it whenever you wanted at the museum."

He turned the chest, so everyone could see. Inside was the silver piece of eight Aunt Amelia had found near the 1715 survivors' camp years ago.

Liz watched the team members pass the coin back and forth in amazement. She was reminded of the gold coin she'd found under Dylan's body. It had been decided that after the state of Florida took their cut, then the licensed salvager, Dylan's mother would give the remaining money to Dylan's charity. Usually, if you found gold on the beach it was finders keepers. However, Liz knew that the coin had originally been found at the bottom of the sea, based on Dylan's photos from the memory card.

Hours later, it was decided the day had been a huge success. Aunt Amelia and Pierre were resting their weary bones in the food tent, while Liz, Ryan, and Greta were cleaning up.

Liz held open a large black garbage bag as Ryan dumped the trash inside. From behind she heard, "Lizzie, I'm so impressed with how successful the day was."

She turned and saw Skylar, Kate's brother, standing outside, the sun highlighting his fair good looks and lean surfer's body. Skylar ran the Barrier Island Education Sanctuary Center but was usually off in Tallahassee or Washington, DC, lobbying for additional funding. Like Kate, Skylar had known Liz since she was five years old. He was two years older than Liz and Kate, and Liz thought of Skylar as the brother she'd never had.

Liz put down the bag and ran to him. She hugged him and gave him a kiss on the cheek. They talked for a few minutes, then Skylar handed her a book. He said, "Hot off the presses. An autographed copy."

She looked down at the book, entitled *Saving Nature—A Blueprint to Success*. The cover was white, with a photo of an underwater green sea turtle. "Oh, Sky, how wonderful. Kate told me you were writing a book, but she didn't say it was already published."

He grinned, dimples appearing on either side of his mouth and laugh lines by his blue-green eyes. The highlights in his sandy blond hair told her that he still had time for surfing. "They moved up the date. I was surprised myself."

They talked for a few minutes, then Skylar left to help load the Barrier Island Sanctuary table into his Save-a-Turtle green van.

When she returned to the food tent, Ryan was missing. She went over to Aunt Amelia and Pierre. Aunt Amelia had taken off her tall black boots and was resting her "dogs," as she called them, on a chair. "Auntie, where did Ryan go? We still have work to do," Liz said.

"He ran out the back. Didn't look too happy—a lot of scowling and stomping of the feet as he charged out."

Liz shook her head. Now what was up? She went out the back flap of the tent and saw Ryan standing on the dock near *Serendipity*. Even from a distance, he didn't look happy. When she reached him, she put her hand on his arm. He immediately pulled away.

"What's up?" she asked, trying to keep it casual.

He turned his dark gaze on her and said, "I don't know, Liz. You tell me."

"I'm sorry, I have no idea what you're pouting about."

He jerked his head back to the dock, his stance cold and stiff as he looked toward the lagoon. It was sunset, and the sky was awash in gorgeous peaches, pinks, and golds.

"Well then, I'll leave you. I'm not a mind reader. I don't deserve the cold shoulder. I haven't done anything wrong." She stomped away.

From behind, she heard Ryan shout, "I see you got your autographed copy. Thought you had no idea your ex was coming to town. No more secrets. Remember?"

Liz slapped her forehead. Ryan thought Skylar was Travis! She stifled a laugh and walked back to him. Yes, Travis and Skylar were both fair and on the thin side, but there was an age difference between the two of about fifteen years, and Travis wore glasses. Then she remembered that the only photo Ryan might have seen of Travis was on the book jacket of *The McAvoy Brothers*. Vain Travis had used a lot of Photoshopping to make himself appear years younger than he was. She supposed without Travis's glasses, there was a slight resemblance between Skylar and Travis.

"You're such a big jerk! If there was a prize for the jerkiest, you'd win it, Ryan Stone." Then she told him who Skylar was.

He looked at her sheepishly. "I've never been the jealous type before. This is all new to me."

"That sounds like an arrogant statement. Do you mean in all your relationships—and I'm sure there were many—you never had a run-in with the green-eyed monster?"

"Not until you, Elizabeth Amelia Holt."

They kissed in the last rays of the sunset. After they pulled apart, Liz said, "I might as well bite the bullet." She went on to tell him about the card with the lingerie-clad, full-figure model she'd found on the floor of his Jeep.

"I wondered where that card had gone to. It's a good thing I'd taken a photo of it with my cell phone."

After Ryan explained, she felt like an idiot. The woman in the poses wasn't his sister or cousin but the daughter of one of his compatriots on the FDNY, who'd asked Ryan to look for his runaway daughter.

"Well, did you find her?" Liz asked

"Yes. She's already back in New York. I got her out before the hurricane." He took his phone out of his pocket and showed her a picture of a gray-haired giant with his arm around the young woman from the card. She looked completely different dressed in an NYU sweatshirt and jeans.

"I'm sorry," Liz said. "I guess we both still have training wheels on in this relationship."

"Oh, this is a relationship, is it?"

He smiled, and she melted into him. "I suppose it is," she said. "So, that was a successful first case as a PI. You're not thinking of leaving my father, are you, and going out on your own? Back to Brooklyn?"

"The thought never crossed my mind."

Chapter 33

The weather for Thanksgiving Day at the Indialantic by the Sea couldn't have been more perfect. The long farm table from the hotel's kitchen had been placed in the shade of a pair of oaks, topped with a white linen tablecloth and set with the hotel's monogrammed china and crystal. In the center of the table, Amelia had placed white ironstone pitchers filled with orange and gold Gerber daises and dahlias from her cutting garden. The scene looked as if it had jumped off the canvas of one of Van Gogh's paintings of Tuscany—except the palm trees swaying in the ocean breeze. Everyone at the table, including Liz, had a lot to be thankful for.

Tom Grayson had been charged with murder. He'd worked out a deal with the DA and the IRS where he would get a life sentence instead of the death penalty if he cooperated with all the aspects of his brother's money-laundering scheme. Tom admitted to killing Gregory after overhearing a conversation between his brother and Jake about Dylan's death, knowing Jake would be the perfect scapegoat. It was Tom who had called in Jake's location. Earlier, he'd taken Gregory's cell phone from his body and dialed Jake's number. Disguising himself as Gregory, he found out Jake's location. The knife Tom had used on Gregory hadn't been one of Jake's. It had been taken from one of the diving lockers in the lower level of *Visions of Gold*.

The afternoon when Liz noticed *Visions of Gold* leaving the dock before its scheduled maiden voyage, Gregory and Tom had gone out to plant treasure at specific coordinates, wanting the next day's *maiden* launch to be a success, thus ensuring future bookings. On the day after Tom killed Gregory, he'd planned to kill Erica because she'd been privy to the fact that Tom had been cooking her ex-husband's books for years. The IRS had followed Tom from Jacksonville and then set up the sting operation with the cooperation of the Brevard County Sheriff's Department. Tom had no idea how to pilot the yacht and luckily, he beached *Visions of Gold* before he had a chance to push Erica overboard. The IRS also made a deal with Erica if she played along. She wouldn't get jail time, but she would lose any assets she'd won in her divorce from Gregory, including a few bank accounts in the Cayman Islands.

No one knew if killing Gregory had been premeditated. But Liz would bet the seed had been planted after Tom found out their father had left everything to Gregory in his will. She remembered the way Tom had reacted to Gregory the day of *Vision of Gold*'s launch, like he was sick of the second-class treatment at his brother's supposedly magnanimous hands.

Liz thought Jake, on the other hand, had gotten off too easily with the charge of accidental manslaughter. She also knew if it wasn't for Jake's testimony and confession, they wouldn't have known what had happened to Dylan on that tragic day at sea. Liz was happy Jake wouldn't be bothering Felicia or any other young women in the near future. Jake had disclosed the whereabouts of the captain and crew of *Poseidon* on the day Dylan went overboard. He'd also revealed the locations where they'd illegally salvaged from the 1715 fleet, leading the authorities to four other fishing trawlers with questionable dealings that were owned by Gregory Grayson's Central Coast Boatworks.

"I'd like to raise a toast to my dear nephew, Fenton," Aunt Amelia said. "Congratulations for getting the Indialantic by the Sea Hotel official historical-site status. Long live the Indialantic by the Sea!" Aunt Amelia wore a paper Native American headdress, the feather's folded and wrinkled from years of storage. Liz had made it for her great-aunt when she was six. Aunt Amelia had worn it to the Thanksgiving table every year thereafter.

Everyone raised their glasses, the sound of the clinking crystal like the wind chimes outside Liz's beach house.

"Auntie," Fenton said, "If it wasn't for you, I don't think we would have gotten approval. So, here's to you." They all clicked glasses again.

If not for Kate's map and Aunt Amelia's idea of burying the treasure for the scavenger hunt, they wouldn't have mistakenly discovered the dugout cypress tree canoe and skeleton. Archaeologists confirmed, using radiocarbon dating, that the canoe was made in the early 1600s and had been used by Native Americans from Florida's Seminole tribe. As for the skeleton, they needed time for the anthropologists to determine its age and ethnicity. The spot where the canoe and skeleton were unearthed was now an official archaeological Florida dig site. The canoe wasn't filled with gold and jewels liked the 1715 treasure, but it was something just as precious to historians.

Ziggy clinked his glass against Amelia's. "Cheers!" The roof of Ziggy's Surf Shack had been damaged by Hurricane Roberta. Luckily, though, all his surfboards had survived unscathed. Aunt Amelia had talked him into renting the empty space in the emporium where Treasure Tours by the Sea once resided. It was now called Zig's Surf Shack by the Sea.

Betty clinked her glass against the debonair Captain Clyde B. Netherton's. "Happy Thanksgiving!" Betty had come back from London excited to get going on her new project. At eighty-three, she had gotten a contract from a British publishing house to write a series of teenage mystery novels set in Sherlockian London. The protagonist in the story was a sixteen-year-old female chimney sweep who dressed as a boy to help take care of her widowed mother and four younger sisters. Sherlock Holmes sent her down the chimneys as a spy to help him with some of his smaller cases.

Captain Netherton was happy to be back piloting *Queen of the Seas*, especially when he heard that Treasure Tours by the Sea was defunct and not able to compete with his sightseeing tours on the Indian River Lagoon.

Chef Pierre clinked his glass against Greta's. "Voltaire said, *Le bonheur est souvent la seule chose qu'on puisse donner sans l'avoir et c'est en le donnant qu'on l'acquiert.* 'Happiness often is the only thing we can give without having it, and we get it when we give it.' Cheers!"

"I'll drink to that!" Greta said.

Kate and the big kahuna, Alex, were on their fourth date and seemed to be inseparable, both tanned and toned from daily weather-permitting surfing dates. Between Ziggy and Alex, Liz thought she might have a future in matchmaking. Time would tell.

Francie and Minna had come to the table without dates. Both divorcees, they liked to play the field and were in between men.

Liz had finished her first draft of *An American in Cornwall*, a very, very rough draft, and was excited to add the research Francie had brought back with her from Cornwall for her second draft.

Fenton had come to the table without Charlotte, who'd been called away on a case, but she promised to join them later for charades in the music room. Liz didn't know if Charlotte's expertise at the game had anything to do with being a homicide detective, but she sure knew how to give good clues.

"I hate to bring this up," Liz said, grabbing onto Ryan's arm, "but I think something has come between us and it's time we dealt with it."

Ryan looked down at Blackbeard, who'd wedged himself between Liz's and Ryan's chairs. He innocently looked up at them. "Turkey, did someone say turkey?" his pleading eyes said.

Liz picked up a few scraps from her plate and fed him from her hand. Blackbeard's head bobbed as he scarfed down the food. Slivers of turkey were caught in his scraggly black beard.

She said, "I think he needs a good haircut."

Ryan removed the pieces of meat from his dog's beard. "He just got one. It took about five hours and cost me a hundred bucks."

"Well, at least trim his eyebrows and beard," she said, laughing. She glanced at the dog's large paws and didn't have the heart to tell Ryan, who'd never been a pet owner, that one day Blackbeard would be a large dog. A very large dog.

Blackbeard woofed his thanks, and Barnacle Bob called out from his cage next to Greta, "Meow. Meow." Unfortunately, at this early stage, Blackbeard wasn't a cat lover like Killer. He charged toward BB's cage before anyone could catch him. Barnacle Bob fluttered around inside in a frenzy.

"Woof, BB. Repeat, woof!" Liz called out.

For once, the parrot listened to her. "Woof! Woof! Woof!" BB repeated in perfect dog.

Blackbeard relaxed into a sitting position at the base of the cage stand, looking up at the macaw as if he'd found a buddy for life.

"Barnacle Bob better keep his meows and woofs straight," Liz said. "Or there could be dire consequences."

Everyone laughed.

Aunt Amelia hit the tip of her knife against her wineglass. "Attention all. I just want to say what a wonderful day this has been. I know we all have a lot to be thankful for. I'm thankful we're all together, new and old friends alike." She looked over at Ziggy, who was grinning like the schoolboy he'd been when Amelia first met him. "I've just learned some exciting news. The production of *The Bat* lives on! Thanks to the recent purchase of the Melbourne Beach Theatre by patron of the arts Samuel Clemens."

"Mark Twain?" Betty asked.

"No. But my mother was a huge fan," Ziggy said, his ponytail swinging to the right as he looked Betty's way.

Susannah Shay appeared at the table like an apparition. She said, "Amelia, dear. Are you saying that Ziggy is the new owner of *our* theater?"

Liz noticed her great-aunt's clenched jaw. With perfect diction, Aunt Amelia said, "Yes, Miss Shay, Ziggy is the new owner of *his* theater, and he's kindly agreed to produce *The Bat*."

Susannah first looked incredulously at Amelia, then Ziggy. "But…will our roles remain the same?"

There was silence. Amelia broke it with, "I'd also like to make another announcement." Amelia picked up her glass and turned to Susannah. "Ms. Susannah Shay will be staying in the Windward Shores Suite and helping Greta and me with the day-to-day operations of the Indialantic. Welcome, Susannah. We couldn't be happier."

"We couldn't?" Liz whispered to Ryan.

"It could be worse," he said. "At least Aunt Amelia is making her work."

"I suppose. That's why we love Auntie, always picking up strays."

Liz looked over at Blackbeard, now asleep at the base of Barnacle Bob's cage stand. Then she glanced at their beautiful surroundings: the ocean, the river, and, finally, into Ryan's dark eyes. It was Liz and Ryan's first Thanksgiving together, and she was already planning the menu for next year in her mind, picturing Ryan in her gourmet kitchen wearing her "Kiss the Cook" apron.

Liz was home. And all was well.

A Trio of Salad Recipes from Deli-casies by the Sea
Deli-casies by the Sea's Corn-Mango Salad

Ingredients:

4 medium fresh ears of sweet corn, cleaned
2 to 3 large mangoes
1 medium red onion
1 tsp. olive oil
4 tbs. olive oil
2 tbs. fresh lemon juice
1 tsp. sugar
Salt and pepper
½ tsp. curry powder
6 cups fresh arugula

Preparation:

Cut kernels from cobs. Seed and peel mangoes; cut in 12 slices. Peel onion; cut in 6 wedges.

Add 1 tsp. oil to a nine-inch cast-iron pan on grill; add corn kernels. Cook and stir two minutes. Divide kernels among six serving bowls. Set aside.

In a bowl, combine mango slices and onion wedges, drizzle with 1 tbs. olive oil. Toss to coat. Put mango and onion slices on grill. Grill mango for 3 to 5 minutes and onion wedges 6 to 8 minutes, turning often. Transfer mango and onion to a bowl.

For dressing, in a bowl combine lemon juice, sugar, curry powder, ½ tsp. salt and ⅛ tsp. pepper. Whisk in remaining 3 tbs. oil until combined. Add 1 tbs. dressing to mango mixture; toss. Spoon mango mixture over corn. Drizzle arugula with remaining dressing and toss. Put on top of each bowl.

Serves 6.

Deli-casies by the Sea's Margarita-Chicken Salad

Ingredients:

4 skinless, boneless chicken breast halves
3 tbs. canola oil or mild tasting oil
1½ cups margarita drink mix *without alcohol*
1 tsp. ground cumin
1 tsp. finely shredded lime peel
½ cup mayonnaise
2 tbs. lime juice
⅛ tsp. cayenne pepper
4 medium tomatoes, sliced
2 medium avocados, halved, seeded, peeled, and sliced
½ medium red onion, thinly sliced
¼ tsp. cracked black pepper

Preparation:
Place chicken in a plastic bag and set in a shallow dish. In a bowl, combine margarita mix, cumin, oil, and lime peel. Pour over chicken and seal bag. Refrigerate 2 to 8 hours. Drain marinade and discard.

Grill chicken for 12 to 15 minutes. Remove from grill and cool slightly.

In a medium bowl, combine mayonnaise, lime juice, and cayenne. Coarsely chop chicken. Add to mayonnaise mixture. Gently toss. Line four salad plates with tomato slices. Top tomatoes with chicken, avocado slices, and red onion. Sprinkle with black pepper.

Serves 4.

Deli-casies by the Sea's Calamari and Grilled Shrimp Salad

Ingredients:

1 medium orange
¼ cup plus 2 tbs. extra-virgin olive oil
2 tsp. chopped fresh thyme
2 tsp. white wine vinegar
Kosher salt and freshly ground pepper
¼ lb. (4–6) cleaned calamari bodies (no tentacles), rinsed and patted dry
16 jumbo shrimp (21–25 per lb.), peeled, deveined, rinsed, and patted dry
1 red bell pepper, quartered lengthwise and cored
1 medium fennel bulb (about 1 lb.), trimmed, quartered, cored, and thinly sliced crosswise
5 oz. baby arugula (about 5 cups)

Preparation:

Prepare medium-high grill.

Finely grate 1 tsp. of zest from the orange and then squeeze ⅓ cup juice. In a small bowl, whisk the juice and zest with ¼ cup of the oil, 1 tsp. of the thyme, the vinegar, ½ tsp. salt, and ¼ tsp. pepper.

Cut open the calamari bodies lengthwise. Put them in a medium bowl with shrimp and red pepper and toss with the remaining 2 tbs. oil, 1 tsp. thyme, ½ tsp. salt, and ¼ tsp. pepper. Thread the shrimp onto 3 or 4 metal skewers.

Grill the shrimp and peppers (skin side up), until they have grill marks, 2 to 3 minutes. Flip both and continue to grill until the shrimp are just firm and opaque, about 2 minutes. Move the shrimp to a clean plate and continue to cook peppers until they're soft and the skin is charred, about 5 minutes more.

Cook calamari until barely cooked through, about 1 minute per side.

When the calamari are done, move them to plate with shrimp. Cut the calamari into quarters lengthwise and remove the shrimp from the skewers. Peel and thinly slice red peppers. In a large bowl, toss the fennel and arugula with half of the vinaigrette. Season to taste with salt and pepper. Distribute greens on 4 plates and top with shrimp, calamari, and red pepper. Drizzle with some of the remaining vinaigrette on top.

Serves 4.
Calories (kcal): 320
Fat Calories (kcal): 190
Fat (g): 22
Saturated Fat (g): 3
Polyunsaturated Fat (g): 2.5
Monounsaturated Fat (g): 15
Cholesterol (mg): 190
Sodium (mg): 480
Carbohydrates (g): 11
Fiber (g): 3
Protein (g): 20

Be sure not to miss the first book in Kathleen Bridge's By the Sea Mystery series,

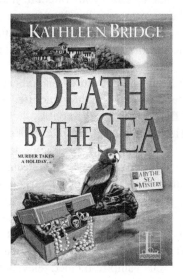

The Indialantic by the Sea Hotel has a hundred-year-old history on beautiful Melbourne Beach, Florida, and more than a few guests seem to have been there from the start. When Liz Holt returns home after an intense decade in New York, she's happy to be surrounded by the eccentric clientele and loving relatives that populate her family-run inn, and doubly pleased to see the business is staying afloat thanks to its vibrant shopping emporium and a few very wealthy patrons.

But that patronage decreases by one when a filthy rich guest is discovered dead in her oceanfront suite. Maybe this is simply a jewel theft gone wrong, but maybe someone—or many people—wanted the hotel's prosperous guest dead. Only one thing is sure: There's a killer at the Indialantic, and if Liz lets herself be distracted—by her troubled past or the tempting man who seems eager to dredge it back up—the next reservation she'll book could be at the cemetery...

Keep reading for a special excerpt.

A Lyrical Underground e-book on sale now!

Chapter 1

"I curse you, Barnabas! May your undeath haunt you through all eternity. I'd rather die a mortal than live year to year preying on innocent blood, watching those I love buried in hallowed ground. You will not take me with you!" She jerked the knife toward her chest and fell to the floor.

After a few beats, Aunt Amelia opened her eyes, cracked a smile, then pulled herself up with the help of a sturdy piano bench. For a minute, Liz feared her eighty-year-old great-aunt had fractured a hip.

"Bravo! Bravo!" Barnacle Bob called out.

Liz applauded. Her great-aunt performed a deep bow, the tip of her bright red *I Dream of Jeannie* ponytail grazing the threadbare Persian carpet. When she stood, her sea-green eyes gleamed under black liner that extended from the corners of her eyes in true sixties style. "Enough theatrics," Aunt Amelia said, adding a schoolgirl giggle. "I must talk to Pierre about dinner." She wrapped a neon-pink scarf around her neck, kissed Liz on the top of the head, and exited the music room.

Amelia Eden Holt, Liz's favorite—and only—great-aunt, had starred in three seasons of the 1960s vampire-themed television soap drama, *Dark Shadows.* "Starred" might be an exaggeration, because she'd only had a small part as a Collinwood maid. However, that was what Liz loved about her paternal great-aunt; she was bigger than life and more colorful than the tail feathers on Barnacle Bob, Aunt Amelia's thirty-year-old macaw.

"Drama queen... Showboater... Diva," Bob squawked.

Her great-aunt adored Barnacle Bob. Liz just hoped Aunt Amelia never heard the parrot's two-faced comments. "Hush, BB, that's not nice." Liz took a seat next to his cage, inhaling Aunt Amelia's signature scent, L'air du Temps.

When Liz was five, after her mother passed away, she and her father came to live with Aunt Amelia in the old family-run hotel. At one time, the Indialantic by the Sea Hotel was Melbourne Beach, Florida's premier ocean-front resort. Unfortunately, the monikers "premier" and "resort" no longer held true. The Indialantic sat on a barrier island sandwiched between the Indian River Lagoon to the west and the Atlantic Ocean to the east. Last fall, Liz's father invested a sizable percentage of his attorney fees from winning a class-action lawsuit into the coffers of the hotel. With Aunt Amelia's and the staff's hard work and dedication, along with the rent coming in from the new shops, the establishment was finally inching its way toward the black, affording them one more year to stave off the bank and real-estate predators.

Aunt Amelia insisted on adding to the old hotel's name by calling it the Indialantic by the Sea Hotel and Emporium. The name was a little long-winded for Liz's taste, but no one dared cross Aunt Amelia.

In 1945, a fire had destroyed the entire midsection of the Indialantic Hotel, and the north and south parts of the resort had been made into two separate buildings, with a large courtyard in between. The south building was the hotel, and the north building housed the emporium shops. The shops consisted of Home Arts by the Sea, a women's lifestyle collective; Deli-cacies by the Sea, a gourmet deli and coffee shop; Sirens by the Sea, a women's clothing boutique; and Gold Coast by the Sea, a rare coin and estate jewelry shop. It had been Liz's idea to have her best friend from childhood, Kate Fields, leave her booth at a local antique mall and rent out the remaining space at the emporium. Kate called her used book and vintage shop Books & Browsery by the Sea.

Before she'd left Melbourne Beach for Manhattan, Liz had considered the hotel too old-school and boringly quaint. Now, after six weeks of being home, she felt cocooned, cozy, and safe when she stepped inside. It was a far different feeling than she'd had in the city, turning the three dead bolts on her SoHo loft's door. Life was simple on the island, and Liz embraced the laid-back beach-town vibe, something she hadn't been able to do at eighteen when she was young and beyond restless.

The upper level of the Indialantic had large guest suites that had become a refuge for Aunt Amelia's occasional "strays," usually senior citizens with small Social Security checks and small pets, "no bigger than a bread basket." Although Liz knew Aunt Amelia made exceptions to her own rule, as evidenced by Killer, the Great Dane who looked longingly at Liz's lap.

"Sorry, pup, don't even think about it. I'll have to spend the next few weeks at the chiropractor." Her father called the upper floor of the hotel Aunt Amelia's Animalia, and chose to live in an apartment next to his law office on the first floor. Liz lived in the Indialantic's former beach pavilion, now turned beach house. It was a nice distance away from the Indialantic and a quiet place to work on her writing career, or more accurately, her *non*-writing career.

Liz glanced around the music room and reminisced about past years with her father at the piano and Aunt Amelia singing, dancing, or replaying one of her scenes from *Dark Shadows* or a myriad of other midcentury television shows in which she'd had small roles. Aunt Amelia had been considered a character actress—and she was quite a character. While some children had

Dr. Seuss and *Goodnight Moon* read to them before falling asleep, Aunt Amelia would tell Liz about the evil witch Angelique and the beautiful Josette who fought each other for the handsome vampire Barnabas's love. "Barnabas didn't want to be a vampire, Lizzy dear, but he had no choice. Sometimes you just have to face who you are and make the best of it..." Liz smiled at the memory and patted Killer's large noggin. She'd been loafing too long. She thought about all the things she had to do to get ready for the Indialantic Spring Fling by the Sea. It had been Liz's idea to have the event on Saturday in the hopes of drumming up more business for the emporium shops. Although Melbourne Beach was, as advertised, a casual, beachy surfer's paradise, Liz knew there were celebrities hiding in nearby ocean-front homes with tons of disposable income who might enjoy an off-the-grid dining and shopping experience.

If Liz was honest with herself, she'd been using her role as her father's and great-aunt's assistant as an excuse not to write. It was amazing that her agent hadn't given up on her, especially after the scandal that had rocked the literati and her life as she knew it.

She got up, walked to the window, and looked out at the Atlantic. The hotel was perched on a sandy cliff, east of State Road A1A. The hotel's property also encompassed the west side of the highway, with its own dock on the Indian River Lagoon. Lost in thoughts of the past, Liz startled when she heard Barnacle Bob squawk, "Places to go. People to see."

Liz moved over to the parrot's cage. "The only place you're going is dreamland. Catch ya later, BB. Time for my dinner. Try to behave yourself."

"Okay, Scarface! Keep it real."

She gave it back to him. "Whatever you say, bald-as-a-billiard-ball Barnacle Bob."

The parrot was missing all the feathers on the top of his head. What remained were little pinholes, like a child's connect-the-dots puzzle.

Liz traced the scar on her right cheek. She'd had two operations with a plastic surgeon in Manhattan, and a week ago, the third procedure with a surgeon in Vero Beach. Each skin graft was an improvement, but she was told that a scar would always remain and that a fourth operation would have to wait for at least another year. She now thought of her life in terms of before-the-scar and after-the-scar. Surprisingly enough, life after-the-scar was the better of the two. Her before-the-scar life had included a tempestuous relationship with Travis Osterman, the Pulitzer Prize–winning author of *The McAvoy Brothers*, a five-hundred-page novel following three generations of brothers and their triumphs and sorrows through countless women and wars.

She'd left Melbourne Beach when she was eighteen and spent six years at Columbia University and then two years writing her novel, *Let the Wind Roar*, while modeling and bartending. After her novel won the PEN/Faulkner award, it flew to the top of the *New York Times* best sellers list. Liz spent the following year living every author's dream. Then she met Travis and her dream turned into a nightmare, due to a scandal and a defamation-of-character lawsuit, not to mention a night of terror she would never forget. Liz had been acquitted of any wrongdoing in the lawsuit, but it was too late. She was branded a pariah and ostracized from every Manhattan literary salon. Liz had returned home to Melbourne Beach, her wings clipped by her father, and rightly so. It was a little embarrassing for a twenty-eight-year-old, but she'd welcomed his broad shoulders to cry on and she loved that her father never questioned her choices, saying instead, "If it wasn't for the contrast in your life, you'd never have known what you truly wanted."

Since Liz had returned to Florida, though, everyone at the Indialantic had been walking on eggshells around her, including Aunt Amelia. Of course, the whole sordid affair had been plastered all over the tabloids, but not even the tabloids knew what had really happened. Only her father, Betty, and her best friend, Kate, knew the entire story. Liz had given Aunt Amelia a kinder, gentler version of the events that had gone down.

Barnacle Bob spun around in his Mercedes of a birdcage and faced the wall, aiming his colorful tail-feathered rear end at Liz. Aunt Amelia had found him after a hurricane at a local pet rescue facility. She'd had her pick of other pets needing a good home, but she always went for the less fortunate, in this case Barnacle Bob. Owing to his colorful language, Barnacle Bob's former owner had probably been a crusty old sailor or a Florida fisherman, no doubt male. Barnacle Bob had a soft spot for Aunt Amelia and he never said anything disparaging to her face, only behind her back. He was less kind to the rest of humanity.

Liz covered the parrot's cage. "Early to bed, early to rise, BB."

As she and Killer walked out of the music room, it was hard to ignore the muffled expletives spewing from Barnacle Bob's foul beak.

About the Author

Kathleen Bridge is the author of the By the Sea Mystery series and the Hamptons Home and Garden Mystery series, published by Berkley. She started her writing career working at *The Michigan State University News* in East Lansing, Michigan. A member of Sisters in Crime and Mystery Writers of America, she is also the author and photographer of an antiques reference guide, *Lithographed Paper Toys, Books, and Games*. She teaches creative writing in addition to working as an antiques and vintage dealer in Melbourne, Florida. Kathleen blissfully lives on a barrier island. Readers can visit her on the web at www.kathleenbridge.com

Printed in the United States
by Baker & Taylor Publisher Services